'The most consistently brilliant sf writer in the world'
John Brunner

'In all his work he wa [illegible]
and very dangerous. [illegible]
time, and perhaps th[illegible]
own, spoken as we c[illegible]

'For everyone lost in the endlessly multiplica[illegible] of
the modern world, remember: Philip K. Dick got there first'
Terry Gilliam

'Dick's plastic realities tell us more than we'll ever want to know about the inside of our heads and the view looking out. In his tortured topographies of worlds never made, we see mindscapes that we ourselves, in our madder moments, have glimpsed and thought real. Dick travelled out there on our behalf. It is our duty to read the reports he sent home'
James Lovegrove

'Dick quietly produced serious fiction in a popular form and there can be no higher praise' Michael Moorcock

'The terror and the humour are fused. It is this rare quality that marks Dick out' Brian Aldiss

Also by Philip K. Dick

Solar Lottery (1955)
The World Jones Made (1956)
The Man Who Japed (1956)
The Cosmic Puppets (1957)
Eye in the Sky (1957)
Dr. Futurity (1959)
Time Out of Joint (1959)
Vulcan's Hammer (1960)
The Man in the High Castle (1962)
The Game-Players of Titan (1963)
The Simulacra (1964)
Martian Time-Slip (1964)
Clans of the Alphane Moon (1964)
The Three Stigmata of Palmer Eldritch (1965)
Dr. Bloodmoney, or How We Got Along After the Bomb (1965)
Cantata-140 (The Crack in Space) (1966)
Now Wait for Last Year (1966)
The Ganymede Takeover (with Ray F. Nelson) (1967)
The Zap Gun (1967)
Counter-Clock World (1967)
Do Androids Dream of Electric Sheep? (1968)
Galactic Pot-Healer (1969)
Ubik (1969)
Our Friends From Frolix 8 (1970)
A Maze of Death (1970)
We Can Build You (1972)
Flow My Tears, the Policeman Said (1974)
Confessions of a Crap Artist (1975)
Deus Irae (with Roger Zelazny) (1976)
A Scanner Darkly (1977)
The Divine Invasion (1981)
Valis (1981)
The Transmigration of Timothy Archer (1982)
Lies, Inc (1984)
The Man Whose Teeth Were All Exactly Alike (1984)
Puttering About in a Small Land (1985)
In Milton Lumky Territory (1985)
Radio Free Albemuth (1985)
Humpty Dumpty in Oakland (1986)
Mary and the Giant (1987)
The Broken Bubble (1988)

SHORT STORY COLLECTIONS

The Variable Man (1957)
A Handful of Darkness (1966)
The Turning Wheel (1977)
The Best of Philip K. Dick (1977)
The Golden Man (1980)
Minority Report (2002)

THE COLLECTED STORIES OF PHILIP K. DICK

1. Beyond Lies the Wub (1987)
2. Second Variety (1987)
3. The Father Thing (1987)
4. The Days of Perky Pat (1987)
5. We Can Remember it for You Wholesale (1987)

SF MASTERWORKS

THE PENULTIMATE TRUTH

Philip K. Dick

This edition first published in Great Britain in 2005
by Gollancz
An imprint of the Orion Publishing Group
Orion House, 5 Upper St Martin's Lane,
London WC2H 9EA

A CIP catalogue record for this book
is available from the British Library

Printed in Great Britain by Clays Ltd, St Ives plc

The Orion Publishing Group's policy is to use papers that are natural, renewable and recyclable products and made from wood grown in sustainable forests. The logging and manufacturing processes are expected to conform to the environmental regulations of the country of origin.

www.orionbooks.co.uk

THE PENULTIMATE TRUTH

ONE

A fog can drift in from outside and get you; it can invade. At the long high window of his library—an Ozymandiasian structure built from concrete chunks that had once in another age formed an entrance ramp to the Bayshore Freeway—Joseph Adams pondered, watched the fog, that of the Pacific. And because this was evening and the world was darkening, this fog scared him as much as that other fog, the one inside which did not invade but stretched and stirred and filled the empty portions of the body. Usually the latter fog is called loneliness.

"Fix me a drink," Colleen said plaintively from behind him.

"Your arm," he said, "it fell off? You can't squeeze the lemon?" He turned from the window with its view of dead trees, the Pacific beyond and its layer in the sky, darkness hanging and approaching, and for a moment actually considered fixing her the drink. And then he knew what he had to do, where he had to be:

At the marble-top desk which had been salvaged from a bombed-out house in the Russian Hill section of the former city of San Francisco he seated himself at the rhetorizor, touched its *on*-tab.

Groaning, Colleen disappeared to search for a leady to fix her the drink. Joseph Adams, at his desk and rhetorizor, heard her go and was glad. For some reason—but here he did not care to probe his own mind too deeply—he was lonelier with Colleen Hackett than without her, and anyhow late on Sunday night he fixed a dreadful drink; it was always too sweet, as if by mistake one of his leadies had dug up a bottle of Tokay and he had used it, not dry vermouth, in the martinis. Ironically, left to themselves, the leadies never made that error . . . was this an omen? Joe Adams wondered. Are they getting smarter than us?

At the keyboard of the rhetorizor he typed, carefully, the substantive he wanted. *Squirrel*. Then, after a good two minutes of sluggish, deep thought, the limiting adjective *smart*.

"Okay," he said, aloud, and sat back, touched the rerun tab.

The rhetorizor, as Colleen reentered the library with her tall gin drink, began to construct for him in the auddimension. "It is a wise old squirrel," it said tinnily (it possessed only a two-inch speaker), "and yet this little fellow's wisdom is not its own; nature has endowed it—"

"Aw god," Joe Adams said savagely, and slapped off the sleek, steel and plastic machine with all its many microcomponents; it became silent. He then noticed Colleen. "Sorry. But I'm tired. Why can't they, Brose or General Holt or Marshal Harenzany, *somebody* in a position of responsibility, put Sunday night somewhere between Friday noon and—"

"Dear," Colleen said, and sighed. "I heard you type out only two semantic units. Give it more to ogpon."

"I'll give it plenty to ogpon." He touched the *no*-tab, typed a whole sentence, as Colleen stood behind him, sipping and watching. "Okay?"

"I just can never tell about you," Colleen said. "If you passionately love your job or hate it." She read the sentence aloud. " 'The well-informed dead rat romped under the tongue-tied pink log.' "

"Listen," he said grimly. "I want to see what this stupid assist that cost me fifteen thousand Wes-Dem dollars is going to do with that. I'm serious; I'm waiting." He jabbed the rerun tab of the machine.

"When's the speech due?" she asked.

"Tomorrow."

"Get up early."

"Oh no." He thought, I hate it even more when it's early.

The rhetorizor, in its cricket's voice, intoned folksily. "We think of rats, of course, as our enemy. But consider their vast value to us in cancer research alone. The lowly rat has done yeoman's service for huma—"

Again, at his savage instigation, it died into silence.

"—nity," Colleen said distantly; she was inspecting the authentic long-ago dug up Epstein bust in the niche that divided the west wall shelves of books, where Joseph Adams kept his reference texts on TV commercials of the last, past, great twentieth century, in particular the religious and the Mars candy bar inspired creations of Stan Freberg. "A miserable metaphor," she murmured. "A yeoman rat . . . yeomen were young villagers during the Medieval period, and I bet even though you're such a pro you didn't know that." She nodded to a leady which had come to the library door at her request. "Get my cloak and have my flapple brought to the main entrance." To Joe she said, "I'm flapping back to my own villa." When he didn't answer she said, "Joe, try it, the entire speech, without that assist; write it in your own words. And then you won't have 'yeoman rats' to make you so cross."

He thought, I don't think honestly I could do it, in my own words, without this machine; I'm hooked on it now.

Outside, the fog had managed a complete success; he saw, with one brief sideways glance, that it inhabited the world right to the window of his library. Well, he thought, anyhow we're spared another one of those brilliant, radioactive-particles-in-suspension-for-all-eternity sunsets.

"Your flapple, Miss Hackett," the leady announced, "is at the main entrance and I hear by remote that your type II chauffeur holds the door open for you. And due to the evening vapors one of Mr. Adams' household servants will shed warm air about you until you are tucked safely inside."

"Jeez," Joseph Adams said, and shook his head.

Colleen said, "You teached it, dear. It got its precious jargony linguistic habits straight out of you."

"Because," he said bitterly, "I like style and pomp and ritual." Turning to her, appealing, he said, "Brose told me in a memo, it showed up at the Agency directly from his own bureau in Geneva, that this speech has to use a squirrel as the operational entity. What can you say about them that hasn't already been said? They save; they're thrifty. We know that. Do they do anything else good that you know of, that you could *hang* a goddam *moral* on?" And he thought, they're all dead. There just isn't such a life form any more. But we still extol its virtues . . . after having exterminated it as a race.

On the keyboard of the rhetorizor he vigorously, with deliberation, punched two new semantic units. *Squirrel*. And—*genocide*.

The machine, presently, declared, "The funniest thing happened to me on my way to the bank, yesterday. I happened to pass through Central Park, and you know how—"

Incredulous, staring at the machine, Joe said, "*You* passed through Central Park yesterday? Central Park's been gone forty years."

"Joe, it's just a machine." Cloak on, she returned momentarily to kiss him goodnight.

"But the thing's insane," he protested. "And it said 'funny' when I fed in *genocide*. Did you—"

"It's reminiscing," Colleen said, trying to explain it to him; she knelt briefly, touched his face with her fingers and peered at him, eye to eye. "I love you," she said, "but you're going to die; you're going to rupture yourself working. Through my office at the Agency I'll file a formal petition to Brose, asking if you can take two weeks off. I have something for you, a gift; one of my leadies dug it up near my villa; legally within the boundaries of my demesne, as per that recent little interchange my leadies had with those of my north neighbor's."

"A book." He felt a flicker within him, the peaked flame of life.

"An especially good book, the real prewar thing, not a Xeroxed copy. Know what of?"

"*Alice in Wonderland*." He had heard so much about that, had always wanted to own it and read it.

"Better. One of those outrageously funny books from the 1960s—in good shape: both front and back covers intact. A self-help book; *How I Tranquilized Myself by Drinking Onion Juice* or some such thing. *I Made a Million Dollars by Leading Two-And-a-Half Lives For the FBI*. Or—"

He said, "Colleen, one day I looked out the window and I saw a squirrel."

Staring at him she said, "No."

"The tail; you can't mistake the tail. It's as round and fat and gray as a bottle brush. And they hop like this." He made a wicket-motion with his hand, showing her, trying to recapture it, for himself, too. "I squalled; I got four of my leadies out there with—" He shrugged. "Anyhow they finally came back and said, 'There's no such thing out there, dominus,' or some darn remark." He was silent a moment. It had, of course, been a hypnagogic hallucination, based on too many drinks and too little sleep. He knew it. The leadies knew it. And now Colleen knew it. "But just suppose," he said, then.

"Write, in your own words, how you felt. By hand on paper—not dictated into a recorder. What finding a thriving, living squirrel would have meant to you." She gestured scathingly at his fifteen thousand dollar rhetorizor. "Not what *it* thinks. And—"

"And Brose himself," he said, "would strike it. Maybe I could get it through the 'vac, to the sim and then on tape; I think it'd go that far. But never past Geneva. Because I wouldn't be saying, in effect, 'Come on, fellas; carry on.' I'd be saying—" He considered feeling peaceful for a moment now. "I'll try," he decided, and rose to his feet, pushing his old-California wicker chair back. "Okay, I'll even do it in longhand; I'll find a—what do you call them?"

"Ballpoint pen. Think of your cousin who was killed in the war: Ken. Then remember you're both men. Then you have it: pen."

He nodded. "And program the 'vac direct from that. You might be right; it'd be depressing but at least it wouldn't make me sick stomachwise; I wouldn't get those pyloric spasms." He began searching around the library for—what had she called it?

Still on rerun, the rhetorizor squeaked to itself, ". . . and that little fellow; inside that head was packed a powerful lot of savvy. Maybe even more than you or I can ever guess. And I think we can learn from him." It droned on. Inside it thousands of microcomponents spun the problem from a dozen drums of info-data; it could go on forever, but Joe Adams was busy; now he had found a pen and all he needed was blank white paper. Hell, he surely had *that;* he beckoned to the leady waiting to escort Colleen to her flapple.

"Get the staff," he instructed it, "to search up paper for me to write on. Go through every room of the villa, including all the bedrooms, even those not currently in use. I distinctly remember seeing a folio or packet of it, however it used to come. It was dug up."

By direct radio contact the leady passed on his command and he felt the building stir, through the villa's fifty-odd rooms, his staff moving into activity from the spot where each had halted after its last task. He, the dominus, sensed, with the soles of his feet, the burgeoning life of this his building and some of the inside fog went away, even though they were only what the Czechs had called *robots,* their crazy word for *workers.*

But, outside, the fog scratched at the window.

And when Colleen left, he knew, it would pluck and scrape, try to get in, more determinedly.

He wished it were Monday and he were at the Agency, in New

York at his office, with other Yance-men around him. And the life there would not be the movement of dead—or rather, to be fair, unliving—things. But the reality itself.

"I can tell you," he said suddenly. "I love my work. In fact I've got to have it; there's nothing else. Not this—" He gestured at the room in which they stood, then at the murky, clouded-over window.

"Like a drug," Colleen said, perceptively.

"Okay." He nodded. "To use the archaic expression, 'I'll purchase that.' "

"Some linguist," she said gently. "It's *buy*. Maybe you ought to use that machine after all."

"No," he said, at once. "You were right; I'm going all the way back to trying it direct, on my own." Any moment now one of his staff of leadies would come clanking in with blank white paper; he was sure he possessed it, somewhere. And if he didn't he could swap some item with a neighbor, make a trip, surrounded and protected, of course, by his entourage of leadies, to the demesne and villa to the south, that of Ferris Granville. Ferris would have paper; he had told them on the open-channel vidline last week, composing his—god forbid—memoirs.

Whatever in, on or over Earth memoirs were.

TWO

Time for bed. The clock said so, but—suppose the power had been off again, as it had for almost a whole day last week; the clock might be hours wrong. It might in fact, Nicholas St. James thought morbidly, really be time to get up. And the metabolism of his body, even after all these years underground, told him nothing.

In the shared bathroom of their cubby, 67-B of the Tom Mix, water ran; his wife was taking a shower. So Nicholas searched about her vanity table until he found her wristwatch, read it; both timepieces agreed, therefore that was that. And yet he felt wide-awake. The Maury Souza affair, he realized; it preyed vulturely on him, made a trough of his brain. This is how it must feel, he thought, to contract the Bag Plague, where those virtues get in and cause your head to expand until it pops like a blown-up paper bag. Maybe I'm sick, he thought. Actually. Even more so than Souza. And Maury Souza, the chief mechanic of their ant tank, now in his seventies, was dying.

"I'm out," Rita called from the bathroom. However, the shower still ran; she was not out. "I mean, you can come in and brush your teeth or put them in a glass or whatever it is you do."

What I do, he thought, is get the Bag Plague . . . probably that last damaged leady they sent down hadn't been 'cided properly. Or I've picked up the Stink of Shrink, and from that he physically cringed; imagine, he thought, having your head diminish in size, features included, to the circumference of a marble. "Okay," he said, reflexively, and began to unlace his work boots. He felt the need to be clean; he would shower, too, despite the severe water ration currently in force at the Tom Mix, and by his own edict. When you do not feel clean, he realized, you are doomed. Considering exactly what we could be made unclean by, the microscopic *things* downfalling to us that some careless ambulatory metal hunk of handmade parts had failed to 'cide out of existence before yanking the drop switch, shooting three hundred pounds of contaminated matter to us, something both hot and dirty at the same time . . . hot with radioactivity and dirty with germs. Great combination, he thought.

And, in the back part of his mind, again he recalled: *Souza is dying*. What else matters? Because—how long can we last without that one grumpy old man?

Approximately two weeks. Because their quota came up for auditing in two weeks. And this time, if he knew his luck and his tank's, it would be one of the Minister of the Interior Stanton Brose's agents, not General Holt's. They rotated. It prevented, the image of Yancy on the big screen had once said, corruption.

Picking up the audphone he dialed the tank's clinic.

"How is he?"

On the other end Dr. Carol Tigh, their G.P. in charge of their small clinic, said, "No change. He's conscious. Come on down; he tells me he'd like to talk to you."

"Okay." Nicholas rang off, shouted—through the noise of running water—to Rita that he was going, and left their cubby; outside in the common corridor he bumped past other tankers on their ways from the shops and recreation rooms to their cubbies for bed: the clocks had been right, because he saw numerous bathrobes and standard issue synthetic wubfur-fuzz slippers. This really is bedtime, he decided. But he knew he still could not sleep.

Three floors down, at the clinic, he passed through empty waiting rooms—the clinic was closed, except for its bed patients—and then passed the nurses' station; the nurse stood up respectfully to greet him because after all Nicholas was their elected president, and then he found himself at the closed door of Maury Souza's room with its *Quiet—Do Not Disturb!* sign on the door. He entered.

In the wide white bed lay something flat, something so squashed that it could only gaze up, as if it were a reflection, something dimly seen in a pool that absorbed light rather than reflected it. The pool in which the old man lay was a consumer of energy of all kinds, Nicholas realized as he walked to the bed. This is only a husk left here; it has been drained as if a spider got to it; a world-spider or for us, rather, a subworld, underspider. But still a drinker of human existence. Even below this far.

From his supine immobility the old man moved his lips. "Hi."

"Hi, you old knurlheaded frab," Nicholas said, and drew a chair up beside the bed. "How do you feel?"

After a time, as if it had taken that long for Nicholas' words to reach him—that great journey across space—the old mechanic said, "Not so good, Nick."

You don't know, Nicholas thought, what you've got. Unless Carol has told you since I last discussed you with her. He eyed the old mechanic, wondering if there was an instinct. Pancreatitis was fatal in almost one hundred percent of its cases, he knew; Carol had told him. But of course no one had or would tell Souza, because the miracle might happen.

"You'll pick up," Nicholas said clumsily.

"Listen, Nick. How many leadies we made this month?"

He considered whether to lie or tell the truth. Souza had been here in this bed eight days; surely he had lost contact, could not check and trip him up. So he lied. "Fifteen."

"Then—" A labored pause; Souza stared upward, never turned his eyes toward Nicholas, as if he were looking away in shame. "We could still make our quota."

"What do I care," Nicholas said, "if we make our quota?" He had known Souza, been shut up with him here at the Tom Mix, for the total war-period: fifteen years. "I care whether—" God, a misspoken word; impossible to amend, too.

" 'Whether I get out of here,' " Souza whispered.

"Naturally I mean *when*." He felt furious with himself. And, now, he saw Carol at the door, looking professional in her white smock, her low-heeled shoes, carrying her clipboard on which, no doubt, she had Souza's chart. Without a word Nicholas rose, walked away from the bed and past Carol and out into the corridor.

She followed. They stood together in the empty corridor and then Carol said, "He'll live one more week and then he'll die. Whether your tongue wags and says 'whether' or if you—"

"I told him our shops had turned out fifteen leadies so far this month; make sure nobody else tells him different."

"I hear," she said, "it's more like five."

"Seven." He told her not because she was their doctor and someone they depended on, but because of The Relationship. Always he told Carol everything; that was one of the emotional hooks that gaffed him, held him to her: she, and this was so rare, could see through any sham, even the little daily innocences. So why try this now? Carol never wanted pretty words; she lived by the truth. Here now she had once again gotten it.

"Then we can't meet the quota," she said. Matter-of-factly.

He nodded. "Partly it's because they've asked for three type VIIs and that's hard; that strains our shops. If it had all been the III or IV types—" But it hadn't; it never was, nor would be. Ever.

So long as the surface lasted.

"You know," Carol said presently, "that on the surface artificial pancreases—artiforgs—are available. You've considered this possibility, of course, in your official capacity."

Nicholas said, "It's illegal. Military hospitals only. Priority. Rating 2-A. We don't qualify."

"There is said to be—"

"And get caught." It would no doubt be a quick kangaroo-court military tribunal session and then execution, if one were caught trading on the blackmarket. In fact if one were caught up there at all.

"Are you afeared to go up?" Carol asked, with her brisk, brilliant hard scrutiny.

"Yep." He nodded: it was so. Two weeks: death by destruction of the red bloodcell-making capacity of the bone marrow. One week: the Bag Plague or the Stink of Shrink or Raw-Claw-Paw and he already felt germphobic; already, a few moments ago, he had quaked with the trauma of it—as did virtually every tanker, although in actual fact not one case of any of the poxes had broken out at the Tom Mix.

"You can," Carol said, "call a meeting of those—you know—those you can trust. And ask for a volunteer."

"Goddam it, I'll go if anyone does." But he didn't want to send anyone because he knew what was up there. No one would return because a homotropic weapon, if not the tribunal, would flush him out of hiding and it would follow him until he died. And that in a matter of minutes, perhaps.

And homotropic weapons were vile things; they did it in a vile way.

Carol said, "I know how badly you want to save old Souza."

"I love him," he said. "Above and beyond the shops, the quota, all of that. Did he ever, in all the time we've been locked up down below here, refuse anyone anything? Any time of the night, a leaking water pipe, break in power, clogged protine chute—he always came and hammered and patched and stitched and rewrapped it back into operation.'' And, since Souza was, officially, Chief Mechanic, he could have dispatched any one of fifty assistants and snoozed on. From the old man Nicholas had learned; you did the job yourself—you did not drop it in the lap of a subordinate.

As, he thought, the warwork's devolved down here to us. Building the metal fighters in eight basic types, and so on, with the Estes Park Government, the functionaries of WesDem and of Brose personally, breathing at us at close, close range.

And, as if the words magically impelled the unseen presence, a gray, faint shape moved urgently down the hall toward him and Carol. Commissioner Dale Nunes, all right; eager, busy, pressed on by his business.

''Nick!'' Panting, Nunes read straight from a slip of paper. ''A big speech in ten minutes; get on the all-cubby circuit and get everyone into Wheeling Hall; we'll watch in unison because there'll be questions. This is serious.'' His fast bird eyes flew in their spasm of alarm. ''Honest to god, Nick, the way I got it over the coax it's all of Detroit; they penetrated the final ring.''

''Jesus,'' Nicholas said. And moved, reflexively, toward a nearby aud-tap of the circuit which ran, speakerwise, throughout each floor and chamber of the Tom Mix. ''But it's bedtime,'' he said to Commissioner Nunes. ''A lot of them are undressing or in bed; couldn't they watch on their own individual cub-sets?''

''The questions,'' Nunes said, agitatedly. ''They're going to up the quotas because of this Detroit fiasco—that's what I'm afraid of. And I want to be sure everyone knows why, if that's the case.'' He did not look happy.

Nicholas said, ''But Dale; you know our situation. We can't even—''

''Just get them into Wheeling Hall. Okay? We can talk later.''

Lifting the microphone Nicholas said, addressing every cubby in the tank, ''People, this is President St. James and I'm sorry but we've all got to be at Wheeling Hall in ten minutes. Come as you are; don't worry about that—a bathrobe is fine. It's grave news.''

Nunes murmured, ''Yancy'll speak. For sure; they told me.''

''The Protector,'' Nicholas said into the mike, and heard his voice boom from each end of the deserted clinic corridor, as it was everywhere else in the great subsurface ant tank of fifteen hundred human souls, "is going to address us, I understand. And he'll accept questions."

He rang off, feeling defeated. It was not a reasonable time to give them bad news. And with Souza and the quota and the audit to come—

"I can't leave my patient," Carol said.

Upset, Nunes said, "But I was told to assemble everyone, Doctor."

"Then," Carol said, with that superlative intelligence that made Nicholas both fear and adore her, "Mr. Souza must get up and come, too. If the edict is to be fully obeyed."

It got through; Nunes, for all his bureaucratic rigidity, his almost neurotic determination to fulfill to the letter each order coaxed down to them—via him—nodded. "Okay, you stay here." To Nicholas he said, "Let's go." He started off, burdened by their mass consciences; his main task was to supervise their loyalty: Nunes was the tank's pol-com, its political commissioner.

Five minutes later Nicholas St. James sat stiffly, formally, in his President's chair, slightly elevated, in row one of Wheeling Hall; behind him they had all assembled, shifted and rustled, murmured and stirred, everyone, including himself, gazing at the floor-to-ceiling vidscreen. This was their window—their sole window—on the above world, and they took rather seriously what was received on its giant surface.

He wondered if Rita had heard the announcement or if she still blissfully loitered in the shower, calling a few remarks to him now and then.

"Any improvement? Nunes whispered to Nicholas. "In old Souza?"

"In pancreatitis—are you kidding?" The Commissioner was an idiot.

"I've passed on fifteen memos," Nunes said, "to them up top."

"And not one of the fifteen," Nicholas said, "was a formal request for an artiforg pancreas that Carol could surgically graft in."

"I just begged for a suspension on the audit." Pleadingly, Nunes said, "Nick, politics is the art of the possible; we might get a suspension, but we won't get on artiforg pancreas; they're just not available. Instead we've got to write off Souza and escalate one of the lesser mechanics like Winton or Bobbs or—"

All at once the great communal screen turned from lusterless gray to beaming white. And the speaker system said, "Good evening."

In Wheeling Hall the audience of fifteen hundred mumbled, "Good evening." It was a legal formality, in that no aud-receptor carried anything up; the lines carried data only one way: down. From above to below.

"News bulletin," the announcer's voice continued. On the screen a stopped-tape: buildings caught and suspended in half-disintegration. And then the tape traveled on. And the buildings, with a roar like the odious tap-tap-tapping of distant, alien drums, pitched into dust and rained down, dissolved; smoke took their place, and, like ants, countless leadies who had inhabited Detroit spilled out and ran, as if from a tipped-over quart jar. They were squashed systematically by invisible forces.

The aud-track grew; the drums drifted foward and the camera, no doubt from an eye-spy Wes-Dem satellite, panned up on one great public building, library, church, school or bank; perhaps all of these combined. It showed, somewhat slowed down, the solidity of the structure as it demolecularized. Objects have been carried back to their dust-origin again. And it could have been us up there, not leadies, because he himself had lived a year in Detroit as a child.

Thank god for all of them, Commies and U.S. citizens alike, that the war had broken out on a colony world, in a hassle as to which bloc, Wes-Dem or Pac-Peop, held the bigger-dog's share. Because in that first year of war on Mars the populations of Earth had been hurried underground. And, he thought, we're still here and it isn't good but it beats *that*; he watched the screen fixedly, saw a flock of leadies melt—hence the name—and, to his horror, still try to run while melting. He looked away.

"Awful," Commissioner Nunes, beside him, muttered, gray-faced.

All at once in the empty seat to Nicholas' right Rita appeared, in bathrobe and slippers; with her came Nicholas' kid brother, Stu. Both, staring at the screen, said nothing to him, as if he weren't there. In fact each person in Wheeling Hall was isolated, now, by the catastrophe on the giant TV screen, and the announcer, then, said it for them.

"This—was—Detroit. May 19th. Year of God 2025. Amen."

It only took a few seconds, once the defensive shield around a city had been broken, to get in and do this.

For fifteen years Detroit had existed intact. Well, Marshal Harenzany, meeting in the thoroughly protected Kremlin with the Supreme Soviet, could pay a painter to paint, as symbol of a direct hit, a tiny spire on the door of their chamber. Chalk up one more U.S. city for their side.

And, in Nicholas' mind, through the horror of seeing this decapitation of one of the few-remaining heads of Western Civilization—which he really did believe in and love—there came the niggling, selfish, personal thought once more. *It means a higher quota*. More must be achieved underground as less, every day, remained above.

Nunes murmured, "Yancy will explain, now. How it happened to happen. So get ready." And Nunes of course was right, because the Protector never gave up; he had that grand turtlelike unwillingness, which Nicholas admired in the man, to admit that this blow was mortal. And yet—

They did get to us, Nicholas realized . . . and even you, Talbot Yancy, our spir-pol-mil leader, brave enough to live in your surface fortress in the Rockies: even you, good friend, can't undo what's just been done.

"My fellow Americans," Yancy's voice came, and it was not even weary. Nicholas blinked, startled by the vigor. Yancy seemed almost unaffected, to have remained true to the *stoa,* to his West Point heritage; he viewed it all, accepted and understood, but no emotion unhinged his calm reason.

"You have seen," Yancy continued in his low, late middle-age voice, that of a seasoned old warrior, ramrod in body, clear in mind; good for a few more years . . . not like the husk, the dying thing in the clinic bed over which Carol watched. "—a terrible thing. Nothing is left of Detroit and as you know a good deal of war material has emerged by her fair autofacs, all these years, and now that is lost. But we have sacrificed no human life, the one commodity which we cannot, will not, relinquish."

"Good point," Nunes muttered, jotting notes.

Beside Nicholas, all at once, Carol Tigh appeared, in her white smock, low shoes; he rose, instinctively, stood to face her.

"He passed away," Carol said. "Souza. Just now. I at once froze him; I was right there at the bed, so there was no time loss. Brain-tissue won't have suffered. He just—went." She tried to smile, and then tears filled her eyes. It shocked him; he had never seen Carol cry, and something in him was horrified, as if it was wicked, this that he saw.

"We shall endure this," the aud-track of the coax transmission from the Estes Park fortress continued, and now, on the screen, Yancy's face appeared and the war, the rolling clouds of matter in suspension or turned to hot gas, faded. And it was a stiff, firm man at a large oak desk in some hidden spot where Soviet, even the awful deadly new Sino-twenty red-dot missiles, had never found him.

Nicholas got Carol seated, got her attention turned to the screen.

"With each passing day," Yancy said, and he spoke with pride, a good and reasonable pride, "we grow stronger. Not weaker. *You* are stronger." And by god he looked, then, directly at Nicholas and Carol and Dale Nunes and Stu and Rita and all the rest of them at the Tom Mix, at every one of them except Souza, who was dead; and when you are dead, Nicholas realized, no one, not even the Protector, can tell you that you are growing stronger. And when you died just now, we also died. Unless that pancreas, at whatever cost, from whatever ugly blackmarket source which robs a military hospital, can be obtained.

Sooner or later, Nicholas realized, despite the law against it, I will have to go up to the surface.

THREE

When the I-am-larger-than-you image of Talbot Yancy's leather and iron face had left the screen and the lackluster gray had returned, Commissioner Dale Nunes hopped to his feet and said to the assembly, "And now, folks. Questions."

The audience remained inert. As inert as it could manage—and get away with it.

Required to by his elected status, Nicholas rose and stood by Dale. "It must be a colloquy between us and the Estes Park Government," he said.

From the back of Wheeling Hall a sharp voice—it could have been male or female—said, "President St. James, did Maury Souza die? I see Dr. Tigh here."

Nicholas said, "Yes. But he's in quick-freeze so there's still hope. Now, people, you've listened to the Protector. Before that you saw the infiltration and demolition of Detroit. You know we're already behind in our quota; we must supply twenty-five leadies this month, and next—"

"What next month?" a voice from the multitude, bitter and dispirited, said. "We won't be here next month."

"Oh yes," Nicholas answered. "We can survive an audit. Let me remind you. The initial penalty is only a cut in food supply of five percent. Only after that can draft notices be served on any of us, and even then it would halt at a decimation—one man from each group of ten. Only if we fail three months running do we face possible—I say *possible*—closure. But we always have legal remedy; we can send our attorney before the High Court at Estes Park, and I assure you we will, before we surrender to a closure."

A voice called, "Have you again asked for a replacement chief mechanic?"

"Yes," Nicholas said. But there are no more Maury Souzas in the world, he thought. Except in other tanks. And out of—what is the number last given?—out of one hundred and sixty thousand ant tanks in the Western Hemisphere none is going to negotiate a release of a really adequate chief mechanic, even if we could somehow make contact with a few of those other tanks. Any more than five years ago when that tank to the north, the Judy Garland, bored that horizontal shaft through to us and pleaded—literally pleaded—just for a loan of Souza. For one month. And we said no.

"All right," Commissioner Nunes said briskly, since no voluntary questions had arisen. "I'll make a spotcheck to see if the Protector's message got across." He pointed to a young married couple. "What was the cause of the failure of our defensive screen around Detroit? Rise and give your names, please."

The young couple reluctantly rose; the husband said, "Jack and Myra Frankis. Our failure was due to the introduction of the new Pac-Peop Type Three Galatea spatter-missile that infiltrated in submolecular particles. I guess. Something like that." He hopefully reseated himself, drawing his wife down beside him.

"All right," Nunes said; that was acceptable. "And why has Pac-Peop technology forged ahead of ours temporarily?" He glanced around, spied a victim to be interrogated. "Is it a failure of our leadership?"

The middle-aged, spinsterish lady rose. "Miss Gertrude Prout. No, it is not due to a failure of our leadership." She instantly sat down again.

"What then," Nunes said, still addressing her, "is it due to? Would you please rise, madam, in giving your response? Thank you." Miss Prout had again risen. "Did *we* fail?" Nunes prompted her. "Not this tank but we tankers, producers of war material, in general."

"Yes," Miss Prout said in her frail, obedient voice. "We failed to provide—" She faltered; she could not recall what they had failed to provide. There was a strained, unhappy silence.

Nicholas took charge. "People, we produce the basic instrument by which the war is conducted; it's because leadies can live on a radioactive surface among a multiform culture of bacteria and chlinesterase-destroying nerve gas—"

"Cholinesterase," Nunes corrected.

"—that we're alive. We owe our lives to these constructs built down in our shops. That's all Commissioner Nunes means. It's vital to understand why we must—"

"I'll handle this," Nunes said quietly.

Nicholas said, "No, Dale. I will."

"You already made one unpatriotic statement. The cholinesterase-destroying nerve gas was a U.S. invention. Now, I can *order* you to take your seat."

"However," Nicholas said, "I won't. These people are tired; this is not the time to badger them. Souza's death—"

"This is *exactly* the time to badger them," Nunes said, "because, and I am trained, Nick, from the Berlin Psychiatric Waffen-Institute, by Mrs. Morgen's own clinicians, to *know*." He raised his voice, addressing the audience. "As you all realize, our chief mechanic was—"

A hostile, jeering voice sounded from the rows. "Tell you what: we'll give you a bag of turnips, Commissioner. Pol-Com Nunes, *sir*. And let's see the bottle of blood you can squeeze out. Okay?" People, here and there, murmured in agreement, in approval.

"I told you," Nicholas said to the commissioner, who had flushed and was strangling his notes with his spasmodically clenching fingers. "Now will you let them go back to bed?"

Aloud, Nunes said, "There is a disagreement between your elected president and I. As a compromise, I will ask only one more question." He paused, surveyed them all; in weary fear they waited. The sole hostile, articulated vocal entity was silent, now; Nunes had them because Nunes, alone in the tank, was not a citizen but an official of Wes-Dem itself and could, if he ordered, have living, human police slide down the chute from above or, if Brose's agents weren't immediately in the vicinity, then a commando team of General Holt's veteran armed leadies.

"The Commissioner," Nicholas announced, "will ask one question. And then, thank god, let's go to bed." He seated himself.

Nunes, reflecting, said in a slow, cold voice, "How can we make up to Mr. Yancy for our failure?"

To himself Nicholas moaned. But no one, not even Nicholas, had the legal power or any kind of power to halt the man whom the hostile, earlier voice from the audience had correctly called their pol-com. And yet under the Law this was not altogether bad. Because through Commissioner Nunes a direct human link existed between their tank and the Estes Park Government; theoretically by way of Nunes they could answer back and the colloquy, even now, within the heart of the worldwide war, could exist between the tanks and the government.

But it was hard on the tankers to be subjected to Dale Nunes' rah-rah tactics whenever Dale—or rather his superiors above ground—saw fit, such as now, at bedtime. But look at the alternative.

It had been suggested to him (and he had promptly, at great and deliberate effort, forgotten forever the names of those who had come to him) that their pol-com be quietly dispatched some night. No, Nicholas had said. It won't work. Because they'll send another. And—Dale Nunes is a man. Not a force. And would you prefer to deal with Estes Park as a *force,* on your TV screen, which you could see and hear . . . but not talk back to?

So as sore as Commissioner Nunes made him, Nicholas accepted the necessity of his presence in the Tom Mix. The radicals who had come slipping up, late one night, with their idea of instant, easy solution to the pol-com problem, had been thoroughly, firmly dissuaded. Or at least so Nicholas hoped.

Anyhow Nunes was still alive. So apparently his argument to the radicals had been convincing . . . and this was three years ago, when Nunes had first put in his eager-beaver appearance.

He wondered if Dale Nunes had ever guessed. Imagined how close he had come to assassination, and that it had been Nicholas who had talked them out of it.

How interesting it would be to know what Nunes' reaction would be. Gratitude?

Or—contempt.

At this moment, Carol was motioning to him, beckoning in sight of the assembled community here at Wheeling Hall. While Dale Nunes looked up and down the rows for someone to answer his question, Carol—incredibly—was indicating to Nicholas that she and he leave together, now.

Beside him his wife Rita saw the gesture, the summons; wooden-faced, she stared straight ahead, then, as if she had seen nothing. And, as he found his target, Dale Nunes saw, too, and frowned.

However, Nicholas obediently accompanied Carol up the aisle and out of Wheeling Hall, into the deserted corridor and seclusion.

"What in god's name," he said to her as he and she stood together, "do you want?" The way Nunes had looked at them as they departed . . . he would be hearing in due time from the commissioner.

"I want you to certify the death papers," Carol said, walking toward the elevator. "For poor old Maury—"

"But why now?" There was more; he knew it.

She said nothing; both of them were silent on the trip down to the clinic, to the freeze locker in which the rigid body lay—he glanced under the wrapper briefly, then emerged from the locker to sign the forms which Carol had laid out, five copies in all, neatly typed and ready to be sent up by vidline to the bureaucrats on the surface.

Then, from the buttoned front of her white smock, Carol brought forth a tiny electronic instrument which he recognized as a you-don't-know-I-have-it aud-recorder. She extracted the spool of tape, unlocked the steel drawer of a cabinet of what appeared to be medical supplies—and exposed to his sight, briefly, other spools of tape and other electronic instruments, none of them related as far as he could see to her medical work.

"What's going on?" he said, this time more controlledly. Obviously she wanted him to witness this, the aud-recorder, the reservoir of tape which she kept locked away from anyone else's sight. He knew her as well, as intimately, as did anyone in the Tom Mix, and yet this was news to him.

Carol said, "I made an aud tape of Yancy's speech. The part I was there for, anyhow."

"Those other spools of aud tape in that cabinet?"

"All of Yancy. Former speeches. Dating back over the past year."

"Is that legal to do?"

Carol said, as she gathered the five copies of Maury Souza's death-forms together and inserted them into the slot of the Xerox-transmitter which would put them on the wire to the Estes Park archives, "As a matter of fact it *is* legal. I looked it up."

Relieved, he said, "Sometimes I think you're nuts." Her mind was always off in some odd direction, flashing and echoing in its fullness, and baffling him eternally; he could never keep up with her, and so his awe of her continually grew. "Explain," he said.

''Have you noticed,'' Carol said, ''that Yancy, in his speeches in late February, when he used the phrase *coup de grâce*, he pronounced it *gras*. And in March he pronounced it—'' From the steel-doored cabinet she brought forth a chart with entries, which she now consulted. ''March twelfth. Pronounced *coo de grah*. Then, in April, on the fifteenth, it was *gras* again.'' She glanced up alertly, eyed Nicholas.

He shrugged wearily, irritably. ''Let me get to bed; let's talk about this some other—''

''Then,'' Carol said, inflexibly, ''on May third in a speech, he once more used the term. That memorable speech in which he informed us that our destruct of Leningrad completely—'' She glanced up from her chart. ''It could well be the *coo de grah*. No *s*. Back to his earlier pronunciation.'' She restored the chart to the cabinet, then, and relocked the cabinet. He noted that it took not only a metal insert key but the pressure of her fingerprints; even with a duplicate key—or her key—the cabinet would remain closed. It would open only for her.

''So?''

Carol said, ''I don't know. But it means something. Who fights the surface war?''

''Leadies.''

''And where are the humans?''

''What is this, Commissioner Nunes all over again, interrogating people at bedtime when they ought to be—''

''They're in ant tanks,'' Carol said. ''Below surface. Like us. Now, when you apply for an artiforg you are told they're available only to military hospitals, presumably on the surface.''

''I don't know,'' he said, ''or care, where the military hospitals are. All I know is that they have the priority and we don't.''

Carol said, ''If leadies are fighting the war, what are in the military hospitals? Leadies? No. Because they send damaged leadies down to shops, our shop for instance. And a leady is a metal construct and it has no pancreas. There are a *few* humans on the surface, of course; the Estes Park Government. And in Pac-Peop, the Soviet. Are the pancreases for them?''

He was silent; she had him completely.

''Something,'' she said, ''is wrong. There can't be military hospitals because there aren't civilians or soldiers who've been maimed in the fighting and who need artiforgs. Yet—they won't release the artiforgs to us. To me, for instance, for Souza; even though they know we can't survive without Souza. Think about it, Nick."

"Hmm," he said.

Carol said quietly. "You're going to have to come up with something better than 'Hmm,' Nick. And soon."

FOUR

The next morning as soon as she awoke, Rita said, "I saw you go off with that woman, last night, that Carol Tigh. Why?"

Nicholas, grubby and confused, not yet shaved, without having had the chance to splash cold water on his face or brush his teeth, murmured, "It had to do with signing the death certificate forms of Souza. Strictly business."

He padded off to the bathroom, which he and Rita shared with the cubby to their right—and found the door locked.

"Okay, Stu," he said. "Finish shaving and unlock the door."

The door opened; there was his younger brother, sure enough, at the mirror, shaving away for all he was worth, guiltily. "Don't mind me," Stu said. "Go ahead and—"

His brother's wife, Edie, said shrilly from their cubby, "We got into the bathroom first this morning, Nick; your wife had it for a whole hour last night, showering. So would you please wait."

Giving up he shut the bathroom door, padded to their kitchen—which they did *not* share with anyone, either to right or left—and started the coffee heating on the stove. Last night's to be reheated; he did not have the energy to brew a fresh pot, and anyhow their allocation of synthetic beans was low. They would be entirely out before month's end anyhow, would be begging, borrowing or bartering with fellow tankers, offering their supply of sugar—neither he nor Rita used much sugar—in exchange for the odd little brown ersatz beans.

And of coffee beans, he thought, I could use an endless amount. If there was such a thing. But, like everything else, the (as marked on invoices) syn-cof-bnz were severely rationed. And after all these years he accepted it—intellectually. But his body craved more.

He could still remember how real coffee, in the pretank days, had tasted. Nineteen, he remembered; I was in my first year of college, just started drinking coffee instead of malted milks, kid stuff. I had just begun to put on maturity . . . and then this.

But, as Talbot Yancy, beaming or frowning, whatever was appropriate, would say, 'At least we weren't incinerated, as we had anticipated. Because we did have that whole year to get under, and we must never forget.' So Nicholas was not forgetting; as he stood reheating last night's synthetic coffee he thought of himself incinerated fifteen years ago, or the cholinesterase of his body destroyed by the hideous U.S. nerve gas weapon, the worst so far conjured up by insane idiots in high places in what had been Washington, D.C., themselves blessed with the antidote, atropine, and hence safe . . . safe from the nerve gas made at the Newport Chemical Plant in Western Indiana as contracted for by the still-notorious FMC Corporation, but not safe from the missiles of the USSR. And he appreciated this and was glad, appreciated the fact that he was here and alive to drink this syn-cof brew, bitter as it was.

The bathroom door opened and Stu said, "I'm finished."

Nicholas started for the bathroom. And then—there was a knock at the cubby's hall door.

Going to it, bowing to the necessity created by his elected office, Nicholas opened the hall door and found himself facing what he recognized at once to be a committee. Jorgenson, Haller, Flanders—again at his door, the activists of the tank and behind them Peterson and Grandi and Martino and Giller and Christenson; their supporters. He sighed. And let them in.

Soundlessly—they knew enough to be that—the committee entered his cubby, filled it up. As soon as the hall door was shut, Jorgenson said, "Here's how we're going to work it, President. We stayed up to four this morning thrashing it out." His voice was low, hard, determined.

"Thrashed out what?" Nicholas said, but he knew.

"We'll handle that pol-com, that Nunes. We'll stage a fracas on floor twenty; access to twenty is hard because of the way those crates of leady components are piled. It'll take him half an hour to break up the fight. And that'll give you time. The time you need."

"Coffee?" Nicholas said, returning to the kitchen.

"Today," Jorgenson said.

Not answering, Nicholas drank his coffee. And wished he were in the bathroom. Locked in where his wife, his brother, his brother's wife and this committee—none of them could get to him. Even Carol, he thought. He wished he could—at least for a minute—lock them all out. And just sit, in the loneliness and silence of the bathroom; just be.

And then if he could just be, maybe he could think. Find himself. Not Nicholas St. James, the president of ant tank the Tom Mix, but himself the man; and then he would know, really know, if Commissioner Nunes were right and the law was the law. Or if Carol Tigh were right, and there was something strange or wrong—whatever she had happened onto with her reservoir of aud-tapes of Yancy's speeches over the last year. *Coup de grace,* he thought. *That's this, right here, for me, the dispatching conk over the head.*

He turned to confront the committee of activists, his coffee cup in hand. "Today," he said, mocking Jorgenson, whom he didn't particularly care for; Jorgenson was a red-necked, heavy-set type, the beer and pretzel sort.

"We know it has to be done in a hurry," Haller spoke up, his voice low; he was conscious of Rita, who stood at the mirror fixing her hair, and it made him nervous—in fact the whole committee was nervous. Afraid, of course, of the cop, the pol-com. And yet they had come here anyhow.

"Let me tell you the situation as regards artiforgs," Nicholas began, but at once Flanders broke in.

"We know all there is to know. All we *want* to know. Listen, President; *we know the plot they've hatched up.*" The six or seven members of the committee glared at him with nervous anger and frustration; the small cubby—or rather, standard-sized—in which Nicholas lived and now stood writhed with their discomfort.

"Who?" he asked.

Jorgenson said, "The bigshot at Estes Park. Who run everything. Tell their mickey mouse size little thugs like Nunes who to put the finger on."

"What's the plot?"

"The plot," Flanders said, almost stammering in his ticlike tenseness, "is they're short on food and they want a pretext to abolish an ant tank here and there; we don't know how many they want to shut down, and force the tankers up to the surface to die—many tanks, maybe, or just a few . . . it depends on how much trouble they're having with rations."

"So see," Haller said beseechingly to Nicholas, his voice rising (the man next to him punched him and he instantly dropped his voice to a whisper), "they need a pretext. They get it as soon as we fail to supply our monthly quota of leadies. And last night after the TV films of Detroit getting it, when Yancy announced that quotas would be upped—that's how we figured it out; they're going to up the quotas and all the tanks that can't meet the new quotas will be abolished. Like us. And up there—" He gestured ceilingward. "We'll die."

Rita, at the mirror, said harshly, "Like you want Nicholas to die when he goes up after that artiforg."

Spinning, Haller said, "Mrs. St. James, he's our president; we elected him—that's *why* we elected him, so he'd—you know. Help us."

"Nick is not your father," Rita said. "Not a magician. Not a wheel in the Estes Park Government. He can't manufacture an artificial pancreas. He can't—"

"Here's the money," Jorgenson said. And handed Nicholas a fat white envelope. "All Wes-Dem fifty notes. Forty in all. Twenty thousand Wes-Dem dollars. Late last night while Nunes was snoozing we went all over the tank, collecting." This sum represented the wages of half the tank for—he could not compute, under the stress of the moment. But for a long, long time. The committee had worked very hard.

Rita said to the committee, her voice harsh, "Then you do it; you collected the money. Draw lots. Don't stick my husband with this." Her voice became gentle. "Nunes is less apt to notice one of you missing than Nick. It might even be several days before he checks up, but once Nick goes Nunes will know, and—"

"And what, Mrs. St. James?" Haller said, determinedly but politely. "There's nothing Nunes can do, once President St. James is out of here up the chute and onto the surface."

Rita said, "When he returns, Jack. Then Nunes will execute him."

To himself Nicholas thought, And the hell of it is, I probably won't even get back.

Jorgenson, with clear, sincere reluctance, reached into the jacket of his work overalls, brought out a small object, flat like a cigarette case.

"Mr. President," he said huskily, in a formal, dignified tone, that of an official bearer of tidings, "Do you know what this is?"

Sure, Nicholas thought. *It's a shop-made bomb. And, if I don't go, and go today, you'll wire it somewhere here in my cubby or my office, set it timewise or booby-trap it wirewise and it'll go off and blow me to bits and also probably my wife and perhaps even my kid brother and his wife or whoever is in my office with me at the time, if it's in my office. And you men—enough of you, anyhow—are electricians; professional wirers and component-assemblers, as we all are to a certain extent . . . you'll know how to do it so it'll have a one hundred percent chance of success. Therefore,* he realized, *if I don't go to the surface your committee absolutely and for sure will destroy me—plus perhaps innocent others around me—and if I do go, Nunes will be tipped off by some stooge among the fifteen hundred citizens of the tank and he'll shoot me when I'm approximately half-way up the chute on my illegal—and this is wartime and military law obtains—journey to the surface.*

Flanders said, "President, listen; I know you think you're going to have to try to make it up the chute, with those leadies always or nearly always hanging around up there with a damaged leady to drop down . . . but *listen.*"

"A tunnel," Nicholas said.

"Yes. We bored it this morning early, as soon as the autofac power-supply came on to drown out the noise of the scoop and the other junk we had to use. It's absolutely vertical. A masterpiece."

Jorgenson said, "It takes off from the roof of room BAA on floor one; a storeroom for reduction gears for type II leadies. A chain goes up it and is staked—securely, I guarantee; I swear—at the surface, hidden among some—"

"Lies," Nicholas said.

Blinking, Jorgenson said, "No, honest—"

"You couldn't bore a vertical tube to the surface in two hours," Nicholas said. "What's the truth?"

After a long, disheartened pause, Flanders mumbled, "We got the tunnel started. We got up about forty feet. The portable scoop is secured there. We figured we'd get you in the tunnel, with oxygen equipment, and then seal it off at the bottom, to deaden the vibrations and noise."

"And," Nicholas said, "I'd lodge myself there in the tunnel and scoop away until I emerged. How long had you calculated it'd take me, working alone and with only that small portable scoop, none of the big gear?"

After an interval someone among the committee murmured. "Two days. We've got food and water already, in fact one of those self-contained spaceman suits they used to use when there were flights to Mars. Compensation for moisture, waste-material—everything. It still beats trying to make it up the chute, with those leadies up there."

"And Nunes," Nicholas said, "at the bottom."

"Nunes will be breaking up the fight on floor—"

"Okay," Nicholas said. "I'll do it."

They gaped at him.

Rita, half to herself, let out a sob, a cry of despair.

To her, Nicholas said, "It beats being blown to bits. They mean it." He indicated the small flat packet which Jorgenson held. *Ipse dixit,* he said to himself; I know *that* much foreign language. An assertion made but not proved. And in this case I don't want to see it proved; even our pol-com, Commissioner Nunes, would be appalled by what that device can do when triggered off.

He went into the bathroom, then, and shut—and locked—the door after him. For this moment, brief as it was, of quiet. Of being a mere biochemical organism, not President St. James of the Tom Mix World War III antiseptic subsurface communal living tank, established in June of 2010. A.D. *Long* A.D., he thought; a hell of a long time After Christ.

What I ought to do, he decided, is come back, not with the artiforg, but with the Bag Plague for you all. Every single last one of you.

His bitterness surprised him. But of course it was superficial. Because, and he realized it as he began running hot water by which to shave, the actuality is that I'm a frightened man. I don't want to lodge myself for forty-eight hours in that vertical tunnel, waiting to hear Nunes cut through below me or a team of Brose's leady police pick up the sound of my scoop from above, and then, if not that, emerge into the radioactivity, the rubble, the war. Into the pox of death from which we've fled, hidden ourselves: *I don't want to emerge on the surface, even for a necessary cause.*

He despised himself for his attitude; it was hard, as he began to lather his jowls, to look at himself in the mirror. In fact it was impossible. So he opened the bathroom door on Stu and Edie's side and called, ''Hey, can I borrow your electric razor?''

''Sure,'' his kid brother said, and produced it.

''What's the matter, Nick?'' Edie said, with unusual—for her—compassion. ''Good lord, you look just awful.''

''I am awful,'' Nicholas said, and seated himself on their rumpled, unmade bed to shave. ''It takes force,'' he said. ''to make me do the right thing.'' He didn't feel like talking about it; he shaved in introverted silence.

FIVE

Over green countryside, the fields, the meadows, the open world of North American forests with occasional clusters of buildings, demesnes at odd, unexpected locations, Joseph Adams flew by flapple from his own demesne on the Pacific where he was dominus to the Agency in New York City, where he was one Yance-man among many. His work day, the longed-for and at last achieved Monday, had come.

Beside him on the seat lay a leather briefcase, initialed JWA in gold, which contained his handwritten speech. Behind him, crowded together in the rear seat, four leadies from his personal entourage.

Meanwhile, by vidphone, he discussed biz with his associate from the Agency, Verne Lindblom. Verne, not an idea man, not a user of words but an artist in the visual sense, was in a better position than Joseph Adams to know exactly what their superior Ernest Eisenbludt in Moscow had in mind scenewise, was up to at the studio.

"It's San Francisco next," Lindblom said. "I'm building it now."

"What scale?" Adams asked.

"No scale."

"*Life*-size?" Adams was incredulous. "Brose has okayed it? This isn't another of Eisenbludt's hare-brained storms of creative—"

"Just a segment. Nob Hill and overlooking the bay. Should take about a month to construct; there's no rush. Hell, they just ran that Detroit sequence last night." Lindblom sounded relaxed. And, as a master craftsman, he could afford to be. Idea men were one-fourth poscred a dozen, but the actual fabricators—they were a closed guild which even Brose, with all his agents, couldn't crack. They were like the red-stained-glass makers of France in the Thirteenth century; if they perished their skills perished with them.

"Want to hear my new speech?"

"God no," Lindblom said genially.

"It's hand-done." Adams spoke with humility. "I kicked out that gadget; it was getting me into a rut."

"Listen," Lindblom said, all of a sudden serious. "I heard a rumor. You're going to be pulled off speeches and put onto a special project. Don't ask me what; my source didn't know." He added, "A Footeman told me."

"Hmm." He tried to look calm, to show poise. But inside he felt queasy. Undoubtedly—since it took priority over his regular job—this emanated from Brose's bureau. And there was something about Brose and his special projects that he did not like. Although just what . . .

"It's something you might enjoy," Lindblom said. "Has to do with archeology."

Adams grinned. "I get it. Soviet missiles are going to destruct Carthage."

"And you're going to program Hector and Priam and all those fellas. Get out your Sophocles. Your pony or cribsheet or whatever."

" 'My friends,' " Adams intoned in solemn parody, " 'I have grave news for you, but we shall overcome. The new Soviet ICBM Hatcheck Girl A-3 missile, with a C-warhead, has strewn radioactive common table salt over an area surrounding Carthage fifty square miles wide, but this only goes to show—' " He paused. "What did Carthage produce, autofac-wise? Vases?" Anyhow that was Lindblom's job. The display of postcards, scanned by the multifax lens-system of the TV cameras at Eisenbludt's mammoth, intricate—in fact endlessly prop-filled—studios in Moscow. " 'This, my good people and friends, is all that remains, but I am informed by General Holt that our own strike, utilizing our newly developed offensive terror weapon, the Polyphemus X-B peashooter, has decimated the entire war fleet of Athens, and with god's help we shall—' "

"You know," Lindblom said meditatively, from the tiny speaker of the flapple's vidset. "You'd feel damn funny if one of Brose's people were monitoring this."

Below, a wide river like wet silver wiggled from north to south, and Joseph Adams leaned out to view the Mississippi and acknowledge its beauty. No reconcrews had accomplished this; what glistened in the morning sun was an element of the old creation. The original world which did not need to be recreated, reconned, because it had never departed. This sight, like that of the Pacific, always sobered him, because it meant that something had proved stronger; something had escaped.

"Let him monitor," Adams said, filled with vigor; he drew strength from the wavering silver line below—strength enough to ring off, cut the switch of the vidset. Just in case Brose *was* monitoring.

And then, beyond the Mississippi, he saw a manmade focus of upright, hard structures, and these, too, gave him a funny feeling. Because these were the Ozymandias-who-he? great conapt dwellings erected by that busy builder, Louis Runcible. That one-man ant army that, in its marches, did not gnaw down with its mandibles but set up, with its many metal arms, one gigantic dormlike structure, including kids' play-grounds, swimming pools, ping-pong tables and dart boards.

Ye shall know the truth, Adams thought, and by this thou shalt enslave. Or, as Yancy would put it, "My fellow Americans. I have before me a document so sacred and momentous that I am going to ask you to—" And so on. Now he felt tired, and he had not even reached 580 Fifth Avenue, New York and the Agency, had not begun his day. Alone, at his demesne on the Pacific, he felt the weedy, twisted fog of loneliness grow by day and by night and clog the passages of his throat; here, in transit across the reconned and not-yet-oh-lord but soon-to-be-reconned areas—and of course the still hot-spots, which lay like ringworm circles every so often—he felt this uneasy shame. He glowed with guilt, not because recon was bad, but—*it* was bad, and he knew who and what *it* was.

I wish there was one missile left, he said to himself. In orbit. And we could touch one of those quaint old-time buttons the brass once had at their disposal, and that missile would go *pfoooooom!* At Geneva. And Stanton Brose.

By god, Adams thought, maybe I will program the 'vac one day not with a speech, even a good speech like the one here beside me that I got off last night finally, but the very simple, calm statement of what gives. I'll get through the 'vac to the sim itself, then onto aud and vid tape, because since that's autonomic there's no editing, unless of course Eisenbludt happens to stroll in . . . and even he, technically, can't touch the speech part of the reading matter.

And then the sky will fall in.

But that ought to be interesting to watch, Adams mused. If you could get far enough off *to* watch.

"Listen," he would program to Megavac 6-V. And all those funny little dingbats that the 'vac had in it would spin, and out of the sim's mouth would come the utterance but transformed; the simple word would be given that fine, corroborative detail to supply verisimilitude to what was—let us face it, he thought caustically—an otherwise *incredibly* bald and unconvincing narrative. What entered Megavac 6-V as a mere *logos* would emerge for the TV lenses and mikes to capture in the guise of a pronouncement, one which nobody in his right mind—especially if encapsulated subsurface for fifteen years—would doubt. But—it would be a paradox, because Yancy himself would be pontificating it; like the old saw, "Everything I say is a lie," this would confound itself, tie its skinny, slippery self into a good hard sailor's knot.

And what would be achieved? Since, after all, Geneva would pounce on it . . . and we are not amused, Joseph Adams articulated within his own mind, the voice which he, like every other Yance-man, had long ago introjected. The super ego, as the prewar intellectuals had called it, or, before that the ayenbite of inwyt, or some such rustic Medieval old phrase.

Conscience.

Stanton Brose, holed up in his castlelike *Festung* in Geneva like some pointed-hat alchemist, like a corrupted, decayed but, as they say, shining and stinking, glowing pale white fish of the sea, a dead mackerel with clouded-over glaucomalike eyes . . . or did Brose look like this?

Only twice in his life had he, Joseph Adams, actually seen Brose in the flesh. Brose was old. What was it, eighty-two? And not lean. Not a stick, ribboned with the streamers of smoked, dried flesh; Brose at eighty-two weighed a ton, waddled and rolled, pitched, with his mouth drizzling and his nose as well . . . and yet the heart still beat, because of course it was an artiforg heart, and an artiforg spleen and an artiforg and so on.

But yet the authentic Brose remained. Because the brain was not artiforg; there was no such thing; to manufacture an artiforg brain—to have done so, when that firm, Arti-Gan Corporation of Phoenix, existed, back before the war—would have been to go into what Adams liked to think of as the "genuine simulated silver" business . . . his term for what he considered with its multiform spawned offspring: the universe of authentic fakes.

And that universe, he reflected, which you would think you could enter the IN door of, pass through and then exit by the OUT door of in say roughly two minutes . . . that universe, like Eisenbludt's prop-heaps in the Moscow film studios, was endless, was room beyond room; the OUT door of one room was only the IN door for the next.

And now, if Verne Lindblom were correct, if the man from the private intelligence corporation, Webster Foote, Limited of London, were correct some new IN door had swung open, given momentum by the hand that reached in all its trembling senility from Geneva . . . in Adams' mind the metaphor, growing, became visual and frightening; he actually experienced the doorway ahead, felt the darkness breathed by it—room lacking light, into which he would soon tread, faced by god knew what task that was not a nightmare, not, like the black, listless fogs from within and without, formless, but—

Too distinct. Spelled out, in graphically unambiguous words, in a memo originating from that damn monster pit, Geneva. General Holt, even Marshal Harenzany who after all was a Red Army officer and not in any sense a Bunthorne sniffing at a sunflower, even Harenzany sometimes *listened*. But the waddling, drizzling, eye-rolling old hulk chuck-full of artiforgs—Brose had greedily ingested artiforg after artiforg of the world's small and dwindling supply—was earless.

Literally. Years ago the organs of that sense had withered away. And Brose had declined artiforg replacements; he *liked* not to hear.

When Brose reviewed each and every TV tape of Yancy's speeches, he did not listen; horribly, or so it seemed to Adams, the fat, semi-dead organism received the aud-portion by direct wire: through electrodes grafted, skillfully implanted years ago, in the proper section of his elderly brain . . . in the one original organ, which *was* Brose, the rest now being, tin-woodmanwise, a mere procession of Arti-Gan Corporation's plastic, complex, never-failing (they had, before the war, proudly carried lifetime guarantees, and in the artiforg business the meaning of the word "lifetime," that is, whether it applied to the life of the object or of the owner was delightfully clear) replacements which lesser men, the Yance-men as a whole had a kind of nominal, formal claim on—in that, while still warehoused in the subsurface storage vaults under Estes Park, the artiforg supplies belonged to the Yancemen as a class and not merely to Brose.

But it didn't quite work out that way. Because when a kidney failed, as had occurred to Shelby Lane, whose demesne up in Oregon Adams had frequently visited—there was no artiforg kidney for Mr. Lane, although in the warehouse three were known to exist. It seemed, and for some reason as he lay in his bed in the master bedroom of his demesne, surrounded by his entourage of worrying leadies, Lane had not seemed convinced by the argument, Brose had put on these three artiforg kidneys what legally was called an *attachment*. He had attached the goddam organs, tied them up, stopped their use, by a complex quasi-legal "prior" claim . . . Lane, pathetically, had taken it to the Recon Dis-In Council which sat perpetually in session at Mexico City, passing judgment on the land-boundary quarrels between demesne owners, a council on which one leady of each type sat; Lane had not exactly lost, but he had quite certainly not won, in that he was dead. He had died while waiting for the issue of attachment to be settled. And—Brose lived on, with the knowledge that he could suffer three more total kidney-failures and survive. And anyone who chose to go before the Recon Dis-In Council would undoubtedly be dead, like Lane, and the litigation would, with the plaintiff, expire.

The fat old louse, Adams thought, and he saw ahead New York City, the spires, the postwar high-rise buildings, the ramps and tunnels, the hovering fruit fly flapples, which, like his own, carried Yance-men to their offices to begin Monday.

And, a moment later, he hovered fruit-fly-like himself, over the especially tall cardinal building 580 Fifth Avenue and the Agency.

The entire city was the Agency, of course; the buildings on each side were as much a part of the machinery as this one omphalos. But here his particular office lay; here he entrenched himself against the competing members of his own class. It was a top job that he held . . . and in his briefcase, which he now picked up expectantly, lay as he well knew top-drawer material.

Maybe Lindblom was right. Maybe the Russians were about to bomb Carthage.

He reached the down ramp of the roof field, touched the hi-speed button, and dropped like a plumb line for his floor and office.

When he entered his office, briefcase in hand, he utterly without a shade or glimpse of warning faced a mound of rubber, winking and blinking, flapping seal-like its pseudopodia and peeping at him while with its slitlike mouth it gaped and grinned, pleased at his dismay; pleased to horrify both by how it physically looked and who it was.

"Mr. Adams. A word with you, sir."

The thing, which had somehow managed to wedge itself into the chair at his desk, was Stanton Brose.

SIX

"Why certainly, Mr. Brose," Joseph Adams said, and under his tongue his salivary glands strained with sickness; he turned his back, then, and set his briefcase down and was amazed at his somatic nausea, his response to finding Brose here in his own office. He was not frightened; not intimidated, not even angered that Brose had managed to walk in despite the elaborate locks, walked in and taken over—none of that counted, because the ill convulsion of his body startled every other reaction out of existence.

"Would you like a moment to compose yourself, Mr. Adams?" The voice, wheedling, thin, like a guy wire plucked by an evil pneumatic spirit.

"Y-yes," Adams said.

"Pardon? I can't hear, you know; I must see your lips."

My lips, Adams thought. He turned. "I need," he said, "a moment. I had flapple trouble." Then he remembered that he had left the four loyal companions, the veteran leadies of his retinue, in the parked flapple. "Would you—" he began, but Brose cut him off, not impolitely but simply as if he were not talking.

"A new project of some importance has arisen," Brose said in his plucked-wire, strumming voice. "You're to do the reading matter on it. It consists of this . . ." Brose paused, then found a vast ugly handkerchief which he dabbled at his mouth with, as if molding the flesh of his face like soft, toothpastelike plastic into proper shape. "No written documents or line transmissions are to exist as to this project; *no records*. All, only, oral face-to-face exchanges between the principals; myself, you, Lindblom who will build the artifacts."

Ha, Adams thought, and exulted. Webster Foote, Limited, the

London-based planetwide private police investigation agency had already snooped, nosed the news into being; Brose, despite his obviously psychopathic security precautions, had lost even as he began. Nothing could have pleased Adams more; he felt the nausea drain away and he lit a cigar, paced about, nodding soberly, showing his willingness to participate in this most vital, secret enterprise. "Yes sir," he said.

"You know Louis Runcible."

"The conapt building man," Adams said.

"Look toward me, Adams."

Looking toward him, Joseph Adams said, "I passed over one of his conapt centers. His dungeons."

"Well," Brose strummed, "they chose to come up. And they didn't have the ability to join us; we couldn't use them so what else but those row-on-row little apts? At least they've got Chinese checkers. And components are more restful to build than assembling complete leadies."

"It is just," Adams said, "that there is a three thousand mile stretch of grass between my demesne and here that I have to pass over every day. Twice. And I wonder sometimes. And I remember how it looked in the old days before the war and before they were induced to go down into those tanks."

"Had they not, Adams, they would be dead."

"Oh," Adams said slowly, "I know they'd be dead; they'd be ash and the leadies would be using that ash to make mortar out of. It's just that sometimes I think of Route 66."

"Whazzat, Adams?"

"A highway. That connected cities."

"A freeway!"

"No, sir. Just a highway; let it pass." And he felt a weariness so strong that he actually thought for a split second that he'd suffered a cardiac arrest or some other fundamental physical collapse; he very carefully stopped inhaling his cigar and seated himself in a guest-type chair facing the desk, and blinked, breathed, wondered what had occurred.

"Okay," Adams continued, "I know Runcible; he's basking in Capetown and he really does try—I know he does—to adequately provide for the tankers who surface; they've got built-in electric ranges, swibbles, wubfur carpeting wall-to-wall, 3-D TV, each group of ten living units has a leady to do chores such as cleaning . . . what's up, Mr. Brose?" He waited, panting with fright.

Brose said, "Recently a hot-spot cooled off in southern Utah, near St. George, where it was . . . the maps still give it. Near the Arizona border. Red rock hills in that area. Runcible's geigers picked up the drop in r.a. before anybody else's, and he got it, staked his claim; the rest." Brose gestured deprecatingly, but with resignation. "In a few days he intends to send in his autonomic 'dozers and start breaking ground for a new constellation of conapts . . . you know, he has all that big primitive heavy-duty construction equipment that he carts all over the world."

"You need that," Adams said, "to build the kind of structures he erects. Those conapts go up fast."

"Well," Brose said, "we want that area."

You liar, Adams thought to himself. He got up, turned his back to Brose and said aloud, "You liar!"

"I can't hear."

Turning back, Adams said, "It's just rock, there. Who wants to put a demesne there? My god, some of us have demesnes that contain a million and a half acres!" He stared at Brose. It can't be true, he said to himself. Runcible got in there first because no one cared enough about that region to want to know the readings; no one paid Webster Foote to have Foote field reps and techs keep tabs on that hot-spot and Runcible got it by default. So don't try to jolly me along, he said to himself, and felt hatred for Brose, now; the nausea was gone and an authentic emotion had replaced it inside him.

Evidently Brose perceived some of this on Adams' face. "I guess that is pretty no-good land, there," Brose admitted. "War or no war."

"If you want me to manage the aud-portion of the project," Adams said, and was almost unhinged to hear himself actually say this to Brose, to the man's face, "you had better tell me the truth. Because I don't feel very good. I was up all night writing a speech—by hand. And the fog bothered me. Fog gets to me; I should never have set up my demesne on the Pacific south of San Francisco. I should have tried down by San Diego."

Brose said, "I'll tell you. Correct; we don't care—no Yance-man with all his marbles could possibly care—about that arid land at the old Utah-Arizona border. Look at these." He managed to flap his pseudopodialike flippers until they connected with a packet which he carried; like a roll of wallpaper samples the document was spread out.

Peering, he saw careful, really lovely drawings. It was like looking over an Oriental silk screen scroll from the—future? Now he saw that the objects depicted were—unnatural. Freak guns with spurious knobs and warts. Electronic hardware that—he intuited from experience—served no purpose. "I don't get it," he said.

"These are artifacts," Brose said, "which Mr. Lindblom will make; superb craftsman that he is he will have no difficulty."

"But what do they do?" All at once Adams understood. These were fake crypto-weapons. And not just that; he saw, as the scroll-like document unrolled in Brose's flippers, additional artifacts.

Skulls.

Some were Homo sapiens.

Some were not.

"All these," Brose said, "Lindblom will manufacture. But you must be consulted first. Because before they are found—"

" 'Found!' "

"These completed objects, made up by Lindblom, using Eisenbludt's studios in Moscow, will be planted on the land Runcible is about to break for his new conapts. However, it must be established in advance that they are of incalculable archeological worth. A series of articles in the prewar scientific journal *Natural World,* which as you know was formerly available to every educated man in the world, must analyze these as—"

The office door opened. Looking wary, Verne Lindblom entered. "I was told to come here," he said to Brose; he glanced, then, at Adams. But said nothing more. However, they both understood; the vid-conversation which had taken place a half hour ago was not to be referred to.

"These," Brose said to Lindblom, "are the scale drawings of the artifacts which you will make to be planted in Southern Utah. At the proper geological stratum." He swiveled the scroll for Lindblom to see; Verne glanced briefly, professionally. "There is a time factor, but I'm sure you can have them ready when needed. The first 'dozer needn't dig them up. Just so they appear before the digging ends and the construction begins."

Lindblom said, "You have someone on Runcible's work crew who'll spot them, if necessary? If they otherwise go unnoticed?" He seemed, to Adams, to understand fundamentally what was going on; someone had already briefed him. He himself, however; he was baffled. But he played along; he continued to study the painstakingly, professionally executed drawings.

"Of course," Brose said. "An engineer named Robert—" He tried to recall; the eighty-two-year-old brain flagged. "Hig," Brose said at last. "Bob Hig. He'll spot them if no one else does, so will you start, then, Lindblom? Eisenbludt knows you're to be given use of every tool and studio facility you need. But he doesn't know what for, and we will keep it limited to as few people as we can, throughout."

"Hig finds them," Lindblom said, "notifies Runcible. Meanwhile—" He glanced at Adams. "You'll have your series in the prewar *Natural World* by some world-famous archeologist regarding artifacts of this sort."

"I see," Adams said, and genuinely did see, now. The articles which he would write would be printed in the journal, backdated, the issues artificially aged so as to appear authentically prewar; on the basis of them, as universally accepted valid scientific opinion, *the Estes Park Government would claim the artifacts to be priceless finds*. They would then go before the Recon Dis-In Council at Mexico City, the high court of the world that stood above both Wes-Dem and Pac-Peop and each Yance-man anywhere in the world—and above the wealthy, powerful builder Louis Runcible. And on the basis of these backdated spurious articles the council would rule the Estes Park Government to be legally correct. For artifacts of such worth automatically made the land government property.

But—Brose did not want the land. So something was still wrong.

"You do not see," Brose said, reading his expression. "Tell him, Lindblom."

Verne Lindblom said, "The sequence is this. Hig, or someone else on Runcible's work crew supervising the leadies and the big autonomic rigs, discovers the artifacts and tells Runcible. And regardless of their worth, U.S. law notwithstanding—"

"Oh my god," Adams said. Runcible would know that, if brought to the Estes Park Government's attention, these artifacts would cost him his land. "He'd conceal the find," Adams said.

"Of course." Brose nodded in delight. "We've had Mrs. Morgen, at the Institute of Applied Psychiatric Research in Berlin, independently analyze the fully documented psych-profile of the man; and she agrees with our own psychiatrists. Why, hell; he's a businessman—he's after wealth and power. What do priceless ancient artifacts made by a nonterran raiding party that landed in Southern Utah six hundred years ago mean to him? These skulls; the ones not Homo sapiens. Your articles will show a photo of this drawing. You will conjecture that these nonterrans landed, conjecture by meager bones and artifacts discovered what they were like, that they were engaged in a skirmish by an Indian war party, and the nonterrans lost, did not colonize Earth—all this is conjecture, and the evidence at the time of your articles, thirty years ago, was incomplete. But further finds were hoped for. These are those."

"So now," Adams said, "we have fully representative weapons and bones. At last. The conjectures of thirty years ago have been verified and this is a moment of vast scientific import." He walked to the window, pretended to look out. The conapt builder Louis Runcible, when notified of the finds, would guess wrong—would suspect that they had been planted on his land so that he would lose that land; and, guessing wrong, would conceal the finds and continue with his digging and construction work.

Whereupon—

Motivated by loyalty to science rather than to his "employer" and that industrial magnate's greed, Robert Hig would "reluctantly" leak the discovery of the artifacts to the Estes Park Government.

Which would make Runcible a felon. Because there was that law, obtaining again and again as the leadies employed by each Yance-man at his private demesne dug and dug for prewar relics of artistic and technological worth. Whatever he found—whatever his leadies found—belonged to him. *If* there was no overriding—i.e., major—archeological worth.

And a nonterran race which had landed on Earth six hundred years ago, fought a pitched battle with local Indians and then retreated, once more departed—it would be a *nolo contendere* plea by Runcible before the Recon Dis-In Council in Mexico City; despite the finest legal help on Earth he wouldn't have the ghost of a chance.

But Runcible would not merely lose his land.

It would be a prison sentence for forty to fifty years, depending on the skill of the Estes Park Government's attorneys before the Council. And the Precious Relics Ordinance, as the law was called, had been tested by a number of Yance-men various times; discoveries of magnitude which had deliberately gone unreported and then been found out—the council would throw the book at Runcible and he would be wiped out; the economic empire which he had built up, his conapts all over the world, would revert to public domain: this was the punitive clause of the Precious Relics Ordinance, the clause that gave it such fierce gnashing teeth. The person convicted under the ordinance not only went to prison—he forfeited his holdings *in toto*.

It all made sense to Adams; he saw now what his articles for *Natural World*, for issues of thirty years ago, were to consist of.

But, and this made him freeze into stupidity; this blotted his mind of its canniness and made him hang vapidly on the colloquy between Brose and Lindblom, both of whom obviously understood the purpose of this—which he did not.

Why did the Estes Park Government want to destroy Runcible? Of what was he guilty—at the very least, what menace did he pose to them?

Louis Runcible who builds housing for tankers who come up to the surface expecting to find the war in progress, only to discover that the war ended years ago and the world's surface is one great park of villas and demesnes for the elite few . . . why, Adams asked himself, must this man be slaughtered, when he is so patently performing a vital service? Not just for the tankers who surface and who must live somewhere, but to us, the Yance-men. Because—and we all know it; we all face it—the tankers living in Runcible's conapts are prisoners and the conapts constitute reservations—or, as the more modern word has it, concentration camps. Preferable to the ant tanks underground, but still camps from which they cannot, even briefly, leave—legally. And, when a couple or a gang of them manage to sneak away illegally, it is General Holt's army here in Wes-Dem or Marshal Harenzany's army in Pac-Peop; anyhow it is an army of very skilled, veteran leadies who track them down and return them to their swimming pools and 3-D TV and wall-to-wall wubfur carpeted conapts.

Aloud he said, "Lindblom, I'm standing with my back to Brose. Therefore he can't hear me. You can. I want you to casually turn your back to him; don't move toward me—just turn so your face is toward me and not toward him. And then for god's sake tell me why."

After a moment he heard Lindblom stir. Then say, "Why what, Joe?"

"Why are they after Runcible?"

Lindblom said, "Didn't you know?"

At the desk Brose said, "Nobody's facing me; please turn so we can continue the mapping of this project."

"Say," Adams grated, staring out the window of the office at the other buildings of the Agency.

"They think Runcible is systematically tipping off one ant tank after another," Lindblom said. "To the fact that the war is over. *Someone* is. They know that. Webster Foote and his field people found that out during routine interviews of a group of tankers who surfaced a month or so ago."

Brose complained with growing peevish suspicion, "What's going on? You two are conversing."

At that, Adams turned from the window to face Brose; Lindblom, too, turned toward the monster concoction wedged somehow into the chair at the desk. "Not conversing," Adams said to Brose. "Just meditating."

On Lindblom's face there was no expression. Only empty, stonelike detachment. He had been given a task; he intended to do it. He recommended to Adams by his manner that Joseph Adams do the same.

But suppose it were not Runcible. Suppose it were someone else.

Then this entire project, the faked artifacts, the articles in *Natural World,* the "leak" of the find, the litigation before the Recon Dis-In Council, the destruction of Runcible's economic empire and his imprisonment:

It was all for nothing.

Joseph Adams trembled. Because, unlike Brose, unlike Verne Lindblom and probably Robert Hig and anyone and everyone else connected with this project—he had a dreadful intuition that it was all a mistake.

And his intuition was not going to halt the project.

Not one bit.

Again turning his back to Brose, Adam said, "Lindblom, they may be wrong. It may not be Runcible."

There was no answer. Lindblom could not respond because he was, at the moment, facing Brose, who now, on his feet, was waddling and groping his way, supported by a magnesium crutch, toward the office door, mumbling as he departed.

"Honest to god," Adams said, staring fixedly out the window,

"I'll write the articles, but if it isn't him, I'm going to tip him off." He turned, then, toward Lindblom, tried to read his reaction.

It was not there to read. But Lindblom had heard.

The reaction would come, sooner or later; Joseph Adams knew this man, this personal friend, had worked with him enough to be sure of it.

It would be a strong reaction. After a great deal of soul-searching Verne Lindblom would probably agree, probably help him find a way of tipping off Runcible without leaving a trail back to the source that Brose's agents could trace; Brose's agents and the private hired talents of the Footemen operating in conjunction. On the other hand—

He had to face it; *was* facing it.

Verne Lindblom was a Yance-man, fundamentally. Before and beyond any other consideration.

His reaction might be to report Adams' statement to Brose.

The agents of Brose would, then, within minutes, show up at Joseph Adams' demesne and kill him.

It was that simple.

And at the moment there was no way he could tell which direction his long-time friend Lindblom would jump; Adams did not possess the services of an international psychiatric profile-analysis organization, as Brose did.

He could only wait. And pray.

And prayer, he thought caustically, went out twenty years ago, even *before* the war.

The field technician of the private police corporation Webster Foote, Limited, crouched in his cramped bunker and said into his aud receiver which transmitted to headquarters in London, "Sir, I have on tape a two-way conversation."

"On that same matter we discussed?" Webster Foote's voice came, distantly.

"Evidently."

"All right. You know who's the acting contact with Louis Runcible; see that he gets it."

"I'm sorry to say that this—"

"Convey it anyhow. We do what we can with what we have." The far-off voice of Webster Foote was authoritative; this, coming from him, was a pronouncement of judgment as well as an order.

"Yes, Mr. Foote, S.A.P."

"Indeed," Webster Foote agreed. "Soon as possible." And, in London, at his end, he broke the aud-transmission.

The Webster Foote, Limited field technician turned at once back to his banks of detection and recording apparatuses, economically operating at low gain but satisfactory output level; he examined the visual, graphic tapes appearing ceaselessly to be certain that during the aud-contact with his superior he had missed nothing. Now was *not* the time to miss anything.

He had not.

SEVEN

And meanwhile, the superb handwrought speech, untouched, remained in Joseph Adams' briefcase.

Lindblom remained, shakily lighting a cigarette and trying not to involve himself—for the moment—in further conversation. He had had enough; he remained because he was too exhausted to go.

"You have it in your power," Adams said as he seated himself at his desk, opened his briefcase and got out his speech, "to get me picked off."

"I know," Lindblom muttered.

Walking toward the door Adams said, "I'm going to 'vac this. Get it to the sim and on tape and then the hell with it. Then—what do we call the new project, this forging of nonterran artifacts to put a man in prison whose whole life is devoted to seeing that decent housing is—"

"The Nazis," Lindblom interrupted, "had no written orders regarding the Final Solution, the genocide of the Jews. It was done orally. Told by superior to subordinate, handed down by word of mouth, if you don't object to an absurd mixed metaphor. You probably do."

"Let's go have a cup of coffee," Adams said.

Lindblom shrugged. "What the hell. *They've* decided it's Runcible; who are we to say it isn't? Show me—conjure up—someone else who would benefit by tipping off tanks."

"I'd be glad to," Adams said, and saw Lindblom look disconcerted. "Any one of the thousands of tankers living in Runcible's conapts. All it would take would be one who got away, wasn't picked up by Brose's agents or Footemen, made his way back to his own ant tank. Then, from it, contacted a neighboring tank, then from that tank to—"

"Yeah," Lindblom agreed, stolidly. "Sure. Why not? Except would his fellow tankers let him back into his tank? Wouldn't they think he was hot or had—what name did we make up to call it?—the Bag Plague. They'd massacre him on sight. Because they believe the reading matter we give them on TV every damn day of the week and twice on Saturday night, just in case; they'd think he was a living missile. And anyhow, there's more you don't know. You ought to hand over a few bucks to the Foote organization now and then; pick up a little inside news. These tankers that had been tipped off about conditions up here—they weren't tipped off by anybody they knew; it wasn't one of their own members coming back."

"Okay, the tanker couldn't reach his own tank; so instead—"

"They got it," Lindblom said, "over the coax."

For a moment Adams failed to understand; he stared at Lindblom.

"That's right," Lindblom said. "On their TV set. For about one minute, and very feeble. But enough."

"Good god," Adams said, and he thought, There are millions of them down there. What would it be like if someone cut into the *main* coax, the chief, sole and central trunk from Estes Park that reaches *all* the tanks. What would it be like to have the earth open and millions of humans, imprisoned subsurface for fifteen years, believing in a radioactive waste above, with missiles and bacteria and rubble and warring armies—the demesne system would sustain a death blow and the great park over which he flappled twice daily would become a densely populated civilization once more, not quite as before the war, but close enough. Roads would reappear. Cities.

And—ultimately there would be another war.

That was the rationale. The masses had egged their leaders on to war in both Wes-Dem and Pac-Peop. But once the masses were out of the way, stuffed down below into antiseptic tanks, the ruling elite of both East and West were free to conclude a deal . . . although, strangely, in a sense it had not been them at all, not Brose, not General Holt who had been C. in C. of Wes-Dem or even Marshal Harenzany, the top officer in the hierarchy of Soviet brass. But the fact that both Holt and Harenzany knew when it was time to use the missiles (and had done so) and when time had come to quit—this was all true, and without it, without their joint reasonability, peace would not have been possible, but underneath this collaboration of the two top military men lay something else, something which to Adams was real and strange and in a sense deeply moving.

The Recon Dis-In Council of leadies in Mexico City/Amecameca. It had assisted in the job of forcing peace on the planet. And as a governing body, a final arbiter, it had not gone away. Man has built a weapon that could think for itself, and after it had thought a while, two years in which vile destruction had occurred, with the leadies locked hip and thigh each with the other, two huge artificial armies from two land masses . . . advanced varieties of leadies, who had been constructed with an eye toward utilizing their analytical brains for planning tactics and finally overall strategy—these advanced types, the X, XI and XII varieties, had figured out that the best strategy was something which the Phoenicians had learned five thousand years ago. It was summed up, Adams reflected, in *The Mikado*. If merely *saying* that a man had been executed was enough to satisfy everyone, why not merely say it instead of doing it? The problem was really—to the advanced leadies—that simple. They were not Gilbert and Sullivan buffs, and Gilbert's words were not in their artificial brains; the text of *The Mikado* had not been programmed into them as operational data. But they had arrived at the same conclusion—and had in addition acted on it, in conjunction with Marshal Harenzany and C. in C. General Holt.

Aloud, Adams said, "But they didn't see the advantage."

"Pardon?" Lindblom murmured, still shaky, still unwilling to engage in any more talk; he looked tired.

"What the Recon Dis-In Council didn't see," Adams said, "and can't see now, because there's no libido-component to their perceptmentation systems, is that the maxim, Why execute someone—"

"Aw, shut up," Lindblom said, and, turning, stalked out of Joseph Adams' office. Leaving him standing there alone, speech in hand, idea in mind; doubly frustrated.

But he could hardly blame Lindblom for being upset. Because all the Yance-men had this streak. They were selfish; they had made the world into their deer park at the expense of the millions of tankers below; it was wrong and they knew it and they felt guilt—not quite enough guilt to cause them to knock off Brose and let the tankers up, but enough guilt to make their late evenings a thrashing agony of loneliness, emptiness, and their nights impossible. And they knew that if anyone could be said to be amending the crime committed, the theft of an entire planet from its rightful owners, it was Louis Runcible. *They* gained by keeping the tankers down, and he gained by luring them up; the Yance-man elite confronted Runcible as an antagonist, but one whom they knew, deep down inside, was morally in the right. It was not a sanguine feeling, at least not to Joe Adams as he stood alone in his office, gripping his superb speech which was to be 'vacked, run through the sim, taped, then castrated from Brose's office. This speech: it did not tell the truth, but it was not a pastiche of cliches, lies, bromides, euphemisms—

And, more sinister ingredients, which Adams had noticed in speeches dreamed up by his fellow Yance-men; after all, he was only one speech writer from among a pack.

Carrying his highly prized new speech—so regarded by him, anyhow, in the absence of a contrary consensual validation—he left his office and, by express elevator, dropped to the floor where Megavac 6-V chugged away; floors, rather, in that the total works of the organism had undergone accretive changes over the years, refinements that had added to it whole new parts occupying entire new layers. Megavac 6-V was huge, but in contrast, the sim itself remained the same as always.

Two uniformed toughs, Brose's hand-picked but oddly effete, physiognomically dainty roughnecks, eyed him as he emerged from the elevator. They knew him; they understood that his presence on Megavac 6-V's programming floor was mandatory in view of his job.

He approached the keyboard of Megavac 6-V, saw that it was in use; another Yance-man, unfamiliar to him, was whacking away at the keys like a virtuoso pianist at the end of a Franz Liszt opus, with double octaves and all, everything but hammering with the fist.

Above the Yance-man his written copy was suspended, and Adams gave in to the impulse; he moved close to inspect it.

At once the Yance-man ceased typing.

"Sorry," Adams said.

"Let's see your authorization." The Yance-man, quite dark, youthful and small, with almost Mexican-like hair, held out his hand peremptorily.

Sighing, Adams got out of his briefcase the memo from Geneva, from Brose's bureau, entitling him to 'vac this particular speech; the document had a stamped code number, entered on the memo as well—the dark, small Yance-man compared the document with the memo, seemed satisfied, returned both to Adams.

"I'll be through in forty minutes." The youth resumed typing.

"So bounce off and leave me alone." His tone was neutral but forbidding.

Adams said, "I rather like your style." He had quickly, briefly, scanned the page of script on top. It was good stuff; unusually so.

Again the Yance-man ceased typing. "You're Adams." Once more he extended his hand, this time for shaking purposes; they shook, then, and the strained atmosphere reduced to a tolerable level. But there was always the I'm-bigger-than-you competitiveness in the air when two Yance-men met, either away from the Agency at their demesnes or here right on the job. It always made the day just that much tougher to get through, and yet Adams thrived on it—if not, he realized, he would long since have gone under. "You've done some good pieces; I've watched the final tapes." Studying him with his sharp, bright, black, deeply-set Mexican-type eyes, the young Yance-man said, "But a lot of your work has been axed at Geneva, or so I hear."

"Well," Adams said stoically, "it's either axed or it's coaxed in this business; there's no such thing as half-transmitting."

"You want to bet?" The youth's tone was brittle, penetrating; it disconcerted Adams.

Guardedly, because after all both of them in essence were competing for the same prize, Adams said, "I suppose a jejune, watered-down speech could be considered—"

"Let me show you something." The dark young Yance-man rose, yanked shut the master circuit breaker so that the 'vac began processing what he had fed it up to now.

Together, Adams and the dark young Yance-man walked over to view the sim.

There it sat. Solely, at its large oak desk, with the American flag behind it. In Moscow another and identical sim sat, with a duplicate of Megavac 6-V, the flag of the USSR behind it; otherwise everything, the clothes, the gray hair, the competent, fatherly, mature but soldierly features, the strong chin—it was the same sim all over again, both having been built simultaneously in Germany, wired by the finest Yance-man technicians alive. And here maintenance men perpetually skulked, watching with trained, narrow eyes for any sign of failure, even a fraction-of-a-second hesitation. Anything which might mitigate the quality striven for, that of free and easy authenticity; this simulacrum, out of all which they, the Yance-men, were involved in, required the greatest semblance of the actuality which it mimicked.

A breakdown here, Adams realized soberly, however minute, would be catastrophic. Like the time its left hand, in reaching out—

A huge red warning light on the wall lit, a buzzer buzzed; a dozen main-men for the simulacrum materialized to scrutinize.

Catastrophic—as the time the reaching left hand went into a spasm of pseudo-Parkinsonism, a neutral-motor tremor . . . indicating, had the tapes been put on the cable, the insidious start of senility; yes, that would have been the tankers' interpretation, most probably. He's getting old, they would have muttered to each other as they sat in their communal halls, overseen by their pol-coms. Look; he's shaky. The strain. Remember Roosevelt; the strain of the war got him, finally; it'll get the Protector, and then what'll we do?

But it hadn't been put on the coaxial cable, of course; the tankers had never seen that sequence. The sim had been opened up, thoroughly gone over, tested and checked and certified; a miniaturized component had been spat on, denounced as the malefactor—and, at a work bench in one of the shops of Runcible's conapts, a workman had been quietly relieved of his duties and possibly his life . . . without ever knowing why or what—because in the first place he hadn't known what the tiny output coil or diode or just plain *thing* had been used for.

The sim began to move. And Joseph Adams shut his eyes, standing as he was, out of range of the cameras, hidden with this small, dark, very young but expert Yance-man, the author of the words about to be uttered. Maybe it'll go out of its mind, Adams thought wildly, and began to recite pornographic ballads. Or, like one of those antique disc records of the previous century: repeat a word repeat a word repeat a word . . .

"My fellow Americans," the sim said in its firm, familiar, near-hoarse but utterly controlled voice.

To himself Joseph Adams said, *Yes, Mr. Yancy. Yes sir.*

EIGHT

Joseph Adams listened to the partial text of the speech, up to the point where the dark young Yance-man had ceased feeding the script to the 'vac, and then, when the sim became rigid and the cameras—at the precise second—shut down, he turned to the man beside him, the author, and said:

"I take off my hat to you. You're good." He had almost been captured himself, as he had stood watching the simulacrum of the Protector Talbot Yancy deliver with absolutely the proper intonation, in the exact and correct manner, the text modified and augmented—meddled with—by Megavac 6-V from what it had received—even though he could see Megavac 6-V and although this was not visible could sense the emanation of the reading matter directed by the 'vac toward the simulacrum. Could in fact witness the true source which animated the purely artificial construct seated at the oak desk with the American flag behind it. Eerie, he thought.

But a good speech is a good speech. Whoever delivers it. A kid in high school, reciting Tom Paine . . . the material is still great, and this reciter doesn't falter or stumble or get the words wrong. The 'vac and all these main-men standing around see to that. *And,* he thought, *so do we. We know what we're doing.*

"Who are you?" he asked this strangely capable young Yance-man.

"Dave something. I forget," the man said, almost mystically absorbed, even now that the sim had become inoperative once more.

"You forget your *name?*" Puzzled, he waited, and then he realized that this was merely an elliptical way by which the dark young man was telling him something: that he was a relatively new Yance-man, not yet fully established in the hierarchy. "Lantano," Adams said. "You're David Lantano, living in the hotspot near Cheyenne."

"That's right."

"No wonder you're black." Radiation-burned, Adams realized. The youth, eager to acquire land for a demesne, had gone in too soon; all the rumors, passed back and forth in the idle hours of evening by the worldwide elite, appeared true: it had been far too soon, and physically young David Lantano was suffering.

Philosophically, Lantano said, "I'm alive."

"But look at you. What about your bone marrow?"

"Tests show there's not too much impairment of red-cell production. I expect to recuperate. And it's cooling daily. I've gotten over the worst part." Wryly, Lantano said, "You should come and visit me, Adams; I've had my leadies working night and day; the villa itself is almost complete."

Adams said, "I wouldn't go into the Cheyenne hot-spot for a pile of poscreds ten miles high. That speech of yours shows how very much you can contribute; why risk your health, your *life?* You could stay here in New York City, live in a conapt of the Agency, until—"

"Until," Lantano said, "the Cheyenne hot-spot cooled down enough in ten years, fifteen years . . . and then someone grabbed it ahead of me." My only chance, he was saying in other words, was deliberately to go in prematurely. As has been attempted in the past by Yance-men in the exact same position, before me. And—so often those premature investments, those hasty, anxious entries into still-hot areas, meant—death. And not a mercifully quick death but a gruesome slow deterioration over a period of years.

Viewing the dark—in truth severely scorched—youth, Adams realized how fortunate he himself was. To be fully established; his villa was long-built, his grounds were fully planted, green throughout. And he had entered the West Coast hot-spot south of San Francisco at a safe time; he had relied on Footemen reports, brought at great cost, and look how it had all worked out. In contrast to this.

Lantano would have his fine villa, his vast stone building made out of the rubble, the concrete that had been the city of Cheyenne. But Lantano would be dead.

And that, according to the Recon Dis-In Council's ruling, put the area up for grabs once again; it would be a rush by eager Yance-men to get in and acquire what Lantano had left behind. An ultimate end to

Adams pathetic irony: the youth's villa, built at such cost—at the expense of his life—would go to someone else who did not have to build, supervise a gang of leadies day after day . . .

"I presume," Adams said, "that you get the hell out of Cheyenne as often as is legal." Twelve out of every twenty-four hours, according to Recon Dis-In Council law, had to be spent within the new demesne area.

"I come here. I work. As you see me now." Lantano returned to the keyboard of Megavac 6-V; Adams trailed after him. "As you say, Adams, I have a job to do. I expect to live to perform it." Once more Lantano seated himself at the keyboard, facing his copy.

"Well, at least it hasn't impaired your mind," Adams said.

Smiling, Lantano said, "Thanks."

For one hour Joseph Adams stood by while Lantano fed his speech to Megavac 6-V, and when he had read it all and then, as it emerged from the 'vac to the sim, had heard it actually delivered by the dignified, gray-haired father-figure Talbot Yancy himself, he felt, overwhelmingly, the futility of his own speech. The dreadful contrast.

What he himself gripped in his briefcase was beginner's prattle. He felt like slinking away. Into oblivion.

Where does a barely grown radiation-burned unestablished new Yance-man get such ideas? Adams asked himself. And the ability to express them. And—the knowhow as to exactly what the 'vac's treatment of the copy would result in . . . how it would ultimately emerge as spoken by the sim before the cameras. Didn't it take years to learn this? It had taken *him* years to learn what *he* knew. To write a sentence and, after examining it, know approximately—that is, sufficiently accurately—how it would in its terminal stage sound, *be*. What, in other words, would appear on the TV screens of the millions of tankers subsurface, who viewed and believed, were taken in day after day by what was fatuously called *reading matter*.

A polite term, Adams reflected, for a substance lacking substance. But this wasn't strictly true; as for instance young Dave Lantano's speech here and now. It preserved the essential illusion—in fact, Adams had grudgingly to admit—the illusion of Yancy's reality was heightened. But—

"Your speech," he said to Lantano, "isn't just clever. It has real wisdom. Like one of Cicero's orations." Proudly, he traced his own work to such eminent ancient sources as Cicero and Seneca, to speeches in Shakespeare's history plays, and to Tom Paine.

As he stuffed the pages of his copy back into his own briefcase, David Lantano said soberly, "I appreciate your comment, Adams; especially coming from you it means something."

"Why me?"

"Because," Lantano said, thoughtfully, "I know that, despite your limitations—" He shot Adams a keen, quick glance, then. "—you have sincerely tried. I think you know what I mean. There are things, easyway things and bad things, that you've scrupulously avoided. I've watched you for several years and I've seen the difference between you and most of the others. Brose knows the difference, too, and despite the fact that he axes rather than coaxes much of your stuff, he respects you. *He has to.*"

"Well," Adams said.

"Has it frightened you, Adams, to see your best work axed at the Geneva level? After getting that far? Do you find it merely frustrating or—" David Lantano scrutinized him. "Yes, it does frighten you."

After a pause Adams said, "I get scared. But at night, when I'm not here at the Agency but alone with my leadies in my villa. Not when I'm actually writing or feeding it to the 'vac or watching the sim itself . . . not here where—" He gestured. "It's busy. But—always whenever I'm alone." He was silent, then, wondering how he had managed to confide his deepest proclivities to this young stranger. Normally, one took care as to what one revealed about oneself to a fellow Yance-man; any personal info could be used against one, in the incessant competition to be *the* speech writer for Yancy; in effect, *the Yancy itself.*

"Here at the Agency," Dave Lantano said somberly, "in New York, we may compete against each other, but underneath we're a group. A corporate body. What the Christians used to call a congregation . . . a very meaningful special term. But then each of us, at six p.m., goes off in his flapple. Crosses an empty countryside to a castle inhabited by mental constructs that move and talk but are—" He gestured. "Cold, Adams; the leadies, even the advanced types who dominate the Council; *they are cold.* Get a couple of your retinue, all the leadies of your household staff that you can cram into your flapple with you, and go visit. Every night."

"I know that the smart Yance-men do that," Adams said. "Are

never at home. I've tried; I've arrived at my demesne, eaten dinner and then gone right out again." He thought of Colleen, and then, when he had lived, his neighbor Lane. "I have a girl," he said deftly. "A Yance-man or I suppose one would have to say a Yance-woman; we visit and talk. But the big front window of the library of my demesne—"

"Don't look out over that fog and coastline of rocks," David Lantano said. "That stretches south of San Francisco a hundred miles; one of the most bleak on Earth."

Blinking, Adams wondered how Lantano had known so exactly what he meant, his fear of the fog; it was as if Lantano had read his deepest mind.

"I'd like to see your speech, now," Lantano said. "Since you've given mine about as thorough a study as possible—and, for you, Adams, that's rather thorough." He glanced toward Adams' briefcase, especially alert, now.

Adams said, "No." He couldn't show his speech, not after the strong, fresh declaration he had just now seen and heard.

The reading matter concocted by David Lantano which had emerged from the Yancy-simulacrum so effectively, dealt with deprivation. Hit at the heart of the tankers' main problem-area . . . at least as he understood it from the reports of the pol-coms in the tanks which the Estes Park Government, the apparatus there, received—received and made accessible as a feedback to all Yance-men, in particular the speech writers. Their sole source of knowledge as to how well they were getting their reading matter through.

Reports from the pol-coms on this speech of Lantano's, when it had been coaxed, would be interesting. It would take at least a month, but Adams made a note of it, noted the official code-designation of the speech, and promised himself to be alert for the feedback responses as they emerged from the ant tanks all over the world . . . Wes-Dem, anyhow, and possibly, if the response was good enough, the Soviet authorities would take the top-copy of the spool from Megavac 6-V which contained the speech, give it to their own 'vac in Moscow to program their own sim . . . and, in addition, Brose in Geneva, if he wished, could sequester the spool, the original, not the top-copy, and decree it officially and formally to be primary source-material from which Yance-men the world over were mandatorily to draw on for later reading matter. Lantano's speech, if it were as good as Adams thought it to be, might become one of those few rare "eternal" declarations, incorporated in permanent policy. What an honor. And the guy was so damn young.

"How can you face it," Adams asked the dark young new Yance-man, who did not even have a demesne, yet, who lived in a lethal hot-spot by night, dying, being scorched, suffering, but still doing this superb job, "how can you openly discuss the fact that those tankers down there are *systematically deprived of what they're entitled to?* You actually said it in your speech." He remembered Lantano's exact words as they had issued from the firm-jawed mouth of the Yancy. What you have, Talbot Yancy, the synthetic and in a sense actually nonexistent Protector, told the tankers—would be telling them in a couple of weeks, when the tape had passed Geneva's scrutiny as of course it would—is not enough. Your lives are incomplete, in the sense that Rousseau had meant when he talked of man having been born in one condition, born brought into the light free, and everywhere was now in chains. Only here, in this day and age, as the speech had just pointed out, they had been born onto the surface of a world and now that surface with its air and sunlight and hills, its oceans, its streams, its colors and textures, its very smells, had been swiped from them and they were left with tin-can submarine—figuratively—dwelling boxes in which they were squeezed, under a false light, to breathe repurified stale air, to listen to wired obligatory music and sit daylong at work-benches making leadies for a purpose which—but even Lantano could not go on here. Could not say, for a purpose you don't know. For each of us here above to augment our retinues with, our entourages which wait on us, follow us, dig for us, build, scrape and bow . . . you've made us barons in baronial castles, and you are the Nibelungen, the dwarves, in the mines; you labor for us. And we give back—reading matter. No, the speech hadn't said that—how could it? But it had admitted the truth, that the tankers were entitled to something they did not have; they were the victims of robbers. Theft had been committed against all the millions of them, and there had been no moral or legal remedy all these years.

"My fellow Americans," the Talbot Yancy simulacrum had said gravely in its stern, stoic, military, leadership, fatherly voice (Adams would never forget this moment of the speech) "there is a certain ancient Christian idea, which you may know, that life on Earth, or in your instance, beneath Earth, is a transition. An episode between a life that came before and an eternal, other-kind-of-life to follow. Once a pagan king in the British Isles was converted to Christianity by the image of this life being the short flight of a nocturnal bird which has flown in through one window of a warm and lighted dining hall of a castle, for a moment passed above a scene of motion and talk, of tangible fellow-life; the comfort of being within a place inhabited by others. And then the bird in its flight has gone on out of the lighted dining hall, out of the castle once more, through a second window. Into the empty, black, unending night on the far side. And it will never see that lit-up, warm hall of murmur and motion and fellow-life again. And—'' And here the Yancy, in all its pomp and dignity, the authority of its words that reached so many, many human beings in so many anywhere in the world tanks, had said, ''—you, my fellow Americans in subsurface shelters, you have not got even this moment to cling to. To remember or anticipate or enjoy, this short flight through the lighted hall. Brief as it is, you are entitled to it, and yet, because of a terrible madness fifteen years ago, a hell-night, you are doomed; you are paying every day for the insanity that drove you from the surface exactly as the whips of the furies drove our two grandparents from the original garden eons ago. And this is not right. Somehow, one day, I assure you, the alienation will end. The abridgment of your reality, the deprivation of your rightful life—with the swiftness said to accompany the last trump's first sound, this terrible calamity, this inequity will be abolished. *When it comes it will not be gradual.* It will hurl you all, expel you, even if you resist it, back to your own land that is waiting for you above, awaiting your claim. My fellow Americans, your claim is staked and we guard it; we are the securing agents only for the present. But everything up here will disappear and you will come back. And even the memory, even the *idea* of us who are up here now, will forever vanish.'' And the Yancy simulacrum had finished, ''And you will not be able to curse us because you will not even recall that we existed.''

God, Adams thought. And this man wants to see *my* speech.

Seeing his reluctance, David Lantano said quietly, ''But I've watched you, Adams. You can take some credit.''

''Damn little,'' Adams said. ''You know, all I've ever tried to do, and it was right, but just not enough—I tried to assuage their doubts. As to the necessity of their situation. But you—my good god, you've actually called it not merely a necessity that they have to live down there but an unjust, temporary, evil curse. There's a big difference between my using the Yancy sim to persuade them that they have to go on because it's even worse up here on the surface, it's germs and radioactivity and death, and what you've done; you've given them a solemn promise—you made a compact with them, gave them your word—*Yancy's* word—that someday it would all be justified."

"Well," Lantano said mildly, "the Bible does say, 'It is God Who shall justify.' Or some such utterance; I forget exactly." He looked tired, more so even than Lindblom had; they were all tired, all of their class. What a great burden, Adams thought, the luxury of this way we live. Since no one makes us suffer we have elected to volunteer. He saw this on Lantano's face, as he had seen it, or something like it, on Verne Lindblom's. But not on Brose's, he thought suddenly. The man with the most power and responsibility feels the least—if he feels any—weight.

No wonder they all trembled; no wonder their nights were bad. They served—and knew it—a bad master.

NINE

His speech still—it seemed eternally—in his briefcase, undisclosed to David Lantano and never fed to Megavac 6-V, Joseph Adams made his way by horizontal express belt from the building at 580 Fifth Avenue to the Agency's titanic repository of reference material, its official archives of every known datum of knowledge from before the war retained and fixed for perpetuity and of course instantly available to the elite, such as himself, whenever needed.

He needed it—some fragment of it—now.

At the great central station he lined up, and when he found himself facing the combination type XXXV leady and Megavac 2-B which acted as ruling monad of the labyrinthine organism of spool upon spool of microtape—whole twenty-six volume reference books reduced to the size of a yo-yo, and merely a yo-yo's shape and width and weight—he said, rather plaintively, it seemed to him as he heard himself speak, "Um, I'm sort of confused. I'm not looking for any one particular source, as for instance Lucretius' *De Rerum Natura* or Pascal's *Provincial Letters* or Kafka's *The Castle*." Those had been instances of his past: sources which had molded him along with the eternal John Donne and Cicero and Seneca and Shakespeare et al.

"Your ident-key, please," the ruling monad of the archives buzzed.

He slid his key into the slot; it registered, and now the ruling monad, after consulting its memory bank, knew and remembered every source item he had ever utilized, and in what sequence; it comprehended the entire pattern of his formal knowledge. From the archives' standpoint, it now knew him without limit, and so it could declare—or so he hoped—the next point on the graph of his growing, organic, mentation-life. The historic development of him as a knowing entity.

God knew *he* didn't have any notion of what the next point on the graph would be; David Lantano's reading matter had completely knocked the slats from under him and he wobbled in a horrid daze—crisis, for the last and critical time, perhaps, in his professional career. He faced, at least potentially, what all speech writers for the Talbot Yancy sim feared: the cessation of their powers. The drying-up of their ability to program the 'vac, in fact to program anything at all.

The ruling monad of the Agency's official archives clicked a few times, as if gnashing its electronic gearteeth, and then it said, "Mr. Adams, do not be alarmed at this."

"Okay," he said, thoroughly alarmed already. Behind him those in line, his fellow Yance-men, waited impatiently. "Let's have it," he said.

The ruling monad said, "You are respectfully referred back to Source One. The two documentaries of 1982, both versions, A and B; with no criticism intended you will, if you step to the counter directly to your right, be handed the spools of Gottlieb Fischer's original work."

The bottom, the support and structure, the form itself, of Joseph Adams' world, fell out. And, as he made his way to the counter to his right, to receive the spools, he died inside, and died in great pain, deprived of the fundamental metabolic rhythm of existence.

Because if he didn't yet understand Gottlieb Fischer's two documentaries of 1982, he didn't understand anything.

For the fabric of Yancy, what he was and how he had come into being—and hence their existence, the hive of Yancy-men such as himself and Verne Lindblom and Lantano, even horrible, powerful old Brose himself—all this rested on documentaries A and B. A, which had been for Wes-Dem; B, produced for Pac-Peop. Beyond these, one could not go.

He had been thrown back years. To the inception of his professional career as a Yance-man. And if it could happen to him the entire edifice could totter; he felt the world he knew melt under his feet.

TEN

Accepting the spools he sightlessly made his way to a vacant table and scanner, seated himself—and then realized that somewhere along the line he had set down his briefcase and not picked it up—had gone on without it; in other words, deliberately, and for good reason, thoroughly lost and parted company forever with his agonized-over, hand-wrought speech of last night.

This proved his thesis. He was in real trouble.

Which, of the two documentaries, he asked himself, must I endure first?

He honestly did not know. At last, more or less aimlessly, he picked Documentary A. Since after all he himself was a Wes-Dem Yance-man. Documentary A, which had been the first of Gottlieb Fischer's two efforts, had always appealed to him more. Because if it could be said that there were any truth to either of them, it lay perhaps here in the A version. Buried, however, under a refuse heap of manufactured fraud so vast as to constitute—and this was the factor which made both documentaries the primal, venerated source for all Yancy-men—an anomaly.

For sheer "the big lie" crust, Gottlieb Fischer had long ago out-classed them all. No one living or who would ever be born, could possibly, with a straight face, tell the yarns of those innocent, halcyon days. The West German film maker Gottlieb Fischer, inheritor of UFA, the older Reichs film trust which had in the 1930s been so deeply interwoven with Dr. Goebbels' office—that really superb, unique fabricator of the convincingly visual had gotten things rolling not with a whimper but with a goddam terrible, awesome bang. But of course Fischer had possessed great resources. Both military establishments, those of Wes-Dem and Pac-Peop, had provided him with financial and spiritual assistance—as well as the fabulous film clips of World War Two which each establishment held in its "classified" film libraries.

The twin documentaries, contrived so as to be released simultaneously, had dealt with World War Two, which, for many people in 1982, lay clearly within memory, it having ended only thirty-seven years before the release of the documentaries. A G.I. of that war who had been twenty in 1945 would, when he sat before his TV set in his living room in Boise, Idaho and saw Episode One (of twenty-five parts) of Documentary A, would have been only fifty-seven years old.

As Joseph Adams fitted his eyes to the spool-scanner he thought to himself that they should have been able to *remember* enough to recognize what they saw on their TV screens to be pure lie.

Before his eyes appeared the tiny, illuminated and clear image of Adolf Hitler, addressing the hired flunkies who constituted the Reichstag of the late 1930s. Der Fuhrer was in a sardonic, jovial, mocking, excited mood. This famous scene—and every Yance-man knew it by heart—was the moment in which Hitler answered the plea from President Roosevelt of the United States that he, Hitler, guarantee the frontiers of a dozen or so small nations of Europe. One by one Adolf Hitler read off the nations comprising this list, his voice rising with each, and with each the hired flunkies jeered in synchronization with their leader's mounting frenzy of glee. The emotionality of it all—der Fuhrer, overcome with titanic amusement at this absurd list (later he was to invade, systematically, virtually every nation named), the roars of the flunkies . . . Joseph Adams watched, listened, felt inside him a resonance with the roars, a sardonic glee in company with Hitler's—and at the same time he felt simple, quite childlike wonder that this scene could ever have truly taken place. And it had. This clip, from Episode One of Documentary A, was—crazily enough, considering its fantastic nature—authentic.

Ah, but now came the artistry of the Berlin film maker of 1982. The scene of the Reichstag speech dimmed, and there segued in, clearer and clearer, another scene. That of hungry, empty-eyed Germans during the Depression of the Weimar days, the pre-Hitler days. Unemployed. Bankrupt. Lost. A defeated nation without a future.

The aud-track commentary, the purring but firm voice of the trained actor whom Gottlieb Fischer had hired—Alex Sourberry or some such name—began to lift into being, to superimpose its aural presence as interpretation of the visual. And the visual, now, consisted of an ocean scene. The Royal Navy of Great Britain, as it maintained the blockade into the year following World War One; as it deliberately and successfully starved into permanent stuntedness a nation which had long ago surrendered—and was now utterly helpless.

Adams halted the scanner, sat back, lit a cigarette.

Did he really need to listen to the firm, purring voice of Alexander Sourberry to know the message of Documentary A? Did he have to sit through all twenty-five hour-long episodes and then, when the ordeal was over, turn to the equally long and intricate version B? He knew the message. Alex Sourberry for version A; some East German professional equal of Sourberry for version B. He knew *both* messages . . . because, just as there existed two distinct versions, there existed two distinct messages.

Sourberry, at the moment the scanner had been shut off, giving Adams a respite which he thanked god for, had been about to demonstrate a remarkable fact: a connection between two scenes set apart in history by twenty-odd years. The British blockade of 1919 and the concentration camps of the starving, dying skeletons in striped clothes in the year 1943.

It was the British who had brought about Buchenwald, was Gottlieb Fischer's revised history. Not the Germans. The Germans were the *victims,* in 1943 as much as in 1919. A later scene in Documentary A would show Berliners, in 1944, hunting in the woods surrounding Berlin, searching for nettles to make into soup. The Germans were starving; all continental Europe, all people inside and outside the concentration camps, were starving. Because of the British.

How clear it was, as this theme emerged throughout twenty-five expertly put-together episodes. This was the "definitive" history of World War Two—for the people of Wes-Dem, anyhow.

Why run the thing? Adams asked himself as he sat smoking his cigarette, trembling with muscular and mental weariness. I know what it shows. That Hitler was emotional, flamboyant, moody, and unstable, but of course; it was natural, the film lied. Because he was pure and simply a genius. Like Beethoven. And we all admire Beethoven; you have to forgive a great world figure genius type its eccentricities. And, admittedly, Hitler was at last pushed over the edge, driven into psychotic paranoia . . . due to the unwillingness of England to understand, to grasp, the looming, *real* menace—that of Stalinist Russia. The peculiarities of Hitler's personal character (after all, he had been subjected to great and prolonged stress during World War One and the Weimar Depression period, as had all Germans) had misled the rather phlegmatic Anglo-Saxon peoples into imagining that Hitler was "dangerous." Actually—and in episode after episode, Alex Sourberry would purr out this message—the Wes-Dem TV viewer would discover that England, France, Germany and the United States should all have been allies. Against the authentic evil-doer, Josef Stalin, with his megalomaniacal plans for world conquest . . . proved by the actions of the USSR in the postwar period—a period in which even Churchill had to admit that Soviet Russia was *the* enemy.

—And had been all along. Communist propagandists, fifth columnists in the Western Democracies, however, had deceived the people, even the governments . . . even Roosevelt and Churchill, and right up into the postwar world. Take, for instance, Alger Hiss . . . take the Rosenbergs, who had stolen the secret of The Bomb and given it to Soviet Russia.

Take, for instance, the scene which opened episode four of version A. Advancing the spool, Joseph Adams halted it at this episode and put his eyes to the scanner, this modern technological crystal ball into which one gazed to know—not the future—but the past. And . . .

Not even the past. Instead, this fake which he now witnessed.

Before his eyes a film sequence, narrated by the maddeningly ubiquitous Alex Sourberry and his oily, skillful murmur. A scene vital to the overall moral of version A which Gottlieb Fischer, backed angelwise by the Wes-Dem military establishment, had wished to drive home—in other words this was the *raison d'être* of the whole twenty-five hour-long episodes of version A.

The scene enacted in miniature before him showed the meeting of the heads-of-state, Roosevelt, Churchill and Stalin. The location: Yalta. Ominous, fateful Yalta.

There they sat, the three world leaders, in adjoining chairs, to be photographed; this was an historic occasion the magnitude of which was intolerable. And no one alive could afford to forget it, because here—Sourberry's voice purred—the momentous decision was made. You are now seeing it with your own eyes.

What decision?

In Joseph Adams' ears the professional smooth voice whispered, "At this spot, at this moment, the deal was hatched which was to decide the future fate of mankind down unto generations yet unborn."

"Okay," Adams said aloud, startling the harmless Yance-man using the scanner across from him. "Sorry," Adams apologized, and then merely thought, did not speak it aloud, *Come on, Fischer. Let's see the deal. Like they say; don't just tell us; show us. Put up or shut up. Prove the basic contention of this great prolonged "documentary" or get out.*

And he knew, because he had seen it so many times before, that the film producer was going to show it.

"Joe," a woman's voice said, close to him, shattering his taut attention; he sat back, glanced up, found himself confronted by Colleen.

"Wait," he said to her. "Don't say anything. For just one second." Again he put his eyes to the scanner, fervid and frightened, like some poor tanker, he thought, who in his phobic terror has caught—imagines, rather—the Stink of Shrink, the olfactory harbinger of death. But I am not imagining this; Joseph Adams knew. And the horror inside him grew until he could stand not a bit more; and yet he continued to watch, and all the time, Alexander Sourberry murmured and whispered away, and Joseph Adams thought, *Is this how it feels down below, to them? If they get the intimation, the scent, of what it truly is they're seeing? That what is given them is our adaptation of this*—and this petrified him.

Sourberry purred, "A loyal American Secret Serviceman took these remarkable sequences with a telescopic-lens camera disguised as a collar button; that is why these particular moments are a trifle blurred."

And, a trifle blurred, as Sourberry had said, two figures moved together along a rampart. Roosevelt and—Josef Stalin, the latter standing, Roosevelt in a wheelchair with a robe over his lap, pushed by a uniformed servant.

"Special long-range microphonic equipment," Sourberry purred, "in the loyal Secret Serviceman's possession, permitted him to pick up—"

Okay, Joseph Adams thought. It seems fine. Camera the size of a collar button; who in 1982 remembered that no such miniaturized spy gadget existed in 1944? So that gets by unchallenged—got by, when this horrible thing was put on the coax to all Wes-Dem. No one wrote in to the Washington, D.C. government and said, "Dear Sirs: Regarding the 'collar button' camera of the 'loyal Secret Serviceman' at Yalta; this is to inform you that—" No, this hadn't happened; or if it had the letter had quietly been buried . . . if not the person who had written it.

"What episode are you looking at, Joe?" Colleen asked.

Again he sat back, stopped the spool. "The great scene. Where FDR and Stalin agree to sell out the Western Democracies."

"Oh yes." She nodded, seated herself beside him. "The blurred, long-distance shot. Who could forget that? It's been drummed into us—"

"You realize," he said, "of course, what the flaw in it is."

"We were *taught* what the flaw was. Brose himself, and since he was alive and Fischer's pupil—"

"Nobody now," Adams said, "makes errors like that. In preparing reading matter. We've learned; we're more expert. Want to watch? Listen?"

"No thanks. I frankly don't care for it."

Adams said, "I don't care for it either. But it fascinates me; it fascinates me in that it got by—and was accepted." Again putting his eyes to the scanner he started the spool up.

On the aud-track the voices of the two blurred figures could be made out. A high background hiss—proof of the long-range aspect of the hidden mike employed by the "loyal Secret Serviceman"—made it a little hard to understand, but not impossible.

Roosevelt and Stalin were, in this version A scene, talking in English; Roosevelt with his Harvard intonations, Stalin in heavy, Slavic-accented, guttural near-grunts.

You therefore could understand Roosevelt better. And what he had to say was quite important, inasmuch as he was saying, candidly, not knowing about the "hidden mike," that he, Franklin Roosevelt, President of the United States, was—a Communist agent. Under Party discipline. He was selling out the U.S. to his boss Josef Stalin, and his boss was saying, "Yes, comrade. You understand our needs; it is arranged that you will hold back the Allied armies in the West so that our Red Army can penetrate deeply enough into Central Europe, in fact to Berlin to establish Soviet mastery as far as—" And then the guttural, heavy accented voice dimmed as the two world leaders passed out of aud range.

Shutting it off again, Joseph Adams said to Colleen, "Despite the one flaw it was a top-notch job that Gottlieb did, there. The guy who played Roosevelt really looked like Roosevelt. The guy who played Stalin—"

"But the flaw," Colleen reminded him.

"Yes." It was a major one, the worst Fischer had made; in fact the only serious one among all the faked sequences of version A.

Josef Stalin had not known English. And, since Stalin could not speak English, this scene could not have taken place. The crucial scene, just now shown, revealed itself for what it was—and by doing so, revealed the entire "documentary" for what *it* was. A deliberate, carefully manufactured fraud, constructed for the purpose of getting Germany off the hook in regard to the deeds done, the decision taken, in World War Two. Because in 1982, Germany was once again a world power, and most important, a major shareholder in the community of nations titling itself "The Western Democracies," or more simply, Wes-Dem, the UN having disintegrated during the Latin American war of 1977, leaving in its place a power vacuum into which the Germans had expertly, eagerly rushed.

"I'm sick," Adams said to Colleen as he shakily picked up his cigarette. To think, he thought, that *what we are now* derives from such crude sleight-of-hand as that scene—Stalin conversing in a language he didn't know.

After a pause Colleen said, "Well, Fischer could have—"

"Easily fixed it up. One, sole, minor interpreter. That's all that was needed. But Fischer was an artist—he liked the idea of them talking tête-à-tête, no intermediary; he felt it would have more dramatic impact." And Fischer had been correct, since the "documentary" *had* been universally accepted as historically correct, as documenting the "sell-out" at Yalta, the "misunderstood" Adolf Hitler who had really only been trying to save the Western Democracies from the Commies . . .. and even the death camps; even that was explained away. And all it took was a few juxtaposed shots of British warships and starving camp victims, a few entirely faked scenes that simply never had actually occurred, some genuine footage from Wes-Dem military archives . . . and the soothing voice which tied it all in together. Soothing—but firm.

Neat.

"I don't see," Colleen said presently, "why it upsets you so. Is it because the error is so glaring? It wasn't glaring then, because who in 1982 knew that Stalin couldn't—"

"Do you know," Adams broke in, speaking slowly, carefully, "what the corresponding central hoax is in version B? Have you ever put your finger on it? Because even Brose, in my opinion, never saw into version B as he did version A."

Pondering, she said, "Let's see. In version B, for the Communist world of 1982 . . ." She continued to introspect, frowning, and then she said, "It's been a long time since I scanned any part of B, but—"

Adams said, "Let's start with the operational hypothesis underlying B. That the USSR and Japan are attempting to save civilization. England and the U.S. are secret allies of the Nazis, of Hitler; they brought him to power for the sole purpose of attacking the Eastern countries, of preserving the status quo against the new rising nations of the East. This we know. In World War Two England and the U.S. only *seemed* to fight Germany; Russia did all the land fighting on the Eastern Front; the Normandy landings—what did they call it? The Second Front?—only took place *after* Germany had been defeated by Russia; the U.S. and Britain wanted to rush in and greedily grab as much of the spoils—"

"Spoils," Colleen said, "which rightfully belonged to the USSR." She nodded. "But where did Fischer commit a technical error in B? The idea is credible, just as the idea in A is; and the genuine footage in B of the Red Army at Stalingrad—"

"Yes. All real. Authentic and properly convincing. The war really *was* won at Stalingrad. But—" He clenched his fist, injuring his cigarette; he then carefully dropped it into a nearby ashtray. "I'm not going," he said, "to scan B. Despite what the master monad told me. So I'm failing; I've ceased to grow and that means I'll be overtaken and that'll be it—I knew that last night before you left. I knew it again today when I heard Dave Lantano's speech and realized how much better it was than anything I can do—or will ever do. He's about nineteen. Twenty at the most."

"David is twenty-three," Colleen said.

Glancing up, Adams said, "You've met him?"

"Oh, he's in and out of the Agency; he likes to get back to the hot-spot of his so he can supervise his leadies, see that his villa is going to come out the way he wants it—in my opinion he's anxious to view it now because he knows he probably won't live to see it completed. I like him but he's so strange and enigmatic; a recluse, actually; comes here, feeds his speech to the 'vac, stands around, talks a little, very little, then is gone again. But what's the error in version B, the Pac-Peop version, that you know about and no one else, even Brose, ever noticed in all these years?''

Adams said, ''It's in the scene where Hitler makes one of his secret flights to Washington, D.C. during the war to confer with Roosevelt.''

''Oh yes. Fischer got the idea from Hess' flight to—''

''The important secret meeting between Roosevelt and Hitler. In May of 1942. Where Roosevelt—with Lord Louis Mountbatten, Prinz Batten von Battenberg, representing Britain—informs Hitler that the Allies will hold back the Normandy landings for at least a year so that Germany can use all her armies on the Eastern Front to defeat Russia. And tells him, too, that the plot-points of all supply convoys carrying war material to Russian northern ports will be regularly made known to the German Intelligence under Admiral Canaris, so that Nazi subs can sink them wolf-packwise. You remember the blurred distance shots that a 'Party comrade employed at the White House' made of that meeting . . . Hitler and Roosevelt seated together on the sofa, and Roosevelt assuring Hitler that he had nothing to worry about; the Allied bombing will be done at night so as to miss their targets, all information from Russia as to their military plans, troop dispositions and so forth will be available to Berlin within twenty-four hours of their entering U.K. and U.S. hands, via Spain.''

''They converse in German,'' Colleen said. ''Right?''

''No,'' he said angrily.

''In *Russian?* So the Pac-Peop audience can understand it? It's been so long since I—''

Adams said harshly. ''It's the arrival of Hitler at the 'secret U.S. Air Force base near Washington, D.C.' that the technical error occurs, and it's incredible that no one's noticed it. First of all, in World War Two there was no U.S. Air Force.''

She stared at him.

''It was still called the Army Air Corps,'' Adams said. ''Not yet a separate branch of the military. But that's nothing; that could be a minor error in the aud commentary—a mere nothing. Look.'' He swiftly removed the spool from the scanner, picked up the spool of version B; eyes to the scanner he deftly ran the spool, on and on, until he arrived at the scene, in episode sixteen, that he wanted; he then sat back and motioned her to follow the scene.

For a time Colleen was silent as she watched. "Here comes his jet now," she murmured. "In for the landing, late at night, at the—yes, you're right; the commentator is calling it a 'U.S. Air Force base,' and I dimly recall—"

"His *jet,*" Adams grated.

Halting the spool, Colleen looked up at him.

"Hitler lands secretly in the U.S. in May of 1942," Adams said, "in a Boeing 707 fan-jet. Those didn't come into use until the mid-1960s. There was only one jet plane extant during World War Two, a German-made fighter, and it never saw service."

"Oh my god," Colleen said, open-mouthed.

"But it worked," Adams said. "People in Pac-Peop believed it—by 1982 they were so used to seeing jets that they forgot that in '42 there were only what they called—" He couldn't remember.

"Prop planes," Colleen said.

"I think I can see," Adams said, "why the master monad of the archives referred me back to these, to the original source. All the way back to the work of Gottlieb Fischer, the first Yance-man; the man in fact who dreamed up the idea of Talbot Yancy." But who, unfortunately, had not lived to see the simulacrum actually built—and brought by the two power blocs into use. "The monad wanted me to see," he said, "that my anxiety about the quality of my work is undue. Excessive, because our work, our collective, historic efforts from the very beginning, starting with these two documentaries, *has been marred*. When you and I go out to fake things you and I and all the rest of us are just plain bound, at some place, sooner or later, to slip up."

"Yes." She nodded. "We're just mortals. We're not perfect."

"But the strange thing is," Adams said, "I didn't have that feeling about David Lantano. I had a fear reaction and now I see why. He's different. He is—or could be—perfect. Not like us. So what does that make him? Not a human?"

"God knows," Colleen said, nervously.

"Don't say that," he said. "For some reason I don't care to think about God in connection with David Lantano." Maybe, he thought, because the man is so close to the forces of death, living there as he does in that hot-spot, seared day after day by the radiation. As if, although it's burning him, killing him, he's imbibing back some mystical power.

He was again aware of his own mortality, the delicate stability of forces that, from the bio-chemical level on up, permitted a human being to exist.

But David Lantano had learned to live at the heart of those forces, and even to draw on them. How had he done this? Lantano, he thought, has a right to draw on something beyond our range; I'd just like to know how he manages it; I'd like to do it, too.

To Colleen he said, "I've learned the thing from these spoils of Fischer's two documentaries of 1982 that I'm supposed to learn, so I guess I can knock off." He rose, picked up the spools. "What I learned was this. Earlier today I saw and heard a speech by a twenty-two-year-old young new Yance-man and it scared me, and then I scanned these two versions of Fischer's 1982 documentary, and what I learned was this."

She waited, expectantly, with feminine, earth-mother patience.

"Even Fischer," he said, "the greatest of us all, couldn't have competed with David Lantano." This was what he had learned, certainly. But he was—at least right now—not sure exactly what it meant.

He had a feeling about it, however. One of these days he and the Yance-man class as a whole, including Brose himself, were going to find out.

ELEVEN

A sensitive rugged little device, operating on a sonarlike principle and attached to his suit, a sort of geologic version of what a submarine might employ, told Nicholas St. James as he labored away with the undersized portable scoop that he had toiled at last to within a yard of the surface.

He ceased work, trying to become at least temporarily calm. Because, he realized, in approximately fifteen minutes from now I will break through and then I will be stalked.

It hardly appealed to him, this instinctive knowledge that very quickly now he would become a quarry.

Something artificial and complicated, with thousands of accurate miniaturized components, with feedback and backup systems, with percept-extensors, power sources that were self-contained and virtually eternal, and, worst of all, tropisms that involved the essential quality of life: the factor called *warmth*.

The unhappy fact was simply this: that by being alive he attracted attention; this was the reality of the surface of Earth, and he had to be prepared for it, because he was going to have to enter into a dodge, a flight. He could not fight. There was no way to win. Either he evaded or he died. And the evasion must begin the instant he broke through, and, here in the stuffy darkness of the narrow tunnel, as he breathed canned air and clung insectlike to the spikes driven into the tunnel side itself, he thought that perhaps it's already too late.

Perhaps already, even before he broke through, he had been detected. The vibrations of his little overworked heated-up, about-to-give-out portable scoop. Or his breathing. Or—and always to this, the grotesque basic malign misuse of the basis of life—his body-heat might have triggered off an autonomic mine (he had seen them on TV) and the mine would already have detached itself from the spot at which it had screwed itself in until it had become invisible . . . detached itself and was now crawling over the rubble that littered Earth's surface like the bad remains of some dirty, gigantic, psychopathic, everybody-stewed-and-falling-down all-night party. Crawling so that it would intersect, meet him at the locus, the exact point, at which he broke through. Utter perfection, he thought, in the synchronization of time and space as coordinates between himself and it. Between what he was doing and what *it* was doing.

He knew it was there. Had known, really, from the moment he entered the tunnel and was, from below, at once sealed in. "You activists," he said, "you committee people; you ought to be here now."

His oxygen mask stifled his voice; it scarcely reached his own ears; he experienced it as a vibration transmitted through his facial bones. *I wish Dale Nunes had stopped me, he thought. How could I know, he thought, that I could be this afraid?*

This must be the neurological spring that sets psychotic paranoia going, he reflected. The acute, unpleasant awareness of being watched. It was, he decided, the most ugly feeling he had ever had; even the fear component was minor; the sense of conspicuousness itself was the overwhelming factor, the unbearable part.

He started up the scoop; it groaned, once more began to dig; dirt and rock gave way above him, and pulverized, burned, converted into energy or whatever the scoop did—a waste product like fine ash filtered from the posterior of the scoop, nothing more. Its mechanical metabolism had used up the rest, and so the tunnel did not simply fill behind him.

Therefore—he could turn back.

But he didn't. He went on.

Whining, the insignificantly sized speaker of his intercom to the committee in the Tom Mix ant tank below said, "Hey, President St. James; are you okay? We've been waiting an hour and you haven't said a word."

He said, "The only word I have to say," and then he shut up; why say it? They had heard the word before and anyhow they already knew how he felt. And anyhow—I am their elected President, he realized, and elected Presidents, even of subsurface ant tanks, don't officially use words like that. He scooped on. The intercom was silent; they had gotten the message.

Ten minutes later light flashed down at him; a mass of dirt, roots and stones tumbled into his face, and although his goggles and mask, in fact his entire helmet-structure protected him, he cringed. Sunlight. Horrible and gray and so sharp that he felt urgent hatred at it; he clawed upward, trying to lacerate it as if it were an eye, an eye that would never close. Sunlight. The diurnal, nocturnal cycle again, after fifteen years. If I could pray, he thought, I would. Pray, I suppose, that the sight of this, one of the oldest of gods, the solar deity, is not the forerunner of death; that I will live long enough to see this rhythm of day and night, not just one scalding, paltry glance.

"I'm through," he said into the intercom.

There was no answer. Either the battery had at last run down—but his helmet light still shone, although minutely, now, in the presence of the overhead midday sky. He shook the intercom savagely; all at once it seemed more important to find his way back to contact with the tank below than to go on—my god, he thought, my wife and my brother, my people; *I'm cut off.*

The urge to scramble back down; it was panic; it made him struggle beetlelike: he tossed dirt and stones up onto the surface and sent others raining down—he tore himself loose from the tunnel, scrabbled and clutched at the clammy, flat earth which was surface earth; horizontal, with no end. And he lay on it, fully, all parts of him pressed down as if he meant to imprint his form; I will leave an impression, he thought wildly. A dent the size of a human; it'll never go away, even if I do.

Opening his eyes he looked north—it was easy to tell north; he found it indicated in the rocks and grass, the dry, brown, desperately sick tufts of weedy grass under and around him; the polar field drew everything, rotated all life toward itself—and then he looked up and was amazed that the sky appeared so gray, not blue at all. Dust, he decided. From, of course, the war; the particles have never completely settled. He felt disappointed.

But the ground. Something alive staggered over his hand; it was a chitinous life form which he admired anyhow, just in his memory and knowledge of it. The ant held some small white particle in its mandibles and he watched it go; they were not bright, as a race, but at least they didn't give up. And—they had stayed up here; fifteen years ago they hadn't run: they had faced the Dies Irae, the Day of Wrath, and were still here. As witness this sample, this representative; he had, in it, seen not one ant but all ants, and eternally, as if it had staggered by him outside of time.

His intercom sputtered on, then. "Hey, President St. James! Are you through?" Jabbering excitement, contained in the miniscule apparatus.

"I'm through."

"Start telling; talk to us about it."

"First of all," he said, "the sky is gray because of the suspension of particles. That's sort of disappointing."

"Yeah, that's a shame!" They scuffled, hovered, at the other end.

Nicholas said, "I can't make out much. The ruins of Cheyenne are to my right; I see a couple of buildings still standing, but otherwise it's pretty bad. It's a long way off, the ruins; on the horizon. Closer to me are boulders. Actually—" It could be worse, and he was puzzled. Because far off he saw what appeared to be trees. "According to TV," he said, "there should be that big military base just across the Nebraska border; as we had planned I'll start northeast and hope—"

"Don't forget," the speaker rattled excitedly, "that according to all the rumors the blackmarket guys are supposed to be living in city ruins, in cellars and old H-bomb shelters. So if it doesn't look promising northeast head up directly north toward the remains of Cheyenne and see if you can contact someone there. I mean, there ought to be a lot of real deep cellars in a big city like that; a lot of local protection you know, on an individual basis, for one or two fellas here and there. And I mean, don't forget; they know how to keep away from the leadies; they'd have to. Right? Can you hear me?"

Nicholas said, "I hear you. All right; I'll—"

"And you have that box of hot-foil scatter particles to throw the thermotropic killing machines off; right? And the pellets for the constructs that are iserntropic—start flinging them around as you go. Ha-ha. Hansel and Gretel; right? Only you *want* the breadcrumbs eaten up."

He got warily, unsteadily to his feet.

And then they had him. He heard them move; released by his change of position they came and he turned with the meager weapon provided him by the smart shop boys from the tank. The first leady soared up as if helium-filled and utterly weightless, so that the beam of his handmade laser pistol passed beneath it; the leady was an old pro and it descended, spiraled so that it was slightly behind him as the other, bent over centipedelike, traveling at enormous speed directly at him, extended something which he could not make out: it was not firing at him, it was trying to nip him. He backed away, fired the miserable handmade laser pistol once more, uselessly, saw a portion of the leady's anatomy go, and then the other one, behind him, hooked him. The hook, he thought, of termination; the hook dragged him and he bounced over the rocks and tufts of weeds, as if caught by a vehicle that would not stop. He tried to disengage the hook; it had his suit and some of the flesh of his upper back and clearly the leady knew that he was helpless; he could not even turn over.

And then he understood why. What they were doing.

They were dragging him away from the tunnel as fast as possible; first, the leady which had gaffed him from behind, and the other, although no longer intact, which was still managing to fill in the tunnel entrance, sealing it; the leady turned some sort of beam on the ground, and the soil and rocks and tufts of weeds bubbled, boiled; steam rose and the entrance was gone, disfigured and obliterated. And then the dragging ceased. The leady halted, shoved him upright, knocked the intercom from his hand and crunched it with its pedal extremity. Systematically, the leady tore everything from him, gun, helmet, mask, oxygen tank, spaceman's suit—it ripped and shredded until, satisfied, it came to a halt. Stopped.

"You're Soviet leadies?" Nicholas said, then, gasping. Obviously they were. Wes-Dem leadies would hardly—

And then he saw stamped on the frame of the leady closest to him, not Cyrillic script, not Russian words, but English. Clearly enameled words, done with a stencil and one swipe of a wide brush—but not done in a tank subsurface; this had been added later, when the leady had risen to the surface by chute. Perhaps it had even been made in the Tom Mix, but that was over, changed, because the weird enameled notice read:

PROPERTY OF DAVID LANTANO
AGENCY IDENT 3-567-587-1
IF RETURNED NO QUESTIONS ASKED
BUT CONDITION MUST VARY BETWEEN
GOOD AND EXCELLENT

TWELVE

As he stood staring at the incomprehensible sign at its chest area the leady said to him, "Excuse us, sir, for our unpardonable treatment of you, but we were anxious to remove you from your tunnel and at the same time, if possible, close it over. Perhaps you can tell us direct, making possible the avoidance of using further detection devices. Are there any more individuals from your tank preparing to or in the process of following you up?"

Nicholas mumbled, "No."

"I see," the leady said, and nodded as if satisfied. "Our next question is this. What caused you to tunnel vertically, in defiance of the familiar ordinance and the grave penalties involved?"

Its companion, the partially damaged leady, added, "In other words, sir, kindly tell us why you are here."

After a time Nicholas said haltingly, "I—came to get something."

"Would you tell us the nature of this 'something'?" the intact leady asked.

For the life of him he could not make out if he should say or not; the whole environment, the world around him and these inhabitants, metallic and yet polite, pressing at him and yet respectful, bewildered him and made him disoriented.

"We will allow you a moment," the intact leady said, "to compose yourself. However, we must insist on your answering." It moved toward him, then, a device in its manual extremity. "I would like you to submit to a polygraphic reading of your statements; in other words, sir, a measuring by an independent percept system of the veracity of your answers. No offense is meant, sir; this is routine."

Before he knew what was happening, the lie detector had been clamped around his wrist.

"Now, sir," the intact leady said. "What description of conditions as they obtain here on the Earth's surface did you provide your fellow tankers below by means of the intercom system which we just now rendered inoperative; please give us ample and specific details."

He said haltingly, "I—don't know."

The damaged leady spoke up, directly to its companion. "There is no need to ask him that; I was near enough to monitor the conversation."

"Please run the playback," the intact leady said.

To Nicholas' aversion and consternation there all at once issued from the damaged leady's voice box the tape recording of his own conversation with those below. Out of the leady's mouth came the squeaky, distant but clear words, as if the leady was now himself, mimicking him horribly.

"Hey, President St. James! Are you through?"

And then his own voice, but slightly speeded-up, it seemed to him, answering. *"I'm through."*

"Start telling; talk to us about it."

"First of all, the sky is gray because—"

He had to stand there, by the pair of leadies, and hear everything once over again in its entirety; and all the time he wondered to himself, again and again, *What is going on?*

At last the total conversation had been run; the two leadies conferred. "He did not tell them anything of value," the intact leady decided.

"I agree." The damaged leady nodded. "Ask him again if they will be coming up." Both metal heads swiveled toward Nicholas; they regarded him intently. "Mr. St. James, will you be followed either now or later?"

"No," he said hoarsely.

"The polygraph," the damaged leady said, "bears out his statement. Now, once more, Mr. St. James; the purpose of your tunneling to the surface. I insist respectfully, sir, that you tell us; you *must* say why you are here."

"No," he said.

The damaged leady said to its companion, "Contact Mr. Lantano and inquire whether we should kill Mr. St. James or turn him over to the Runcible organization or the Berlin psychiatrists. Your transmitter is operative; mine was destroyed by Mr. St. James' weapon."

After a pause the intact leady said, "Mr. Lantano is not at the villa; the domestic staff and yard workers say that he is at the Agency in New York City."

"Can they contact him there?"

A long, long pause. Then, at last, the intact leady said, "They have contacted the Agency by vidline. Mr. Lantano was there, using the 'vac, but he has left since and no one at the Agency seems to know where or when he will turn up; he left no message with them." It added, "We will have to decide on our own."

"I disagree," the damaged leady said. "We must contact the nearest Yance-man, in Mr. Lantano's absence, and rely on his judgment, not our own. By means of the vidline at the villa we can perhaps contact Mr. Arthur B. Tauber to the east, at his demesne. Or if not him, then anyone at the New York Agency; the point is that Mr. St. James has told no one below in his tank anything as to the conditions on the surface and hence his death would be regarded by them as a bona fide war casualty. They would be satisfied."

"Your last point is well made," the intact leady said. "I think we should go, then, and kill him, and not bother the Yance-man Mr. Arthur B. Tauber who anyhow would be at the Agency and by the time we—"

"Agreed." The damaged leady brought forth a tubelike apparatus, and Nicholas knew that this was the dealer out of death; this would be it, for him, with no further debate: the colloquy between the two leadies—and he kept thinking over and over again, *we made them, ourselves, down in our shops; these are the products of our own hands*—this conversation was over and the decision had been made.

He said, "Wait."

The two leadies, as if out of formal, correct politeness, waited; did not kill him quite yet.

"Tell me," he said, "why, if you're Wes-Dem and not Pac-Peop, and I know you're Wes-Dem; I can see the writing on both of you—why would you kill me?" Appealing to them, to the extraordinary perceptive and rational neural equipment, the highly organized cephalic capabilities of the two of them—they were type VI—he said, "I came up here to get an artiforg pancreas, so we can fulfill our quota of war work. An artiforg; you understand? For our chief mechanic. For the war effort." But, he thought, I don't see the signs of any war. I see the remains, indication of a war that has passed . . . he saw ruins, but they were inactive; there was a quality of age about the landscape, and far off he did actually see trees. And the trees looked new and young and healthy. Then that's it, he thought. *The war is over*. One side won or anyhow the fighting has ceased and now these leadies belong not to Wes-Dem, are not part of a governmental army, but are the property of the individual whose name is stamped on them, this David Lantano. And it is from him that they take their orders—when they can find him. But he is not at the moment around to appeal to. And because of that, I have to die.

"The polygraph," the damaged leady said, "indicates great mentation on Mr. St. James' part. Perhaps it would be humane to inform him—" It broke off. Because it had been pulverized; where it had stood a heap of disconnected fragments teetered, an upright column that toppled and rapidly came apart. The intact leady spun about, spun full-circle, like a tall metal top; it sought in a veteran expert way the origin of the force that had obliterated its companion, and while it was doing that the concentrated beam of murder touched it, too, and it ceased to whirl. It collapsed, broke apart and settled and Nicholas found himself alone, facing nothing that lived or spoke or thought, even artificial constructs; the silence, everywhere, had replaced the feral activity of the two leadies who had been about to dispatch him and he was glad of that, intensely and absolutely relieved that they had been destroyed, and yet he did not comprehend; he looked in every direction, as the intact leady had done, and he, like it, saw nothing, only the boulders, the tufts of weeds, and, far off, the ruins of Cheyenne.

"Hey," he said loudly; he began to walk up and down, searching, as if he might stumble over it, the benign entity, any moment, as if it might be fly-sized, a bug at his feet, something insignificant that he could only locate by almost stepping on it. But—he found nothing. And the silence went on.

A voice, magnified by a power-driven horn, boomed, "Go to Cheyenne."

He hopped, turned; behind one of the boulders the man lurked, speaking but concealing himself. Why?

"In Cheyenne," the booming voice said, "you'll find ex-tankers who came up previously. Not from your tank, of course. But they'll accept you. They'll show you the deep cellars where there's minimal radioactivity, where you'll be safe for a while until you can decide what you want to do."

"I want an artiforg," he said, doggedly, like some reflex machine; it was all he could think of. "Our chief mechanic—"

"I realize that," the booming, horn-amplified voice said. "But I still advise, *go to Cheyenne*. It'll take you hours of walking and this area is hot; you must not stay up here too long. Get down into the Cheyenne cellars!"

"And you can't tell me who you are?"

"Do you have to know?"

Nicholas said, "I don't 'have to know.' But I'd like to. It would mean a lot to me." He waited. "Please," he said.

After a pause of overt, genuine reluctance a figure stepped from behind a boulder—so close to him that he leaped; the mechanical reinforcement of the voice had been a technical deception to distract efforts to locate the origin of the sound—it had successfully given a totally false impression of great vastness and distance to both him and the latter of the two leadies. And all spurious.

The figure who stood there was—

Talbot Yancy.

THIRTEEN

Standing at the far end of the table Verne Lindblom said, ''I think these are enough.'' He indicated the several weapons objects and then the neatly plastic-wrapped bones and skulls. Terran and nonterran; two distinct varieties, separate now, but soon to be mingled in the soil of Utah.

Joseph Adams was impressed. It had not taken Lindblom, the artisan, long. Even Stanton Brose, coasting up in his special wheeled chair, seemed surprised. And of course immensely pleased.

The other person present had no reaction; he was not permitted to: he loitered in the background. Adams wondered who he was and then he realized, with a jolt of aversion, that this was the Brose today who had infiltrated Runcible's staff; this was Robert Hig, who would find one or more—begin the process of turning up—these artifacts.

''My articles,'' Adams said, ''aren't even in rough, yet. And here you have all the completed artifacts themselves.'' He had, in fact, merely begun page one of article one; it would be days before he finished the batch of three, turned them over to the Agency's shops to be printed up into their magazine form, combined with other, probably authentic, scientific articles of thirty years ago, in prewar issues of *Natural World*.

''Don't fret,'' the ancient sagging mass in the motor-driven chair which was Stanton Brose muttered at him. ''We don't need to produce the issues of *Natural World* until our legal staff hauls Runcible up before the Recon Dis-In Council, and that'll take time; do them as quickly as you can, but we can go ahead and have these objects buried—we don't need to wait on you, Adams.'' He added, gratuitously, ''Thank god.''

"Do you know," Lindblom said to Adams, "that we've established this: Footemen, employed by Runcible, have warned him—or will warn him shortly—that *something* is being planned. Something roughly of this sort. But Foote's people won't really know what. Unless one of the four of us in this room is an agent for Webster Foote, and that's unlikely. After all, only we four know."

"One more," Brose corrected. "The girl who did the original drawings, especially the very authentic skull remains of the nonterrans. It required enormous anthropological and anatomical knowledge to make these specs; she had to know just what alterations from Homo sapiens to indicate . . . greater ridge bones over the eye sockets, undifferentiated molars, no incisors, less of a chin, but much greater frontal area of the skull so as to indicate a highly organized brain of far more than 1,500 c.c. capacity; in other words, a race more advanced evolutionwise than ours. And the same goes for those." He pointed to the leg bones. "No amateur could sit down and draw fibula and tibia like she did."

"And what about her?" Adams asked. "Would she leak any of this to Runcible or to Webster Foote's people?" As, he thought, I myself may well still do . . . as you, Verne Lindblom, know.

Brose said, "She's dead."

There was silence.

"I'm out of this," Lindblom said. He turned, started like a somnambulist toward the door.

Suddenly two Brose agents in shiny jackboots with their dainty cold faces materialized, blocking the door; god in heaven, where had they come from? Adams was appalled; they had actually been in the room all this time, but, no doubt due to some technological piece of witchcraft they had been absolutely inconspicuous. Cammed, he realized; an old-time much-used espionage assist . . . chameleoned into the fabric of the room's walls.

Brose said, "No one killed her; she had a coronary. The pressure of work; she overtaxed herself, unfortunately, because of the deadline we gave her. Christ, she was valuable; look at the quality of her work." He jabbed a flabby, pudgy finger at the Xeroxed copy of the original scroll of specs.

Hesitating, Lindblom said, "I—"

"It's the truth," Brose said. "You can see the medical report. Arlene Davidson; her demesne is in New Jersey. You knew her."

"That's true," Lindblom said, finally, speaking to Adams. "It is a fact that Arlene had an enlarged heart and had been warned not to overtax herself. But they—" He glowered futilely at Brose. "They pushed her. They had to have their material by due date, on schedule." To Adams he said, "Like with us. I got mine done; I can work fast under pressure. How about you? Are you going to live through those three articles?"

Adams said, "I'll live through it." I don't have an enlarged heart, he said to himself; I didn't have rheumatic fever as a child, like Arlene. But if I had, they'd push me anyhow, as Verne said, as they did with Arlene, even if it killed me; just so long as I died *after* I delivered the goods. He felt weak, powerless and sad. Our fake-producing factory, he thought, demands a lot from us; *we may be the ruling elite, but we are not idle*. Even Brose himself needs to be tireless. And at his age.

"Why didn't Arlene get an artiforg heart?" Robert Hig spoke up, astonishing them all. His tone was diffident, but it remained a good question.

"No hearts left," Brose murmured, displeased that Hig had entered the conversation. And in such a way.

"I understood that at least two—" Hig went on, but Brose cut in harshly.

"None *available,*" Brose amended.

In other words, Adams realized, they exist there in that subsurface warehouse in Colorado. But they're for you, you hulking, wheezing, dribbling, rotting old sack of fat; you need every artiforg heart there can be, to keep that carcass functioning. Too bad we can't duplicate the processes that sole licensed prewar manufacturer had developed . . . too bad we can't produce heart after heart here at the Agency's shops, or send an order by coax to one of the bigger ant tanks for them to put together a batch for us.

Oh hell, we could produce a heart, here, he thought. But—it'd be a simulated heart; it would look like the real thing, beat like it . . . but when you had it surgically installed it would turn out like everything we make turns out. And the patient wouldn't get much life out of *that*.

Our products, he realized soberly, could not sustain life for even a second. Commentary on us, on our efficacy. Good lord. And his sense of sadness grew; that vast, awful internal fog plucked at him as he stood here in this busy chamber of the Agency with his fellow

Yance-man. Verne Lindblom, who was also his friend, and his employer, Stanton Brose, and the nullity, Robert Hig who, surprisingly, had asked the one pointed question; good for Hig, Adams thought. For having the guts to ask it. One never knows; you can never write off a person entirely, no matter how colorless and empty and bought he seems.

Lindblom, with gravity and reluctance, at last returned to the table of new-looking artifacts. His tone was low and slowed-down; he spoke mechanically, without effect. "Anyhow, Joe, since Runcible will immediately carbon-date these, they must not only look six hundred years old—they'll have to *be* six hundred years old."

"You understand," Brose said to Adams, "that otherwise we'd hardly have had Verne here produce shiny new artifacts? Like your magazine articles, they'd have had to be aged. And you can see; these are not."

Because aging, Adams realized, as Brose said, can't be faked; Runcible would ferret it out. So—it's true, then. To Brose he said, "The rumors. About a time scoop of some sort. We always heard, but we didn't—couldn't be sure."

"It'll carry them back," Brose said to him. "It can move objects into the past but not return anything; it's one-way only. Do you know why that is, Verne?" He eyed Lindblom.

"No," Verne Lindblom said. To Joseph Adams he explained, "It was a wartime weapon, developed by a relatively small firm in Chicago. A Soviet missile got the firm, including all its personnel; we have the time scoop, but we don't know how it works or how to duplicate it."

"But it does work," Brose said. "It'll carry very small items back; we'll feed these artifacts, skulls, bones, all this on the table, piece by piece, into the scoop; that'll be done late at night on Runcible's land in Southern Utah—we'll have geologists present to show us how deep to sink them, and a leady team to dig. This part has to be highly precise, because if they're too deep Runcible's autonomic 'dozers won't turn them up. You see?"

"Yep," Adams said. And thought, What a use to put an invention like that to. We could shoot back scientific data, constructs of unfathomable value, to civilizations in the past—formulae for medicines . . . we could be of infinite aid to former societies and peoples; just a few reference books translated into Latin or Greek or Old English . . . we could head off wars, we could provide remedies that might halt the great plagues of the Middle Ages. We could communicate with Oppenheimer and Teller, persuade them not to develop the A-bomb and the H-bomb—a few film sequences of the war that we just lived through would do that. But no. It's to be for this, to concoct a fraud, one implement in a series of implements by which Stanton Brose gains more personal power. And originally the invention was even worse than that; it was a weapon of war.

We are, Adams realized, a cursed race. Genesis is right; there is a stigma on us, a mark. Because only a cursed, marked, flawed species would use its discoveries as we are using them.

"As a matter of fact," Verne Lindblom said, and bent to pick up another of the bizarre "nonterran" weapons from the table, "based on what I know of the time scoop as a weapon—that little Chicago firm called it a Reverse Metabolic Distributor or some such thing—I've based this on its design." He held the tubelike device out to Adams. "The Reverse Metabolic Distributor never saw action in the war," he said, "so we don't know how it would have functioned. But anyhow I needed a source for—"

"I can't see your lips," Brose complained; he swung his power-driven chair rapidly, so that he now sat where he could watch Lindblom's face.

Lindblom said, "As I was explaining to Adams, I needed a source for 'nonterran' weapons; obviously I couldn't merely put a grotesque outer-frame on our own familiar weapons from World War Three, because Runcible's experts might find enough components intact to pinpoint the resemblance. In other words—"

"Yes," Brose agreed. "It would be an odd coincidence indeed if the 'nonterrans' who invaded Earth six centuries ago just happened to have employed weaponry precisely like our own of the last war . . . the only difference being, as Verne says, the outer case; what Arlene drew."

"I had to fill them with components unfamiliar to our time," Verne Lindblom said. "And there wasn't the opportunity for me to invent them, so I turned to the advanced weapons archives here at the Agency that contains prototypes that never saw use." He glanced at Brose. "Mr. Brose," he said, "provided me entree. Otherwise I couldn't have gotten in." The advanced weapons archives of the Agency was one of the many sections of New York which Brose had "attached," just as he had attached the artiforgs in the Colorado subsurface warehouse. Everything spurious was available to all Yance-men. But the real thing—this was reserved for Brose alone. Or, in this case, by extension, to a small staff working under his immediate direction on a secret project. Unknown to the class of Yance-men as a whole.

"So these really are weapons," Adams said, absorbed in an almost frightened contemplation of the bizarrely shaped artifacts. *The fakery had gone that deep*. "I could then pick up one of these and—"

"Sure," Brose said genially. "Shoot me. Take any one of them, point it at me, or if you're tired of Verne, get him."

Verne Lindblom said, "They don't work, Joe. But after six centuries of being buried in the soil of Utah—" He grinned at Joseph Adams. "If I could make them really work I could take over the world."

"That's right," Brose chuckled. "And you'd be working for Verne, instead of me. We had to get the—what did they call it?—the Reverse Metabolic Distributor prototype out of the advanced weapons archives in order to make use of it retrograde scoopwise, so Verne had a good long opportunity to open it up and fuss—" He corrected himself. "No, that's right; you were forbidden to fuss, weren't you, Verne? My memory's slipping."

Woodenly, Verne said, "I got to look. But not to touch."

"It hurts a manual type like Verne," Brose said to Adams. "To be limited to just looking; he likes to feel things with his fingers." He chuckled. "That must have been painful, Verne, that glimpse you had of the prototype weapons from the war, the advanced hardware that never got into production, never reached our autofacts or the Soviets'. Well, someday my brain will give out . . . arteriosclerosis or some such thing, a clot or a tumor, and then you can beat out every other Yance-man and replace me. And *then* you can go into the advanced prototypes section of the weapon archives and putter and fuss and fondle with your fingers all day long."

From his respectfully distant place, Robert Hig said, "I'd like to be sure of a couple of points, Mr. Brose. Now, I find one or two of these objects. All corroded and decayed, of course. Should I recognize them as nonterran? I mean, when I take them to Mr. Runcible—"

"You tell him," Brose said harshly, "that you know, because you're an engineer, that what you have is *not* terran-made. No American Indians of the year 1425 made objects like that—hell, anybody would know that: you won't have to back up your report to Runcible with any engineering or scientific jargon; you show him the weapons and tell him they came from the six-hundred-year stratum and look at them—are these flint-tipped arrows? Are these unbaked clay pitchers or granite hollowed-out grinding stones? You say that and then you get the hell right back to the 'dozers and see that more and more, especially the non-Homo sapiens skulls, get turned up."

"Yes, Mr. Brose," Robert Hig said, and nodded obediently.

Brose said, "I certainly would like to see Louis Runcible's face when you show him those finds." His rubbery old eyes were wet with anticipation.

"You will," Lindblom reminded him. "Since Hig will have one of those shirt-button cameras going, complete with aud track. So when the litigation begins we can supply proof that Runcible was not ignorant of either the discoveries or their scientific value." His voice was faintly edged with contempt—contempt for an aging brain which could not retain all the facts, which had already forgotten this vital part of the project. To Joseph Adams, Lindblom said, "You know those little action cameras. Gottlieb Fischer always used them in his documentaries; that's how all the 'blurred fuzzy secret espionage shots' were obtained."

"Oh yes," Adams said somberly. "I know." How little chance there was that *he* would forget the existence of the famous shirt-button camera. Circa 1943, he thought acidly, according to Fischer. "Are you sure," he said, "you haven't made these finds *too* valuable? Of such fantastically great scientific worth that even Runcible—"

"According to the Berlin psychiatrists," Brose said, "the more the scientific worth the more fear he'll have of losing his land. So the more he'll be inclined to hide the find."

"You'd have gone to a lot of work for nothing," Adams said, "if your Berlin psychiatrists have guessed wrong." And he felt within him the hope that they had. The hope that Runcible would do the reputable thing, would at once proclaim the finds to the world—instead of delivering himself over to his enemies via his weaknesses, his fears and lusts, his greed.

But he had a feeling that the Berlin psychiatrists were right.

Unless someone—and god knew who that might be—came to Louis Runcible's aid, the man was doomed.

FOURTEEN

In the sun that filtered through the vine-entangled latticework of the patio of his Capetown villa, Louis Runcible lay prone, listening to the report by the Footeman, the abstract-carrier representative from the international private police corporation originating in London, Webster Foote, Limited.

"On Monday morning," the Footeman said, reading from his compiled documents, "our monitoring devices picked up a vidcall between two Yance-men, Joseph Adams who is in Ideas and Verne Lindblom who is in Construct, that is, a builder for Eisenbludt, generally speaking, although of late Brose has had him at the Agency in New York."

"And this conversation," Louis Runcible said. "It mentioned me?"

"No," the Footeman admitted.

"Then for chrissake—"

"We feel—that is, Mr. Foote himself personally feels that you should be given this data. Allow me to summarize it."

Dully, Runcible said, "Okay. Summarize." Hell, he thought; I know they're out to get me. I better be receiving something from you for my money besides just knowing *that*. Because I don't need Webster Foote to tell me *that*.

The Footeman said, "Adams and Lindblom discussed the next visual project which Eisenbludt will film at his Moscow studios; it will be the destruct of San Francisco. Adams mentioned a new speech which he had written to be 'vacked and then programmed to the sim. 'Hand done,' he described it."

"And for this I'm paying you—"

"A moment please, Mr. Runcible," the Footeman said frostily in his English manner. "I will now quote the direct words of the Yance-man Lindblom, as our monitors picked them up. 'I heard a rumor.' He was speaking, you understand, to his friend. 'You're going to be pulled off speeches and put onto a special project. Don't ask me what; my source didn't know. A Footeman told me.' " The Footeman was silent, then.

"What next?"

"Then," the Footeman said, "archeology was mentioned."

"Hmm."

"They joked about the destruct of ancient Carthage and the war fleet of Athens. It was amusing, but of no relevance. Allow me, however, to make this point. What the Yance-man Lindblom said was untrue. No one from our corporation informed him of any 'special project.' He undoubtedly told Adams that so that Adams would not press him for details. Obviously his source came from within the New York Agency. However—"

"However," Runcible said, "we know there's a special project being inaugurated and that an idea man and one of Eisenbludt's fake city builders are involved, and that it's top secret. Even within the Agency."

"Correct. This is indicated by Lindblom's unwillingness to—"

"What's Webster Foote's theory about it?" Runcible asked. "What's he think might be going on?"

"Since this vidphone conversation on Monday the builder Verne Lindblom has been perpetually at work; he has slept either at the Agency or at Eisenbludt's studios in Moscow—he has not had time to return to his demesne and take his leisure. Second. No speech by Adams has been 'vacked this week. In other words, before he could 'vac the speech which he—"

"And that," Runcible said, "is *all* you guys have found out? That's it?"

"We know only one more item which might pertain. Brose left Geneva several times and flew by high-velocity flapple to the Agency. And at least once—and possibly twice—conferred with Adams, Lindblom, and possibly one or two others; we're not sure, frankly. As I say, Mr. Foote believes that this 'special project' is connected with you in some manner, and, as you know, Mr. Foote relies on his mild but quite helpful parapsychological hunches, his precog ability to foresee coming events.

"He does not, however, in this instance, foresee anything clearly.

But he wants to emphasize this point; *please notify him of anything unusual that occurs in your business operations.* No matter how trivial. And contact Mr. Foote immediately, before you do anything else; Mr. Foote is quite frankly, on an extrasensory level, concerned as to your welfare."

Runcible said tartly, "I wish Webster's concern had brought more actual data to light."

With a deprecatory, philosophic gesture the Footeman said, "No doubt so does Mr. Foote himself." He shuffled and reshuffled his documents, in an effort to conjure up something more. "Oh. One item. Not related that we know of, but interesting. A Yance-man, female, named Arlene Davidson, who has a demesne in New Jersey; the Agency's top draftsman. Died of a massive coronary during the past weekend. Late Saturday night."

"Any effort made to obtain an artiforg heart for her?"

"None."

"The skunk," Runcible said, meaning Brose. Hating him—if it were possible to hate Brose any more than he did already.

"She was known," the Footeman said, "to have a weak heart. Enlarged, from childhood, due to rheumatic fever."

"In other words—"

"She may have been given a deadline for something major; overworked. But that's conjecture. It is *not* usual, however, for Brose to go so often out of Geneva to New York; he is, after all, in his eighties. This 'special project'—"

"Yeah," Runcible agreed. "It must really be something." Again he pondered, and then he said, "Brose has, of course, penetrated deep into my enterprise."

"Correct."

"But I don't know and you don't know—"

"We have never been able to tag the Brose agent or agents in your operations. I'm sorry." He looked, too, genuinely unhappy; it would have been a major coup of Webster Foote, Limited, to have unearthed the Brose-creatures on Runcible's payroll.

"What I'm wondering about," Runcible murmured, "is Utah."

"Pardon?"

"I'm all ready to give the signal to my auto-rigs and leady teams near what used to be St. George to go ahead." This was pretty widely known.

"Mr. Foote is aware of that, but he has no recommendation; at least none he passed on to me."

Raising himself up, then turning over and getting to his feet, Louis Runcible said, "I guess there's no use in waiting. I'll vid them to go ahead and start digging. And hope."

"Yes sir." The Footeman nodded.

"Fifty thousand people," Runcible said.

"Yes, it'll be large."

"Who will be living where they ought to be, under the sun. Not down in a septic tank. Like a salamander at the bottom of a dried-up well."

Still shuffling his documents, trying to come up with something of use, trying and unhappily failing, the abstract-carrier Footeman said, "I wish you good luck. Maybe next time . . ." And he wondered if, for Runcible, there would *be* a further report. This inadequate—admittedly so—one today might well be the last, if his employer Webster Foote's extrasensory intimation were at all correct.

And generally they proved to be.

FIFTEEN

From the mangled, badly distributed chunks that once had been high buildings, streets, the intricate, strong structures of a major city, four men rose to intercept Nicholas St. James. "How come," the first of them said, and all were bearded, ragged, but evidently healthy, "no leadies detected you?"

Utterly weary, Nicholas stood for a time and then he seated himself on a broken stone, fished futilely in his coat pocket for a cigarette—the pack had been ripped away by the leady—and then said, "Two did. When I broke through. They must have picked up the vibrations of the scoop."

"They're very sensitive to that," the leader of the group agreed. "To any machinery. And any radio signals, if you for instance—"

"I was. An intercom to below. They recorded the whole thing."

"Why'd they let you go?"

"They were destroyed," Nicholas said.

"Your fellow tankers came up after you and got them. That's what we did: there were five of us originally, and they got the first one up. They weren't killing him; they were going to drag him off to one of those—you wouldn't know. Runcible's conapts. Those prisons." He eyed Nicholas. "But we got them from behind. Only, they killed that first man, or actually what happened was he got killed when we fired on the leadies. I guess it was our fault." The man paused. "My name's Jack Blair."

One of the other bearded men said, "What tank are you from?"

"The Tom Mix," Nicholas said.

"And that's near here?"

"Four hours' walk." He was silent. They, too, seemed not to know what to say; it was awkward, and all of them stared at the ground and then at last Nicholas said, "The two leadies who had me were destroyed by Talbot Yancy."

The bearded men stared at him fixedly. Unwinkingly.

"It's god's truth," Nicholas said. "I know it's hard to believe, but I saw him. He hadn't intended to come out; he didn't want to, but I got him to. I got a good close look at him. There was no doubt." Around him the four bearded men continued to stare. "How could I not recognize him?" Nicholas said, then. "I've seen him on TV for fifteen years, three or four and even five nights a week."

After a time Jack Blair said, "But—the thing is, there is no Talbot Yancy."

One of the other men spoke up, explaining. "See, what it is, is that it's a fake; you know?"

"What is?" Nicholas said, and yet he did know; he sensed the enormity of it in a flash: a fake so vast that it could not even be described. It truly beggared description; it was hopeless for these men to try and he was going to have to see, to experience it, for himself.

Jack Blair said, "What you're looking at on your TV screen every night, down there in—what'd you say? The Tom Mix?—down in your tank, what you call 'Yancy,' the Protector, that's a robot."

"Not even a robot," one of the other bearded men corrected. "Not even independent, or what they call intrinsic or homeo; it's just a dummy that sits there at that desk."

"But it talks," Nicholas said, reasonably. "It says heroic things. I mean, I'm not arguing with you. I just don't understand."

"It talks," Jack Blair said, "because a big computer called Megavac 6-V or something like that programs it."

"Who programs the computer?" Nicholas asked presently. The whole conversation had a slow, dreamlike, heavy quality to it, as if they were trying to talk under water; as if a great weight filled them all. "Someone," he said, "would have to feed those speeches to it; the computer didn't—"

"They have a lot of trained guys," Jack Blair said. "Yance-men, they're called. The Yance-men who are idea men, they write the speeches and feed them to Megavac 6-V and it does something to the words, adds the right intonations and gestures for the dummy to do. So it looks authentic. And it all goes on tape, and it's reviewed in Geneva by the top Yance-man who runs it all, a jerk named Brose.

And when he approves the tape then it's put over the coaxial cable and transmitted to all the ant tanks in Wes-Dem."

One of the other men added, "There's one in Russia, too."

Nicholas said, "But the war."

"It's been over for years," Jack Blair said.

Nodding, Nicholas said, "I see."

"They share film studios in Moscow," Blair said. "Just like they share the New York Agency. Some talented Commie producer named Eisenbludt; he stages all the scenes of destruct you see on your TV screen. Usually it's in min—done in scale. Sometimes, though, it's life-size. Like when they show leadies fighting. He does a good job. I mean, its convincing; I remember and sometimes, when the TV set we have up here is working, we manage to catch it. We were fooled, too, when we were below. He, that Eisenbludt, and all the Yance-men; they've fooled everybody almost, except sometimes tankers do come up anyhow. Like you did."

Nicholas said, "But I didn't come up because I guessed." Carol began to, he said to himself; Carol was right. She's smarter than I am; *she knew*. "Is all the world like this?" He gestured at the ruins of Cheyenne around them. "Radioactive? Just rubble?"

"Oh hell no," Blair said agitatedly. "This is a hot-spot; there now aren't very many left. The rest is a park. They've made the world into a great park and it's split up into their demesnes, their estates; they, the Yance-men—they each have entourages of leadies. Like Medieval kings. It's sort of interesting." His voice died away. "But I mean, it's not fair. At least I don't think so."

The other bearded men nodded vigorously; they agreed. It was not fair. No doubt of that.

Nicholas said, "How do you people live?" He pointed at the four of them. "Where do you get food?" And then he thought of something else. "Are there more of you?"

"In our bunch there's two hundred ex-tankers," Blair said. "Living here in the ruins of Cheyenne. We're all supposed to be in prisons, in huge condominium apartment buildings that this guy I mentioned named Runcible builds; they're not bad, not like the tanks—I mean, you don't feel like a rat trapped in a tin box. But we want—" He gestured. "I can't explain it."

"We want to be able to come and go," one of the other bearded men explained. "But actually we can't, living this way. We can't risk leaving the Cheyenne area, because then leadies would catch us."

"Why don't they come here?" Nicholas said.

"They do," Blair said, "but they sort of don't—try very hard; you know what I mean? They just go through the motions. Because see, this is part of a new demesne that's being formed; the villa, the building, isn't finished yet or anything, and it's still hot. But a Yance-man has moved in here, taking a chance. Trying to live, and if he does, if the r.a. fails to kill him, then this is his; it becomes his demesne and he's the dominus."

Nicholas said, "David Lantano."

"Right." Blair stared at him oddly. "How'd you know?"

"It was two of his leadies," Nicholas said, "that hooked me."

"And they were going to *kill* you?"

He nodded.

The four bearded men exchanged apprehensive, disconcerted glances. "Was Lantano at his villa? Did he okay it?"

"No," Nicholas said. "They tried to contact him but they weren't able to. So they decided on their own."

"The dumb saps," Blair said, and cursed. "Lantano wouldn't have let them; I'm positive. He'd have been sore. But they were built to kill; I mean, a lot of leadies are veterans of the war: they have the reflex to destroy life. Unless their dominus tells them otherwise. But you're lucky to get away; that's dreadful—I mean, that gets me. It does."

"But," one of the other men said, "what he said about Yancy; how can that be?"

"I saw him," Nicholas repeated. "I know it was him."

Jack Blair said, quoting an obscure text, " 'I saw God. Do you doubt it? Do you dare to doubt it?' What kind of weapon did he, this guy who saved you, use? A laser pistol?"

"No. The leadies were pulverized. Into dust." He tried to make it clear, how violent and sudden an abolition of the two leadies it had been. "Just mounds," he said. "Of old dry flakes, like rust. Does that make any sense?"

"That's a Yance-man advanced type weapon, all right," Blair said, nodding slowly. "So it was a Yance-man who saved you; no ex-tankers have that weapon; I don't even know what it's called but it's left over from the war I suppose—they've got a lot, and every now and then a couple of Yance-men who're neighbors get into a beef over the property line, you know, where one's land ends and the next guy's starts. And they make a dive for the open section of the weapons archives at the Agency in New York—that's where all that reading matter is put together—and they come flying back to their demesnes as fast as hell aboard those little flapples. And they lead their retinues of leadies into battle; it's really funny—they plug away at each other, potshot like mad, destroy a dozen or so leadies or maim them, and even a Yance-man now and then gets it. And then they send the maimed leady down below to the nearest tank to fix it up in its shops. And they're always sequestering the brand-new leadies made down below, to add to their retinues."

Another of the bearded men chimed in, "Some Yance-men at their demesnes have like two thousand leadies. A whole army."

"Brose for instance," Blair said, "he's supposed to have ten or eleven thousand, but technically *all* the leadies in Wes-Dem are under the military command of General Holt; he can pre-empt, you know: supersede the orders of any Yance-man, any dominus of a demesne, and call for its leadies. Except of course Brose." His voice sank. "No one can supersede Brose. Brose is above them all, like for instance he's the only one who has access to the weapons archives where the advanced types, the ones that never saw action, the really terrible prototypes are, that if they had used there'd be no planet. The war just barely stopped in time. Another month and—nothing." He gestured.

"I wish," Nicholas said, "I had a cigarette."

The four bearded men consulted, and then, reluctantly, a pack of Lucky Strikes was held out to Nicholas; he carefully took only one of the cigarettes, let them regain the remainder of the precious pack.

"We're short on everything," Blair said apologetically as he lit Nicholas' cigarette for him. "See, this new dominus who's starting his demesne here, this David Lantano; he's not a bad guy. He sort of, like I said, holds his leadies back, when he's around to do it, so they don't wipe us out or get us into one of those conapts; he sort of looks out for us. He gives us food." Blair was silent for a time, then; his expression, to Nicholas, was unreadable. "And cigarettes. Yeah, he's really trying to help us. And pills; he personally drops by with anti-radiation pills; they help restore the red blood cells or something. He takes them himself. I mean, he really has to."

"He's sick," another bearded ex-tanker added. "He's badly burned; see, the law requires he's got to be here on the hot-spot twelve hours out of every twenty-four; he can't get down subsurface into cellars like we can; we stay below—we just came up because we spotted you."

To Blair he said, nervously, "In fact we better get back to the hovel right now. We've been exposed long enough for one day." He gestured at Nicholas. "And him, especially; he's been walking on the surface for hours."

"You're going to take me in?" Nicholas said. "I can live with you fellas; is that what I'm to understand?"

"Sure." Blair nodded. "That's how our colony formed, here; you think we're going to boot you out? Why would we?" He seemed genuinely angry. "For some leady to kill, or—" He broke off. "Some charity that would be. You're welcome to stay here all you want. Later, after you know more, if you want to turn yourself in, you can go live in a conapt; must be hundreds of thousands of ex-tankers in those conapts—that's up to you entirely. But *wait*. Get your bearings." He started off along a meager trail among the rubble, a sort of goat path; the others, including Nicholas, followed single file. "It takes weeks sometimes," Blair said, over his shoulder, "to really sober up, to shake off what you've been fed over what they call the 'coax' for fifteen years." Pausing, halting for a moment and turning, he said earnestly, "Intellectually maybe you accept it, but I know; emotionally you can't right away, it's just too much. There's no Yancy and never was—*never* was, Mr. St. Nicholas—"

"No," Nicholas corrected. "Nicholas St. James."

"There never was a Yancy. There *was* a war, though, anyhow, at first; as you can see." He gestured at the miles of ruins ahead of them. At Cheyenne. "But Yancy was made up by Stanton Brose, based on an idea of a West German film producer of the last century; you probably have heard of him, only he died before your time, but they still were showing his documentary, *The Winning in the West,* that twenty-five part series on TV about World War Two. I remember it when I was a kid."

"Gottleib Fischer," Nicholas said. "Sure." He had seen that great classic documentary, not once but several times; it was considered in the same category with *The Blue Angel* and *All Quiet On the Western Front* and *The Dizzy Man*. "And he made up Yancy? Gottleib Fischer?" He followed the four of them, eager and anxious; perplexed. "But why?"

"To rule," Blair said, without stopping; the four of them hurried, now, eager to get back down into what they called their hovel, their deep-chamber which had not been contaminated by the H-bombs that had made this region what it was.

" 'Rule,' " Nicholas echoed, understanding. "I see."

"Only as you maybe remember, Fischer disappeared on that ill-fated flight to Venus; he was eager to be one of the first travelers into space, he just had to go, and that was that, because—"

"I remember," Nicholas said. The event had made huge headlines in the homeopapes at the time. Gottlieb Fischer's untimely tragic death; his spaceship's fuel igniting during reentry . . . Fischer had died in his late thirties, and so there had been no more documentaries, no more films equal to *The Winning in the West*. After that only nonentities had followed, except, slightly before the war, the interesting experimental films of some Russian, a Soviet film producer whose work had been banned from Wes-Dem . . . what had been his name?

As he struggled to keep up with the swiftly moving bearded men, Nicholas remembered the Russian film producer's name. Eisenbludt. The man Blair had just now said did the faking of the war scenes for the tankers, in both Wes-Dem and Pac-Peop, the visual "confirmation" of the lies that comprised Yancy's speeches. So at last the people of Wes-Dem had gotten to see Eisenbludt's films.

Obviously there was no more hostility between East and West. Eisenbludt was no longer an "enemy" film producer as he had been at the time Nicholas St. James and his wife Rita and his kid brother Stu had been prodded virtually at gun-point into descending into the Tom Mix for what they had believed, at the time, to be for perhaps a year at the longest . . . or, as real pessimists had forecast, two years.

Fifteen. And out of that fifteen—

"Tell me exactly," Nicholas said, "when the war ended. How many years ago?"

"It's going to make you hurt," Blair said.

"Say. Anyhow."

Blair nodded. "Thirteen years ago. The war lasted only two years on Earth, after the first one year on Mars. So—thirteen years you've been snow-jobbed, Nicholas, or whatever you said; sorry, I forgot again. Nick. How's that: Nick."

"Fine," Nicholas murmured, and thought of Carol and Rita and old Maury Souza and Stu and all the others, Jorgenson and Flanders and Haller, Giller and Christenson, Peterson and Grandi and Martino and on and on, even to Dale Nunes; even to the Tom Mix's pol-com. Did Nunes know? Nicholas thought. If Nunes knows, I swear; I affirm; I will in god's name kill him—I will do it with my hands so as to feel it, and nothing will stop me. But it was impossible, because Commissioner Nunes had been shut up there with them. But—not for all that time. Only for—

Nunes had known. He had only a few years ago descended the chute, from the "Estes Park Government," from Yancy.

"Listen, Mr. James," one of the bearded men said, "I was wondering; if you didn't guess, then what'd you come up for? I mean, you'd expect to find nothing but the war, and they tell you on TV—boy, how I remember—they'd shoot you on sight—"

"And that's what practically happened to him," Blair said.

"—because of the Bag Plague and the Stink of Shrink, neither of which exists in reality; that's another fink snow-job they made up, those two bacterial plagues, although there really was that hideous nerve gas we invented, that New Jersey Chemical Corporation or whatever its name was; a Soviet missile got it, I'm glad to say, right off, including everyone in it. But it's radioactive in this spot, although the rest of the surface—"

"I came up," Nicholas said, "to buy an artificial pancreas. An artiforg. From the blackmarket."

"There aren't any," Blair said.

Nicholas said, "I'm prepared to—"

"There aren't any! Nowhere! Even the Yance-men can't get them; Brose has them attached; he owns them all, legally." Blair turned, his face wild with rage; distorted like a handpuppet writhing from the twisting fingers contained within. "All for Brose, who's eighty-two or -three and's full of artiforgs, all but the brain. The company's gone and now nobody knows how to make them; we're degenerate, I mean, that's what war does. The Yance-men tried, but they didn't work, grafted in, for more than a month or so. A lot of very specialized techniques depending on what they call 'highly sophisticated' equipment, you know, delicate tools and all—I mean, it was a *real war* while it lasted; don't forget that. The Yance-men have their demesnes, and you guys down below make leadies for them, and they fly around in their goddam little flapples, the Agency in New York cranks out speeches and Megavac 6-V is kept functioning but—sheoot." He gave up, walked on in silence.

Nicholas said presently, "I've got to get the pancreas."

"You'll never get it," Blair said.

"Then," he said, "I've got to get back to the Tom Mix and tell them. They can come up; they can forget the quota and the threat of having the tank abolished.''

''Sure they can come up. And be prisoners above ground. It's better; I agree. Runcible is starting a whole new constellation of conapts in the Southern Utah region; see, we hear a lot of news because David Lantano gave us a wide-band radio receiver, just aud, not vid, but we pick up the stuff that's transmitted not to the ant tanks but like between demesnes; they're always blabbing away to each other in the evening because they're lonely. Just maybe one guy in his fifty-thousand-acre demesne with his leadies.''

''No families?'' Nicholas said. ''No children?''

''They're most of them sterile,'' Blair said. ''See, they were on the surface during the war, remember. Mostly at the Air Arm Academy at Estes Park. And they lived; they were the elite of the U.S., the young Air Arm cadets. But—they can't reproduce. So in a way they paid. Real high. For what they've got. For having been the elite cadets in that great bomb-proof structure in the Rockies.''

''We paid, too,'' Nicholas said. ''And look what *we* got.''

''You wait a while,'' Blair said. ''Think it over about trying to get back to your ant tank to tell them. Because the way the system up here is run—''

''They'd be better off,'' one of his bearded compatriots put in, defiantly. ''You've forgotten what it's like down there; you're getting senile like old Brose. Runcible's made sure they're better off; he's a darn good construction man, they have ping-pong and swimming pools and wall-to-wall carpet of that funny plastic imitation—''

''Then how come,'' Blair said, ''you're squatting here in these ruins instead of lounging at a swimming pool in one of those conapt constellations?''

The man grunted, gestured. ''I just—like to be free.''

No one commented; it did not require it.

But another topic did seem to require additional comment, and Blair, musingly, supplied it. To Nicholas he said, ''I just don't get it. Nick. How could Talbot Yancy have rescued you if Talbot Yancy doesn't exist?''

Nicholas said nothing. He was too weary to speak.

And anyhow he did not know.

SIXTEEN

The first giant autonomic 'dozer groaned like a stiff old man. And, as it dipped stink-buglike head down, tail up, the first scoop of earth—and a huge scoop, too—was gathered, pried loose, swung up and then off to one side; the scoop of dirt was dropped into a waiting converter, also on autocircuit, operating homeostatically, without human attention. Within its field the dirt was transformed into energy, and that energy, which did not deserve to be wasted, was carried by cable to a major storage meta-battery assembly a quarter mile away. The meta-battery, a development which had come shortly before the war, could store up power which, when read off as ergs, consisted of billions of units. And—it could store that power for decades.

The energy from the meta-battery would provide electricity to run the completed dwelling units of the conapt buildings; it would be the source for everything that lit up, heated, cooled or turned.

Over the years Runcible had made his modus operandi a highly efficient one. Nothing was discarded.

And the real profit, Robert Hig reflected as he stood near the automatic 'dozer—or rather near the first one; twelve had gone into operation simultaneously—came ultimately from the people who would live in the conapts. Because, as they had worked below ground in their ant tanks, assembling leadies to augment the entourages, the private armies of the demesne owners, now they would work for Runcible.

The lower floors of each conapt building consisted of shops, and in these shops the components for the leadies were made. The components, turned out by hand—the intricate network of the surface autofac system having been wiped out by the war. Below ground the tankers of course did not know this, had no idea where their supply of components originated. Because to let them know this would have been to let them know—god forbid—that humans could live on the surface.

And the whole point, Hig reflected, is to see that they don't know, because just as soon as they come up we will have another war.

At least so he had been told. And he did not question this; he was, after all, not a Yance-man; he was merely an employee of the Agency, of Brose. Someday, if he were lucky and did his job properly, Brose would advance his name as candidate; he would be legally entitled to seek out a hot-spot for his demesne . . . assuming any hot-spots still existed by then.

Perhaps, Hig thought, as a result of this one job, this major special Agency project, I'll be a Yance-man. And then I can start paying those private cops of Webster Foote to keep readings going for me in the hot-spots that remain; I can start the long vigil like David Lantano did up until just recently. If he could do it, so can I, because who ever heard of him before?

"How's it look, Mr. Hig?" a human workman yelled at him, as all the 'dozers dug, dropped their dirt into the converters, dug again.

"Okay," Hig yelled back.

He walked closer to examine the exposed hard brown dirt; the 'dozers were to go down fifty feet, create a flat depression five square miles wide. In no sense was this an unusual excavation task, in terms of what Runcible's rigs could accomplish; the problem here at the start was merely to produce level ground, rather than excavate as such. Surveying teams, high-type leadies, could be observed here and there, utilizing their tripod-mounted theodolites to determine the true horizontal plane. The digging, then, would not take much time; this was not like the days before the war when the ant tanks had been buried—this was nothing in comparison.

Hence the buried artifacts had to appear soon. Or they would not be found at all. In less than two days in fact the digging would be done.

I hope, Hig thought, *there's been no foul-up, that the damn things aren't too deep. Because if they are, then so ends the special project; it's over as soon as the first load of concrete is poured, the first vertical steel shafts go in; in fact when the first plastic forms are laid to contain the concrete.* And already the forms were arriving by air-lift. From the site of the last construction job.

To himself he said, *So I better be ready. Any minute. To halt the 'dozers, stop the scooping and digging and whirring and wheezing; bring it all to a grinding halt. and then—*

Begin to yell my head off.

He tensed himself. Because, within the brown hard surface, below the level of dead tree roots, he already saw something glint, something smeared and dark, that would have passed unnoticed except for his vigil. The leadies wouldn't notice; the rigs wouldn't notice; even the other human engineers wouldn't notice—they all had their jobs.

As he had his. He peered. Was it just a rock, or was it the first of the—

It was. A rusted dark weapon; hard to believe, but the same that he had seen last night, shiny and new, just out of Yance-man Lindblom's expert hands. What a change six centuries had brought: Hig felt a terrible forbidding distrust of his senses—it *couldn't* be what Lindblom had made, what he and Adams and Brose and Lindblom had stood together viewing on the table. It was barely recognizable . . . he walked toward it, squinting in the sun. Rock or artifact? Hig waved to the 'dozer nearby, which automatically backed, leaving the area vacant for a moment. Descending into the depression, Hig walked to the spot, stopped by the embedded, dark, formless object.

He knelt, "Hey," he yelled, looking around, trying to find another human—not just rigs and leadies. There was Dick Patterson, another human, an engineer employed by Runcible, like himself. "Hey Patterson!" Hig began to yell. And then he discovered that, goddam it, the thing was not an artifact; he had made his move too soon. Oh christ! He had flubbed it!

Approaching, Patterson said, "Whazit?"

"Nothing." Furious, Hig strode back, out of the depression; he signaled the 'dozer to start up again and it did; it groaned back into operation and the black object—nothing but a rock—disappeared under the tread of the rig.

Ten minutes later the 'dozer exposed something that shone white and metallic in the early-morning sun, and this time there was no doubt; at the ten foot level the first artifact had come to light.

"Hey, Patterson!" Hig yelled. But Patterson, this time, was not within sound of his voice. Reaching, Hig picked up a nearby walkie-talkie, started to broadcast a general call. Then he changed his mind. I better not cry wolf again, he realized. So he waved the 'dozer back—it seemed reluctantly, grumpily, to retreat under protest—and this time, when he strode over to the object he saw with furious excitement that yes; this was it—a gun of a peculiar sort, deeply stuck, thoroughly lodged in the soil. The mouth of the 'dozer's scoop had actually shaved off the top layer of rust, of soft corrosion, exposing still hard metal beneath.

Goodbye, Mr. Runcible, Hig said to himself in exultation. Now I will be a Yance-man—he felt intuitively positive of it—and you are going to learn what prison is like, you who've been building prisons for others. Again waving to the 'dozer, this time to shut down entirely, he strode with vigor toward the walkie-talkie; it was his intention now to broadcast the code which would halt all operations—and would bring every engineer on the site and half the leadies on the run, demanding to know what was up.

Secretly, he switched on his shirt-button camera and, at the same time, started the aud recorder. Runcible was not here, but Brose had at the last moment decided he wanted the entire sequence recorded, from the moment Hig first called attention to the find.

He bent, picked up the walkie-talkie.

A laser beam cut him, severed the right lobe of his brain and the skull and passed on through his scalp and he dropped to the ground, the walkie-talkie falling and shattering. There he lay. There he died.

The autonomic 'dozer, which he had halted, waited patiently for a signal to resume work. At last, from another human engineer on the far side, the signal came; the 'dozer, with a grateful roar, started up.

Under its treads the shining, small metal object embedded in the earth at the ten foot level, exposed briefly to the sun after six hundred years, disappeared.

And in the next scoop it disappeared along with the dirt, into the converter.

Without hesitation the converter transformed it, with all its intricate wiring and miniaturized components, along with rocks and dirt, into pure energy.

And, noisily, the digging continued.

SEVENTEEN

In his London office Webster Foote studied with a jeweler's loupe—old-fashioned gadgets fascinated him—the gradually unreeling photographic record which eye-spy satellite 65, owned by Webster Foote, Limited of London, had taken during its pass 456,765, Nor-Hem-W.

"Here," his photo expert, Jeremy Cencio, said, pointing.

"All right, my boy." Reaching, Webster Foote stopped the unreeling of the continuous positive; he swung a 1200x microscope into position at the locus, manually adjusted first a coarse and then the fine focus—he had a slight astigmatism in his right eye, so he utilized the left—and saw, on the film, what Cencio wanted him to see.

Cencio said, "This is roughly the region where Colorado and Nebraska and Wyoming come together. South of what once was Cheyenne, before the war, a major city of the United States."

"Oh indeed."

"Shall I animate this segment?"

Webster Foote said, "Yes. Please. And project it wallwise."

A moment later, as the room lights darkened, a square appeared on the wall, projection of the segment of film. Cencio started the animating equipment, which altered the film from a still into a sequence of several minutes.

Enlarged by way of 1200x microscope, which intervened between the film and the animating construct, a scene, looked down at from above, of course, could be made out. A man and two leadies.

As he watched, Webster Foote saw one of the leadies prepare to kill the man; he saw the unmistakable move of its right manual extremity toward what he, as a professional, knew it carried at that spot of its mechanical anatomy. The man was about to be extinguished.

And then, like a puff, a sneeze of dust, one leady whisked out, and its companion whirled frantically in what technically was called a circus-motion pattern, all circuits at peak-velocity as it strove to locate the source of the destruct beam—and then it, too, condensed into disconnected motes that floated and drifted.

"That's all," Cencio said, and turned on the room light.

"That would be the demesne area of—" Foot consulted one of the police corporation's reference works. "A Mr. David Lantano. No, not a demesne; still in preparation. Not a full year, yet; so legally it remains technically a hot-spot. But under Lantano's jurisdiction."

"Presumably those are—were—Lantano's leadies."

"Yes." Foote nodded absently. "I tell you, my boy. Go over all the adjoining segments with the 400x lens until you find the source of the destruct beam that took out those two leadies. See who—"

The vidcom in his office pinged; it was his secretary, Miss Grey, and the signal, three winks of light along with the ping, meant that the call was urgent.

"Excuse me," Foote said, and turned to the full size vidset on which the call would be, by Miss Grey, relayed for his attention.

The face of Louis Runcible appeared, heavy, rather ruddy and fleshy, the old-fashioned rimless glasses . . . the dome of his head a little more bald since Foote had last seen him; a little less of the fine white hair combed across, ear to ear. "Your field rep," Runcible said, "told me to call you the instant anything unusual occurred in my business operations."

"Yes!" Foote leaned eagerly toward the screen, grabbed at the key of the aud-vid recorder to be sure this call was permanently registering. "Go ahead, Louis. What turned up?"

"Somebody murdered one of my engineers. Lasered him in the back of the head, while he was at the new site in Southern Utah. So your extrasensory perception was right; they're out to get me." Runcible, on the vidscreen, looked more indignant than frightened, but that, for him, would be natural.

"You can continue your ground-breaking without this man?" Foote asked.

"Oh sure. We're digging away. We didn't even find him until evidently an hour or so after it happened; no one noticed, with all the work in progress. Hig was his name. Bob Hig. Not one of my best, but not too bad, either."

"Keep digging, then," Foote said. "We'll of course send a field rep to the spot to examine the body of Hig; he should be there within half an hour, released by one of our substations. And meanwhile keep in touch. This may be their first move in a sequence." He did not need to specify who "they" were; both he and Runcible understood perfectly.

The call terminated, Foote returned to the examination of the continuous film-strip made by the satellite.

"Any luck on pinpointing the origin of that destruct beam?" he asked Cencio. He wondered if there were any connection between the murder of Runcible's engineer and the taking out of these two leadies. It always appealed to him, tying separate events together; he enjoyed a pattern which wove all strands into harmony. But as the connection between these two despiteous events, however, even his extrasensory vision did not provide him with any knowledge. Perhaps in time . . .

"No luck," Cencio said. "So far."

"Are they trying to scare Runcible into stopping work in Utah?" Foote asked rhetorically, aloud. "Because that's hardly the way; Louis can lose engineer after engineer and survive. My god, with the weapons they have at the Agency, especially the advanced prototypes that Brose has access to—they could wipe out the entire site, all the men, leadies and machinery that loiter around there. And not just an engineer . . . not a top one at that." It made no sense.

"No hunch?" Cencio asked him. "No Psionic foresight?"

"Yes," Webster Foote said; he had an odd inkling. It grew in his mind until it amounted to a true precog revelation. "Two leadies dissolved," he said. "Then one of Runcible's construction crew in Utah lasered in the back of the head, the moment they start breaking ground . . . I foresee—" He broke off. Another death, he said to himself. And soon. He examined his round, ancient pocket watch. "It was the *back* of the head. Assassination. Look for someone in the Yance-man class."

"A Yance-man—murdered?" Cencio stared at him.

"Very soon now," Foote said. "If not already."

"And we'll be called."

"Oh yes," Foote said. "And this time not by Runcible but by Brose. Because—" And his extrasensory talent told him this; plainly. "It'll be someone Brose is depending on; this will upset Brose extravagantly—we'll get quite an agitated call."

"Let's wait and see," Cencio said, skeptically, "if you're right."

"I know I'm right as to what's going to happen," Foote said. "The question is—*when?*" Because his talent was very bad on timing, and he recognized this; he could be days, even a week off. But not much more than that. "Suppose," Foote said thoughtfully, "the murder of this person was not directed at Runcible. It just doesn't hurt Louis enough; he can't be the target." *Suppose*, he thought, *although Hig was an employee of Runcible's, this is directed at Stanton Brose.*

Was that so bad?

"Do you like Brose?" he asked his photo expert assistant in charge of all visual satellite-tracking data.

"I never thought about it one way or another," Cencio said.

Foote said, "I have. I don't like Brose. I wouldn't lift my left little finger to help him. If I could avoid it." But how could he avoid it? Brose, acting through General Holt and Marshal Harenzany, had an army of veteran leadies at his disposal, plus the advanced weapons archives at the Agency. Brose could get at him, at Webster Foote, Limited of London, any time he wanted.

But perhaps there was someone else, someone not afraid of Brose.

"We will know whether such a person exists," Foote said, "when and only when a Yance-man valuable to Brose is killed." As, with his parapsychological talent, he foresaw.

"What sort of person?"

"A new sort," Foote said. "Of the kind we have never seen." That, as far as he knew, did not exist.

I will sit here at my desk, Foote said to himself, *and wait and hope to get a vidcall from fat, horrid old spiderish Stanton Brose. Telling me in lugubrious terms that an essential Yance-man in his immediate circle has been dispatched, and in no crude, barbaric but on the contrary highly—as they like to phrase it—sophisticated manner. And when that call comes, I will go out on a two week binge.*

He began the wait as of now. By his round, archaic pocket watch, nine a.m., London time. And, in just a minuscule way, he initiated the celebration: he took one small pinch, one for each nostril, of Mrs. Cluny's Superfine Preferred Mixture high-grade snuff.

On the main floor public corridor of the New York Agency, Joseph Adams, seeing no one in sight, stepped rapidly into a pay vidphone booth. He shut the door, managed to deposit the metal poscred coin.

"Capetown, please. The villa of Louis Runcible." He was shaking so badly that he could barely hold the aud receiver to his ear.

"Seven dollars for the first—" the operator said; it was a leady, highly efficient and brisk.

"Okay." Quickly he shoved a five and two ones into the slot, and then, as the connection was put through, Adams, with a convulsive, hasty but thorough motion, covered the vidscreen with a handkerchief; he had now blocked the visual portion of the transmission, leaving only the aud.

In his ear a female voice said, "Miss Lombard, Mr. Runcible's secretary; who is calling, please?"

Joseph Adams said hoarsely, not having to alter deliberately his voice to make it unrecognizable; it emerged that way on its own, "I have an absolutely urgent message for Mr. Runcible's ears alone."

"Who is this, please? If you—"

"I can't do it," Joseph Adams grated. "Maybe the line is tapped. Maybe—"

"What is it, sir? Could you speak up, please? And the visual signal doesn't seem to be coming through at all. Could you reconnect in a better channel?"

"Goodbye," Joseph Adams said. *I just can't take the chance*, he thought in fear.

"I'll put you through, sir; if you'll just wait—"

He hung up the receiver.

Removing the handkerchief, still shaking, he got to his feet, left the public vidphone booth. Well, he almost had done it. Tried; I did try, he said to himself. So close.

Then a wire? Or a special registered 'stant mail letter, no name signed, letters cut from homeopapes.

Can't, he realized; can't ever do it. Darn sorry, Louis Runcible; the bonds are too strong. The ties; they're too long, old, tight. I have introjected them and now they act as a part of me; they live here inside, within me. Life-long. Now and now on.

He walked unhastily, feeling a membrane of numbness transport itself with him, hovering as he walked up the corridor away from the vidphone booth. Back to his own office. As if nothing had happened.

Nothing had. It was gall-bitter truth: nothing, nothing at all.

So it would progress on its own, the thing. Force he did not understand, substantial but remote, eluding, butterflylike, his perception even at the edge: shapes that winged across the sky of his life and left no trail, no sensation; he felt blind and afraid and helpless. And still he walked. Because it was natural. And, for him, there was nothing else.

And as he walked, it moved. Stirred; he felt it roll forth. Coasting in a direction which was unveering: straight ahead.

EIGHTEEN

Across the cropped green lawn, temporarily abandoned now because this was night and the leady gardeners had gone off elsewhere into storage sheds and immobility, the machine coasted on rubber, hard wheels; it made no noise, orienting itself by the rebound of the radarlike signals which it emitted at a frequency not customarily utilized. The signals had begun to return now in a succession which informed the machine that the large stone building—the tropism of phase one of its homeostatic but many-sectioned journey—lay properly on its path, and it began to slow until at last it bumped soundlessly against the wall of the building, came to rest for a moment as the next stage of its cycle rotated, in the form of a cam, into position.

Click. Phase two had begun.

By means of suction discs extended from stiff radii of a power-driven revolving central shaft the machine ascended the vertical surface until it arrived at a window.

Entering the building by means of the window posed no problem, despite the fact that the window, in its aluminum frame, was securely locked; the machine simply subjected the glass to sudden enormous heat—the glass became molten, dripped away like honey, leaving a wide, empty hole dead center, where the core of the heat beam had been directed. The machine, with no difficulty, traveled off the vertical, over the aluminum frame—

And, poised momentarily on the aluminum frame, it performed phase four of its total operation; it exerted the precise pressure on the rather soft metal that a two-hundred-and-twenty pound weight, if resting there, would create; the frame yielded, bent until warped—satisfied, the machine then crawled on vertically once more by means of its radii of suction cups, until it reached the floor of the room.

An interval passed in which the machine remained inoperative, at least from external appearances. But within it seletoidal switches opened and shut. At last an iron oxide tape moved past a playback head; through an audio system current passed from transformer to speaker and the machine abruptly said in a low, muffled, but whiny voice, "Damn it." The tape, expended, fell into a reservoir within the machine and was incinerated.

The machine, on its small hard-rubber wheels, again rolled forward, again orienting itself batlike, by its radar emanations. To its right lay a low table. The machine halted at the table and seletoidal switches once more opened and shut. And then the machine extended a pseudopodium, the end of which it pressed firmly against the edge of the table, as if, for a moment, it had involuntarily eased itself of the burden of its own excessive weight, had rested there before going on. And now it went on. Carefully. Because the ultimate tropism, the man, was not far off. The man slept in the next room; the machine had picked up the sound of his respiration and the emanations of warmth from his body. Attracted by both, tropisms of each sort operating in synchronicity, the machine turned in that direction.

As it passed a closet door it paused, click-clicked, and then released an electrical impulse corresponding to the Alpha wave of a human brain—of, in fact, one particular human brain.

Within the closet a recording instrument received the impulse, deposited it as a permanent record sealed within a locked case buried deep within the wall, inaccessible except through extensive drilling or by the proper key. The machine, however, did not know that and if it had it would not have cared; it did not inquire into these ramifications; they were not its proper concern.

It rolled on.

As it passed through the open doorway into the bedroom it halted, reared back on its hind wheels, extended a pseudopodium which deftly—but at the loss of several seconds—lodged a single strand of artificial cloth-fiber into the brass lock fittings of the frame. This done to its satisfaction it again continued on, pausing once to excrete three hairs and a fleck of dried scalp material; otherwise it had no need to interrupt its double tropism toward the man asleep in the bed.

At the edge of the bed it stopped entirely. The most intricate part of its overall cycle now came, by means of a rapid series of switch openings and closings, into play. The case forming the hull of the machine radically changed shape as a slow, fastidiously regulated warmth softened the plastic; the machine became thin, extended, and then, this accomplished again tipped back onto its rear wheels. The effect, had anyone seen it, would have been comic; the machine now swayed like a snake, barely able to maintain its balance—it came to the verge of falling first to one side and then to the other, for, slender and elongated as it was, it no longer possessed a wide resting base. However, it was too busy to preoccupy itself with the problem of its lateral oscillations; the master circuit which controlled it, the *clock*, as the wartime technicians who had built it had called that assembly, endeavored to obtain something more vital than upright balance.

The machine, having completed its mobile, ambulatory phases, based on the doubly reinforcing tropisms of heat and respiratory rhythm, was attempting to locate exactly the beating heart of the man asleep in the bed.

This, after an interval of minutes, it accomplished; it locked its percept system, focused on the beating heart: the stethoscopic effect of its sensors registered deep within it, and then the next phase came swiftly. It could not hesitate, now that the beating heart had been located; it had to act at once or not at all.

It released, from an aperture at its upper lid, a cyanide-tipped self-propelling dart. Traveling at extremely slow speed, so that corrections of its trajectory could be achieved even at the last fractional second, the dart made its way from the upended machine, veered slightly as signals from the machine indicated the need of a minor correction—and then its needle nose penetrated the chest of the sleeping man.

Instantly the dart ejected its freight of poison.

The man, without waking, died.

And, at his throat, a complicated but extremely fine band, as fine as gold wire, but containing a variety of functioning electronic valves and surge gates, emitted an elaborate series of radio signals which were without time lapse accepted by larger units bolted to the underside of the bed. These larger units, triggered off by the fine-spun collar which had reacted immediately upon the cessation of blood circulation and heart action, at once sent out their own signals.

An alarm—audibly—sounded; the room clanged with the racket. In other parts of the villa leadies hopped into activity, churning windmill-like at full throttle toward the upstairs bedroom. A further signal tripped an automatic coded call to leadies stationed on the grounds outside the building; they, ceasing to be immobile, sprinted toward the building, lined up at the wall by the bedroom window.

The man's death rattle had awakened fifty diverse leadies comprising his entourage, and every leady, guided by the rapid impulses from the larger units bolted to the underside of the bed, thanostropically converged on the scene of the assassination.

The machine, having released its dart, now registered the cessation of heartbeat; it thereupon again warmed its frame, sank back, became square as before. It began to roll away from the bed, its job done.

And then—minute cilialike antennae on its anterior surface detected the radio signals emitted by the large unit bolted to the underside of the bed. And it knew it would never get away.

From outside, below the window with its empty, fused-away entry hole where glass had been, a type VI leady called up at full voice-amplification, "Sir, we are aware that you're in there. Make no attempt to escape. A police agency individual is on the way; please remain where you are until he comes."

The machine rolled on its small wheels away from the bed in which the dead man lay; it detected the leadies beyond the bedroom door, waiting out in the hall, and the leadies below the window, leadies everywhere, deployed in precise and expert pattern; it reentered the room adjoining the bedroom, the first room through which it had traveled. There, pausing, as a sort of ejaculatory afterthought, it released one drop of blood which fell to the carpet—the machine swiveled, started first in one direction, then another, then at last all switches operated by the *clock* within it shut down as the master circuit accepted the totality of the situation; all exits were barred and no motion was possible. Hence, one final—optional—phase of its circuit clicked into play.

Once more the plastic form which housed the components of the machine warmed, flowed, reshaped. This time into the conventional figure of—a portable television set, including handle, screen, v-shaped antenna.

In that form the machine settled into inertness; every active portion of its electronic anatomy closed down in finality.

Nothing remained; the end had been reached. A neurotic oscillation between two opposing impulses—the tropism toward flight, the tropism toward camming—had been settled in favor of the latter; the machine, in the darkness of the room, appeared externally to be an ordinary television receiver, as its wartime makers had intended, under such conditions as these: when, due to overly rapid defensive response on the part of the defenders, the machine, although having completed its task of assassination, could not then—as had been hoped for—escape.

There, in the darkness, the machine remained, while below the empty window the type VI leady in charge shouted its message over and over again, and, in the hall outside the dead man's bedroom, the solid phalanx of leadies stood watchful guard, prepared to bar the departure of any person or thing that might be attempted from the scene of the murder.

There it remained—until, one hour later, Webster Foote, in his official capacity, was admitted past the phalanx of leadies guarding the hall door to enter the bedroom.

NINETEEN

He had been summoned by a frantic, half-insane vidcall from the ancient Stanton Brose; hysterically, Brose's image on the screen wavered with the kind of pseudo-Parkinsonism agitation possible only in a neurologically damaged structure, one bordering on senility.

"Webster, they killed one of my men, my best men!" Near-sobbing, Brose confronted Foote, completely out of control, the random spasms of his limbs fascinated Foote, who watched fixedly, thinking to himself, *I was right. My precog hunch. And right away.*

"Of course, Mr. Brose, I'll go personally." He held his pen poised. "The name of the Yance-man and the location of his demesne."

Brose spluttered and blubbered, "Verne Lindblom. I forget; I don't know where his demesne is. They just called me, his death rattle; it went off the second they got him. So his leadies trapped the killer, he's still there in the villa—the leadies are outside the doors and windows, so if you get there you'll find him. And this isn't the first assassination; this is the second."

"Oh?" Foote murmured, surprised that Brose knew about the death of Runcible's engineer, Robert Hig.

"Yes; they started with—" Brose broke off, his face rolling and unrolling, as if the flesh, starved, were shriveling away and then seeping back, refilling the emptiness, the hollows of the skull. "My agents on Runcible's staff reported it," he said, more controlled, now.

"Hmm."

"Is that all you can say? Verne Lindblom was—" Brose snorted; he wiped at his nose, his eyes, dabbed at his mouth with loose, wet fingers. "Now listen, Foote; pay attention. Send a commando team of your best people to California, to the demesne of Joseph Adams so they don't get him next."

"Why Adams?" Foote knew, but wanted to hear what Brose had to say. The participants of the special project—the existence of which he knew, the nature of which he did not—were being taken out, one by one; Brose saw the pattern, so did Foote. With his pen, Foote made the note out: *c-team for A's dem. Now.*

"Don't inquire of me," Brose said, in his deadly ancient voice, " 'why' anything. Just do it."

Correctly, stiffly, Foote said, "Immediately. I'll come to the Lindblom demesne; a commando team, my best, to support Yance-man Adams. We will be with Adams from now on, unless, of course, he has already been destroyed. Did he, like Lindblom—"

"They all," Brose quavered, "have death rattles. So Adams is still alive, but he won't be unless you get there right away; we're not set up—my people are not prepared—any more to protect themselves. We thought it went out when the war ended; I know their leadies clash over boundaries, but nothing like this, like the *war*—it's the war all over again!"

Webster Foote agreed, rang off, dispatched a commando team of four men from his substation in the Los Angeles area; then ascending to the roof of his corporation's building, followed by two of his specially trained leadies who lugged heavy cases of detection equipment.

On the roof a high velocity inter-hem heavy-duty old wartime military flapple waited, already chugging, started by remote from Foote's office; he and his two specially trained leadies boarded it and, a moment later, he was on his way across the Atlantic.

By vidphone he contacted the Yance-man Agency in New York City and from it learned the location of the dead man's demesne. It lay in Pennsylvania. By vidphone to his own GHQ in London he asked for and obtained—presented visually to the screen for him directly to examine—the folio on Yance-man Verne Lindblom, to refresh his memory. No doubt about it; Lindblom had not been merely *a* builder, one of many, but *the* builder of the Yance-organization. The man had had absolute come-and-go use of Eisenbludt's facilities in Moscow . . . this, of course, Foote had ascertained in the original investigation of the "special project" of which Lindblom had been a vital part. The investigation, he thought tartly, which had failed to turn up any useful thing.

Except that Brose's despair and babyish concern, extended to anticipate the sequential next-step death of Joseph Adams, confirmed that the assassinations so far, Hig's and then Lindblom's, were the result of the involvement of both men in the special project; Foote perceived this clearly, perceived the weaving strand that passed from Hig to Lindblom and now, potentially, next to Adams—and, he reflected, may have involved a deliberately fatal assault on Arlene Davidson, last Saturday, but in a manner which at the time had seemed natural. In any case Brose had blubbered the admission that this was a sequence involving the participants of the special Agency project—Brose's project—and this meant that Hig was, obviously now, a Brose agent on Runcible's staff. So Foote's insight had been authentic; the murder of Hig had not been directed toward Runcible at, say, the instigation of Brose; the murder of Hig, as proven by the death of Yance-man Lindblom, had aimed at Brose for its ultimate target. The ruling Yance-man himself. All this now ceased to be conjecture; it had become history.

And still Foote had no idea what the special project was . . . or rather had been. For now, it would appear, the project had been properly aborted. Evidently it had *not* involved great numbers of members; perhaps Adams was the last, excluding Brose himself, of course.

That clanged loudly in Foote's professional mind. Adams, a part of the project, now under the protection of Footemen commandos, might under the stress of these circumstances be persuaded to blab to one of Foote's expert personnel the nature of the special project . . . a venture, Foote had no doubt, which was intended to make Runcible the target. Runcible was to have been the slaughtered goat, but—it had not quite worked out that way. The 'dozers in Southern Utah continued; Runcible had not been interrupted. But Brose had been: completely so.

In fact Foote could not recall ever having seen Brose—or anybody—so messy in their emotionality. So out of control. Foote thought, *This special project must have been a critical endeavor. Could it conceivably have been directed at the absolute and total elimination of Louis Runcible? In other words, could we have witnessed here the instigation of the final showdown between Brose and the fabulous empire-building conapt constructor? Instigation—and rapid collapse!*

My lord, Foote thought mildly, *my field rep, in talking to Louis Runcible, and I myself in vidphone conversation with him, obtained no impression that he was preparing such enormously precise and effective steps by which to protect himself. Louise Runcible had seemed utterly unaware—even unconcerned—as to what was being prepared to ensnare him . . . how then could he have responded so decisively, and in such short a time?*

And Runcible had not comprehended the meaning of the death of his employee, Robert Hig; that had been apparent on the vidphone.

Therefore, Foote realized, it is possible, even probable, that Hig and then the Yance-man Lindblom, and before that the Yance-man-woman Arlene Davidson—none of these were dispatched at Runcible's instigation, or even with his knowledge.

The safety of Louis Runcible is being shored up, Foote decided, but not by the man himself.

An additional figure unglimpsed by me, by Runcible, by Brose—*the* additional figure—has entered the arena and is competing for power.

He thought, I'm glad I'm content with what I have. Because, had I begun to overreach myself, as Brose has done in this special project, I might have found myself the target—*and the marksman, if this is accurate*.

TWENTY

Within the hour Webster Foote descended to the roof of the dead Yance-man's villa. Shortly, followed by his two expert leadies who lugged the heavy cases containing his detection equipment, Webster Foote made his way down the deep-pile carpeted hall to the top floor of the villa. Ahead he made out a forlorn sight: a phalanx of alert leadies, guarding a closed door. Within lay the body of their dominus, the lord of the demesne. And, if the type VI leady in charge were correct—that leady still keeping watch outdoors in the night darkness—the murderer had been trapped within the room, at the spot at which the killing had taken place.

Thus, Foote reflected, does the death rattle function. History has proven, tragically, that one cannot, no matter how highly placed, insure oneself against assassination. But one can threaten—and carry out the threat—*that the killer will be trapped*. At the instant of Verne Lindblom's death the machinery of apprehension, encircling the killer, had gone into operation, and so it could be presumed, as the type VI leady so did, that when he, Webster Foote, opened the bedroom door he would face not only a corpse (he hoped unmangled) but an armed, professional assassin as well—ready to fight it out to save his life.

Foote came to a halt before the phalanx of leadies, who, loyal dogwise, waited, guarded in dignified silence. Turning to his own two leadies he said, "A weapon." He pondered as they set down their heavy loads, opened the cases, waited for a more exact instruction. "One of the ephemeral nerve gasses," Foote decided. "To produce dysfunction temporarily. I doubt the individual within has an oxygen tank and mask in his possession." One of his two leadies obediently handed him the long, slender cylinder with its intricate tip. "Thank you," Foote said, and, passing through the phalanx of silent Lindblom leadies he reached the closed bedroom door.

Presenting the tip of the cylinder to the wooden surface of the door—clearly the door had been lovingly salvaged from some old mansion—he pondered for a moment as to the vanity of life, the fact that all flesh was grass and so forth, and then squeezed the trigger.

The tip of the cylinder rotated at high velocity, bored in an instant through the wooden but solid, not hollow-core, door, broke through, sealed the hole with plastic slime so that none of the gas could back up to affect the weapon's user, and then, on its own cycle, shot a fragile sphere of neurologically disjunctive synapse-depotentiating gas into the room beyond; the sphere landed in the darkness of the room and no power on earth could have intervened to prevent its fracturing; the distinctive noise meant to be audible reached Webster Foote and he then examined his round pocket watch and prepared to wait. The gas would be active for five minutes and then, due to its own constituents, would turn benign. Entry, in safety, could then be made.

Five minutes passed. "Now, sir," one of his leadies said.

Webster Foote withdrew the cylinder, returned it to the nearer of the two leadies, who placed it in the carrying case once more. However, it was within the realm of possibility that the killer had been provident, had come equipped to counter this weapon with a neutralizing agent. So, from the case, Foote selected a funny-gun, as an offensive weapon, and then, after some deep thought, the kind that tended, over past circumstances, to save his hide, he asked for a plastic protective shield which he unfolded, draped awkwardly but effectively over himself; one of his leadies assisted him so that at last the shield, capelike, covered him except for his shins and English wool socks and London-fabricated Oxfords. Then, carrying the funny-gun, which was not funny at all, he again passed through the phalanx of Lindblom leadies. And—opened the bedroom door.

"A flare," he ordered instantly. The room was dark; no time to grope for—grope and miss—the switch.

One of his two superbly trained leadies without hesitation obligingly lobbed a safe-style indoor flare into the bedroom; the flare lit up, a warm, comforting yellow light that did not dazzle but clearly illuminated each object. There was the bed; on it, under his covers, lay the dead man, Verne Lindblom, eyes shut. Peaceful, as if unaware; as if he never had been informed of, made acquainted with, the fact of his painless and instantaneous death. Because this was obvious to Foote; the relaxed supine state of the dead man indicated that one of the tried and true, long-tested, much-used cyanide instruments had been employed. Probably a homeostatic dart directly into the brain or the heart or the upper ganglia of the spinal column. *Merciful, anyhow*, Foote said to himself, and he glanced around for what he anticipated: a completely helpless adult male, unable to move or talk, twitching in paroxysms of arrhythmial neurological reflex arc activity; unable to protect himself or escape.

But the bedroom contained no such man. In that or any other state. The dead man, peaceful, under his covers, was alone in the room—he and Webster Foote: no one else. And, as Foote made his way cautiously into the adjoining room, through which entry, by the window, had originally been made, he saw no one there either. Behind him his two trained leadies followed; he saw no one there and they saw no one there and they at once began opening side doors, poking into a bathroom with wondrous mosaiclike tile, then two closets.

"He got away," Foote said, aloud.

His two leadies said nothing; no comment was indicated.

Returning to the phalanx of Lindblom leadies guarding the bedroom hall door, Foote said, "Inform your type VI below that they came too late."

"Yes, Mr. Foote," the in-charge leady said, and did so. "The response," it informed him in its metallic, gracious manner, "is that such could not be. The killer of Mr. Lindblom is in the bedroom area; anything else is impossible."

"According to your kind of deduct leady logic, perhaps," Foote agreed. "But empirical fact says otherwise." He turned to his own two leadies. "I will ask you now," he instructed them, "to begin collecting data. Assuming that the assassin was a human, not a leady, pay special attention for the presence of organic traces. Dermal deposits, hair."

One of the higher-type Lindblom leadies said, "Mr. Foote, there is, within the wall, a brain pattern receptor. Access to which we have the key."

"Good," Foote said. "I'll gather its readings."

"Plus an audio recorder. This also in continuous operation."

"Very good." *If* the assassin had been a human. *If* he had said something. And *if* he had passed near the percept-extensors of the brain pattern receptor. Webster Foote thoughtfully walked back into the bedroom, then into the adjoining room to examine the window through which entry had been made.

On the floor rested a portable TV set.

Bending, he took hold of it by the handle, ignoring the possible loss of fingerprints; it was unlikely that the murderer had involved himself in moving a TV set around.

The TV set was too heavy. He could lift it, but with difficulty. Aloud, Foote said, "This is it."

Within the room's closet, engaged in unlocking the unit which contained the brain-pattern record, if any, one of Lindblom's leadies said, "Pardon, sir?"

Foote said, "This is the killer. This TV set."

"Sir," the Lindblom leady said and snickered, "a portable television set is not an instrument by which a human death can be—"

"Do you want to take over the job," Foote said, "of finding your lord's slayer? Or will you leave it to me?"

"You, of course, Mr. Foote, are in charge."

"Thank you," Webster Foote said acidly. And wondered how, if at all, he was going to manage to pry open this object masquerading—chameleoned, as it was called—as a portable TV receiver. Because if he were right, it would resist being pried apart, had been built to withstand every sort of forced, hostile inspection.

He had, then, a bleak precog hunch. It was going to take days, even weeks, to get at the works within this "TV set." Even under the pressure of his many, varied shop assists.

Here in his hands he had the death instrument. But a hell of a lot of good it was going to do him.

TWENTY-ONE

The clues. The trail, beginning at the bent aluminum frame of the room's window, where the glass had been melted away; Webster Foote's two leadies crouched at the frame, photographed and analyzed the exact extent of the warpage of the metal, recorded its misalignment, calculated the pressure, in terms of pounds, which would have produced such a warp.

Foote's leadies gathered data like the good and successful machines they were. But he himself felt nothing, stared sightlessly; he was not interested, not involved.

"Spot of blood, Mr. Foote," one of the leadies informed him.

"Good," he said tonelessly.

The Lindblom leady which had opened the deeply embedded case set within the closet wall now informed him, "The brain pattern recept shows on its permanent record, in its repository, the presence of—"

"A man," Foote said. "Who passed by it and emitted an Alpha-wave pattern."

"The aud recorder, too, contains—"

"The man spoke," Foote said. "He came here to kill a sleeping victim and yet he spoke, loudly enough to get his voice on the iron oxide tape."

"And not only loudly," the leady said, "but distinctly. Would you care to have that sequence of tape rerun for you right now?"

Foote murmured, "No, I'll wait. Later."

One of his own leadies exclaimed in shrill, metallic triumph, "Three human hairs, not those of the victim."

"Keep going," Foote said. There'll be more clues by which to identify the murderer, he said to himself. We've got his unique brain wave pattern, his distinctive voice; we know his weight, we have hairs from his head, a drop of blood—although it seems rather strange that he should all at once have, for no reason, bled *a* drop, right in the middle of the room: a drop and no more.

Within the next few minutes a fragment of cloth fiber was found. And then, on a low table, fingerprints, not those of the victim.

"You can stop, now," Foote said to his two leadies.

"But sir," one of them said, "we may also find—"

"That's all," Foote said. "All which the standard model 2004 Eisenwerke Gestalt-macher produces. Voice, fingerprints, hairs, drop of blood, fiber of clothing, indication of body weight and idiosyncratic Alpha-wave brain emanation pattern—that's the extent and that's sufficient. Based on those, any reasonably adequate computer can pop a signal card; *you've got seven factors of delineation.*" And actually six were unnecessary. The brain-emanation pattern alone—if not the fingerprints—was adequate.

This was what annoyed him about this wartime West German invention; it overdid its job. Ninety percent of its circuitry, its activities, could have been left out—in which event as portable TV receiver it would have tended to possess the proper weight. But that was the German mentality, their love of the *Gestalt*, the complete picture.

Now, with the trail of clues, the data which made the Gestalt, in his possession, the question arose as to which population-catalog computer to consult. Actually he had his choice of three, and each possessed an enormous memory bank, an adequate library of cross-indexed reference aspects; in fact, by an odd coincidence, the exact aspects which his team of leadies had for the last hour been gathering in these two rooms

He could go to Moscow. The big BB-7 would probably find him the reference card to which these seven aspects, this Gestalt, pertained. Or the 109-A3 at Estes Park. Or even Megavac 6-V at the Yance-man Agency in New York; he could utilize it, relatively small and specialized as it was, in that its memory file consisted solely of Yance-men past and present. Because, Foote intuited, the Gestalt depicted a Yance-man and not one out of all the millions of subsurface tankers; the existence of reference cards representing them was not required. So why not Megavac 6-V?

One very good reason presented itself to Webster Foote immediately. His client, Stanton Brose, would automatically, at his *Festung* in

Geneva, be notified of the event, would be handed a duplicate first of the data fed to the computer and then the computer's response.

And it might serve the interests of all parties concerned that Brose have that information.

Therefore the big BB-7 in Moscow, which was the furthest removed from Brose's control.

As Foote and his two leadies, each of them again lugging a heavy case, got back into their flapple, he said to himself, I wonder whose card the computer will pop . . . and, theoretically anyhow, set the wheels of punitive justice turning. What individual, within the Yance-man class, was this Gestalt-macher programmed to indict? Carefully, as he set the ersatz television set on the seat beside him, again conscious of its inordinate weight—the quality which it could not conceal and hence that which had given it away . . . it could mimic any object of its general size but it could not decide to cease being affected by Earth's gravity.

He had, already, an idea of whose card would emerge. But it would be interesting to have his precog hunch verified.

Three hours later, after happily napping while his flapple made the trip by means of its automatic circuit, Webster Foote arrived in Moscow.

Below him lay the you-kicked-the-toy-basket-over-so-you-pick-it-all-up installations of Eisenbludt's film studios; interested, as he always was, to view this immense factory of the counterfeit, Foote peered down, noting that subsequent to his last trip here the studios had once more expanded: several new buildings of pasted-together rubble had sprung up, leady-built and probably already buzzing off-key with the industrious activity of cranking out fake destructs of cities . . . as he recalled, San Francisco came next on the Agency's agenda and this no doubt meant bridges, water, hills—a nice multisided entity to be erected by all the artisans concerned.

And there, where the original Kremlin had once stood—before the U.S. Queen Dido self-guiding missile of World War Three had abolished it down to the last particle of old red brick—lay Marshal Harenzany's villa, the second largest demesne on Earth.

Brose's demesne, in Geneva, of course was by far the larger. Yet still this vast park with its mighty and palacelike, look-on-my-works-ye-mighty-and-despair central buildings was impressive. And

Harenzany's demesne did not have that black, befouled quality of Brose's, the sense of some evil thing hanging upside down with ragged, aged wings. Like his counterpart in Wes-Dem the marshal was underneath it all a soldier, not a pol-com *ex mero motu* sybarite. Just the ordinary stag-party extraordinary sybaritic type. A man who liked to live.

But also, like General Holt, he remained, despite his nominal control of an army of veteran leadies, under the yoke of Brose.

As his flapple landed, Foote asked himself the question, *How really does an eighty-two-year-old semisenile but still cunning colossal abnormality, weighing god knows how many pounds, manage to keep his power? Is it the fact that at Geneva he maintains—owns and operates—an electronic contraption, a fail-safe gimcrack which, in a crisis, pre-empts Holt and Harenzany in their management of the totality of the world's leadies? Or is there something deeper and less crude?*

It may be, he decided, what the Christian sect calls "apostolic succession." The process of reasoning would be this: before World War Three the military establishments of Pac-Peop and Wes-Dem held ultimate power; all the civilian governmental bodies were so many league-of-nations relics. And those twin, competing establishments ruled through a demigod, the fakes-factory of Gottlieb Fischer; they ruled through their cynical and professional manipulation of all media of information, including the sides of country barns, but it was not they, the military, who knew precisely *how* to manipulate these media; it was Fischer. And then the war came, the two establishments struck a deal. And by then Fischer was dead anyhow, but leaving one pupil. Stanton Brose.

But even below that there seemed something more. Charisma, perhaps? That magic aura that great leaders in history such as Gandhi, Caesar, Innocent III, Wallenstein, Luther, F.D.R. have had? Or maybe it's simply that *Brose is Brose*. He has ruled since the termination of the war; the demigod this time made it, usurped ultimate authority. And even before that he was powerful; he inherited—literally, in the courts—the studios and instruments that had been Fischer's. The fakes-factory *sine qua non*.

Odd, Fischer's death, so sudden and tragic, out in deep space.

I wish, Foote wished, *I had that time scoop gadget that Brose, by means of the advanced weapons archives, has access to. I'd send back a packet of tracers, detection meters to make aud and vid tracks . . . I'd have electronic tails pinned onto the posteriors of both Brose and Fischer in those days, from 1982 on; especially I'd have a monitor following Gottlieb Fischer up to the moment of his death, just to see what really happened there when that ship, landing on Venus, tried to fire its retrojets—fired them and exploded.*

As he disemflappled, the vidset of the ship said *pinnngggg*. A call for him from the corporation's London GHQ; probably Cencio, who was in charge during his absence.

Stepping back into the flapple, Foote turned on the vidset. "Yes, my boy."

Cencio, face appearing in miniature, said, "I've got an animation of the sector from which that destruct beam emanated."

"What destruct beam?"

"That destroyed those two leadies of Yance-man David Lantano. You don't remember."

"Now I do. Go ahead. Who or what fired the destruct beam? A Yance-man, but which one of them?"

Cencio said, "Our shot, of course, is from directly above. So we can scarcely make out the figure. But—" He was silent.

"Go ahead, darn it," Foote said. "I'm just about to go into Marshal Harenzany's office and—"

"The man who fired the destruct beam," Cencio blurted, "according to the film our satellite took, is Talbot Yancy." He waited, Foote said nothing. "I mean," Cencio said, "it *looks* like Yancy."

"How much like him?"

"Exactly. We've enlarged it to life size. It's exactly what you, I mean *they*, see on their TV screens. No mistake."

And I've got to go into Harenzany's office, Foote thought, *with that piece of news in my mind*. "All right, my boy," he said. "Thank you. And by the way; god bless you for very fine psychological timing in giving me that piece of news just now. When I need it most." He broke the vid connection, hesitated, then went on away from his parked flapple, leaving his two inert leadies aboard.

Yancy did it, he said to himself. Killed Arlene Davidson, then Bob Hig, then Verne Lindblom, and next he'll kill Joseph Adams and after that probably Brose himself and possibly, as a chaser, me as well.

A dummy, bolted to an oak desk, programmed by Megavac 6-V. Stood behind a boulder in the Cheyenne hot-spot and fired a destruct beam at two veteran leadies. To save the life of what was undoubtedly just another poor tanker who had bored his way to the surface for a breath of fresh air and a glimpse again, briefly, of the sun. An ex-tanker, now, squatting in the ruins of Cheyenne with the rest of them, living for, waiting for, god only knows what. And then this dummy, this simulacrum called Talbot Yancy, without anyone at the Agency noticing, returned to its oak desk, rebolted itself back in place, resumed its computer-programmed speech-delivering existence.

Resigned—accepting the insanity of it all—Webster Foote continued on to the down-ramp of the roof field, to Marshal Harenzany's office.

Half an hour later, with a large legal document granting permission to use the computer, supplied by one of Harenzany's clerks, he stood before the big Soviet computer BB-7, and, with the help of the friendly, correct Russian technicians, fed in the seven spurious data elements which his team of leadies had uncovered, the trail of cover clues laid down by the Gestalt-macher.

BB-7, looming ceiling-high before him, began to process, to sort through its human catalog. And presently, as Foote had anticipated, one single punched elongated card slithered from the slot and came to rest in the wire basket.

He picked up the card, read the name typed on it.

He precog hunch had been correct; he thanked the helpful Russian technicians, found an up-ramp, ascended to his parked flapple.

The card had read, BROSE STANTON.

Exactly as he had anticipated.

Had the machine, the Gestalt-macher, which now rested beside him in its cammed form of portable TV set, managed to get away—had Lindblom not possessed a death-rattle—the evidence would legally speaking be pure and absolute in the direction to which it pointed. It would appear beyond a reasonable doubt that Stanton Brose, the man who had hired Foote to look into this felony was the killer. But of course Brose was not; the object beside Foote proved it.

Unless he was wrong. Suppose this was *not* a Gestalt-macher. He would not know for certain—could not *prove* it—until he got the machine open, actually saw its works.

And meanwhile, as he and his shopmen struggled to open the machine, and what a good, hard, long struggle it would be, Brose would be on the vidphone relentlessly, demanding to know what the clues, picked up at Lindblom's villa, indicated. Whom did they point to?

I can see myself saying, "To thyself, Mr. Brose," Foote thought to himself archly. "Thou art the murderer and hence I abominate thee and I now put thee under arrest and will see that thou art arraigned before the Recon Dis-In Council."

Hilarious thought.

However, he felt no mirth. Neither by that nor by the recognition of the fight he had on his hands to get open the object beside him. There were plastics so tough, so beyond the power of ordinary drills and thermo fields. . . .

And all the time in the back of his mind he was thinking, Is there a Talbot Yancy? And if so, *how?*

He did not understand it at all.

And yet his job demanded that he, of all people, make sense out of this. If *he* couldn't who could?

Meanwhile, Foote decided, I will tell Brose nothing. Or rather, as little as I can get away with.

His intuition, his Psionic hunch, remained; it was not to anyone's benefit—including his own—to tell Stanton Brose the facts at this point ascertained.

Because Brose—and this was what made him so personally uneasy—might know what they meant *and might know what to do with them.*

TWENTY-TWO

To Nicholas the bearded ex-tanker Jack Blair said dolefully, "I guess we don't have a cot for you to sleep on, Nick. Not right away. So you'll have to bed down on the cement."

They stood in the dim basement of what had once been an insurance company's central offices. The insurance company had long ago vanished, along with its mighty concrete and steel structure; the basement, however, remained. And was much appreciated.

And all around, on every side, Nicholas saw other ex-tankers, now residents in a sense of the surface. But still so completely, palpably deprived; so devoid, in the most literal physical sense, of what was theirs.

"Not much of a way," Blair said, seeing his expression, "of inheriting the Earth. Maybe we haven't been meek enough."

"Maybe too meek," Nicholas said.

"You're beginning to feel that hate," Blair said acutely. "The desire to get back at them. It's a fine idea. But how? If you think of a way, tell us; all of us. Meanwhile—" He began searching around. "A more immediate issue is your need for bedding. Lantano gave us—"

"I'd like to see this Lantano," Nicholas said. "This one Yance-man that seems to have a decent gene or two." And through him, he thought, bargain for the artiforg.

Blair said, "You should get to, pretty soon. This is usually just about the time he drops by. You'll recognize him because he's so dark. From the radiation burns." He glanced up and then said quietly, "Here he is now."

The man who had entered the basement shelter had not come alone; behind him a file of leadies lurched under their loads, supplies for the ex-tankers squatting here in the ruins. And he was dark; his skin shone a reddish-black. But, Nicholas realized, not from radiation burns.

And, as Lantano made his way through the basement, among the cots, stepping over people, their meager stores, saying hello here, smiling to someone there, Nicholas thought, *My god, when he came through the entrance he looked like an old man, weathered, dried-out, but now, closer, Lantano appeared middle-aged; the aura of extreme age had been an illusion due to the scrawny quality of the man and the peculiar stiffness in the way he walked; it was as if he were delicate, feared an injury, a fall.*

Going up to him, Nicholas said, "Mr. Lantano."

The man with the retinue of leadies—who were now opening their bundles and spreading out the contents for distribution—stopped, glanced at Nicholas. "Yes?" he said, with a ragged, burdened and quite fleeting smile of greeting.

Blair plucked at Nicholas' sleeve. "Don't keep him long; remember he's sick. From the burns. He's got to make it back to his villa so he can lie down." To the dark man, Blair said, "Isn't that right, Mr. Lantano?"

Nodding, the dark man continued to gaze at Nicholas. "Yes, Mr. Blair. I am sick. Otherwise I would get here oftener." Lantano turned, then, to be sure his leadies were distributing their goods as rapidly and efficiently as possible; he turned his attention away from Nicholas.

"He was oppressed and despised," Nicholas said.

At once Lantano turned back, eyed him intently; his eyes, black, deep-set, burned as if overpowered, as if the surge of energy within him had gone beyond the safe limit—the blaze seemed to consume the actual organ of sight through which it found expression, and Nicholas felt awe. "Yes, my friend. What was it you asked me for? A bed to sleep on?"

"That's right," Blair chimed in eagerly. "We're out of cots, Mr. Lantano; we could use ten more, in fact, just to be on the safe side, because there's always somebody like this Nick St. James here every day, it seems like. More and more all the time."

"Perhaps," Lantano said, "the illusion is wearing thin. An error here and there. A weak video signal that interrupts . . . is that why you came up, Nick?"

"No," Nicholas said. "I want a pancreas. I have twenty thousand dollars." He reached into what remained—after the mauling by the leady—of his coat. But the wallet was gone. It had fallen then, when the leady had clawed him, or when it had hooked and dragged him, or during the hours of walking . . . any time. He had no idea. He stood, empty-handed, with no idea what to say or do; he simply stood facing Lantano in silence.

After a time Lantano said, "I couldn't have gotten it for you anyhow, Nick." His tone was faint but compassionate. And the eyes. They still burned. Still overpowered by the flame that was not mere life; it was archetypal—it went beyond the individual, the mere animal-man as such. It drew from whatever final source energy of this sort sprang; Nicholas had no idea about it, no understanding: he had never seen it before.

"Like I said," Blair reminded him. "That Brose has got—"

Lantano said, "Your quote was wrong. 'He was despised and rejected of men.' Did you mean me?" He indicated his retinue of leadies, who by now had finished distributing their stores to the ex-tankers. "I'm not doing too badly. Nick; I have forty leadies, not bad for a start. Especially not bad considering this legally is still only a hot-spot and not a demesne."

"Your color," Nicholas said. "Your skin."

"Chrissakes!" Blair grated, grabbing at him, drawing him away from Lantano. In an angry low voice he said into Nicholas's ear, "What do you want to do, embarrass him? He knows he's burned; my god, he comes here and keeps us alive and you go and—"

"But he's not burned," Nicholas said. *He's an Indian*, he said to himself. *A full-blooded Cherokee, from the looks of his nose. And he's explained his skin color away as radiation burns; why? Is there some law that would bar him from being . . . he could not remember the term. Yance-man. Part of those who ruled; the insiders. Maybe it was strictly white, as back in the old days, the previous prejudiced centuries.*

Lantano said, "Mr. St. James, Nick—I'm sorry you had such a traumatic first-meeting with my retinue, today. Those two leadies; they were so militant because—" His voice was calm; he seemed tranquil, not disturbed by anything Nicholas had said: he was not really sensitive about his skin; Blair was completely wrong. "—other demesne owners," Lantano was saying, "bordering this hot-spot. They'd like to acquire it. They send their leadies in to make Geiger counter readings; they're hoping it's too hot, that it'll kill me, and then this area will be open once more." He smiled. Grimly.

"*Is* it too hot?" Nicholas asked him. "What do their readings give?"

"Their readings give nothing. Because they never survive. My own metallic companions destroy them; how hot this area has become is my business alone. But—you see, that makes my leadies dangerous. Try to understand, Nick; I had to pick those who were old vets of the war; I needed their toughness, their training and ability. Yance-men—you understand that term?—prize the new, undented, undamaged leadies being minted below. But I have such a special problem; I must defend myself." His voice, hauntingly melodic, was almost a chant, as if only half-uttered; Nicholas had to strain to hear it. As if, he thought, Lantano was becoming unreal. Fading.

And, as he looked once more at the dark man he again made out the lines of age, and this time, with those lines, a familiar configuration. As if, in aging, Lantano had become—someone else.

"Nick," Lantano said softly, "what was that about my skin?"

There was silence; he did not say.

"Go ahead," Lantano said.

"You're a—" He scrutinized Lantano intently and now, instead of age he saw—a youth. A supple man, younger than himself; no more than nineteen or twenty. It must be the radiation, Nicholas thought; it consumes him, the very marrow of his bones. Withers, calcifies, speeds up the destroying of cell-walls, of tissue; he is sick—Blair was right.

And yet the man rehealed. Visibly. It was as if he oscillated; he swung into degeneration, into submission to the radioactivity with which he had, twelve hours a day, to live . . . and then, as it ate him, he pulled himself back from the edge; he was recharged.

Time curled and poked at him, tinkered insidiously at the metabolism of his body. But—never totally overtook him. Never really *won*.

" 'Blessed,' " Nicholas said, " 'are the peacemakers.' " He then was silent. That seemed to be the extent of his contribution. He could not say what he knew, what his hobby of years, his interest in North American Indians and their artifacts and culture, had provided him as a basis for understanding what these other ex-tankers around him had not, could not; their own phobias about radiation, phobias developed while still below in their tanks, and now augmented, had misled them, concealed from them what was to his eyes obvious.

And yet he was still puzzled, because obviously Lantano had allowed them to think of him this way, as injured, burned. And—he did seem to be wounded. Not, perhaps, in regard to his skin, but more deeply. And so, fundamentally, the ex-tankers' view was correct.

"Why," Lantano said, "are the peacemakers blessed?"

That stumped Nicholas. And it was he who had said it.

He did not know what he meant; the idea had arisen as he contemplated Lantano; that was all he knew, just as a moment ago another outside-of-time observation had risen, unsolicited to his conscious mind, that about the man who was despised and rejected. And that man had been—well, in his own mind he knew who that man had been, even though most persons at the Tom Mix had attended the Sunday services as a mere formality. For him, however, it had been real; he had believed. Just as he had also believed—although *feared* was a more accurate word—that someday they might need to know how the North American Indians had survived, because they themselves might need to know the art of chipping flint arrowheads and processing animal hides.

"Come and see me," Lantano said to him, "at my villa. Several rooms are complete; I am able to live comfortably while the noisy metal men bang away at the job of hauling concrete slabs and chunks which once made up bank buildings and freeway ramps and drive-ins and—"

Nicholas interrupted, "Can I stay there? Instead of here?"

After a pause Lantano said, "Of course. You can see that my wife and children are safe from the predations of the leadies of the four neighboring demesnes while I'm at the Agency; you can strawboss my little defensive police force." Turning, he signaled to his retinue; it began to file from the basement.

"Well I see," Blair said enviously, "you made it big."

Nicholas said, "I'm sorry." He did not know why Lantano awed him, why he wanted to go with him. A mystery, he thought; there is an enigma about this man who when you first catch sight of him is old, then not so old, is middle-aged, and then when you are up close he is all at once a youth. A wife and child? Then he can't be as young as he now seems. Because David Lantano, striding out of the basement ahead of him, moved like a man in his early twenties, in the full vigor of youth before it became weighed down by the responsibilities of wife, children: of marriage.

Time, Nicholas thought. *It's as if a force that grips us all in a one-way path of power, a total power on its part, none on ours, has for him divided; he is moved by it and yet simultaneously, or perhaps alternately, he seizes it and grips it and he then moves on to suit his own needs.*

He followed after Lantano and his file of leadies, out of the basement, up into the gray light of a partial day.

"There are colorful sunsets," Lantano said, pausing and glancing back. "Which make up for the dinginess of the daytime atmosphere. Did you ever see Los Angeles in the days of the smog?"

"I never lived on the West Coast," Nicholas said. And then he thought, *But smog ceased to afflict Los Angeles by* 1980; *I wasn't even born, then.* "Lantano," he said, *"how old are you?"*

There was no answer from the man ahead of him.

In the sky something passed slowly, very high. From east to west.

"A satellite," Nicholas said, excitedly. "My god, I haven't seen one in all these years."

"An eye-spy," Lantano said. "Taking photographs; it's reentered the atmosphere to get a clearer shot. I wonder why. What would interest anyone here? Rival demesne owners? Domini who'd like to see me a corpse? Do I look like a corpse, Nick?" He halted. "Answer me. Am I here, Nick, *or am I dead?* What's your opinion? Is the flesh that hung—" He became silent, then; all at once he turned and continued on.

Nicholas, despite his fatigue from the four-hour hike to Cheyenne from the tunnel, managed to keep up. Hoping, as he trudged on, that it was not far.

"You've never seen a demesne villa, have you?" Lantano said.

"I've never even seen a demesne," Nicholas said.

"Then I'll fly you over a few of them," Lantano said. "By flapple. It will interest you, the view from above; you'll think it's a park—no roads, no cities. Very pretty, except that the animals are all dead. All gone. Forever."

They trudged on. Overhead, the satellite had almost disappeared beyond the line of the horizon, into the gray smoglike haze that, Nicholas realized, would remain in suspension for generations to come.

TWENTY-THREE

Poring over the segment of positive, Cencio, the loupe in his right eye, said, "Two men. Ten leadies. Walking through the Cheyenne ruins in the direction of Lantano's incomplete villa. Want a blowup?"

"Yes," Webster Foote said, instantly. It had been worth instructing the corporation's satellite briefly to reenter; they would possess a much better picture, now.

The room darkened and then the square of white appeared on the wall, and then that square was modified as the film segment was fed into the projector which at the same time, at 1200x, magnified. The animator, his dearly prized gadget, began to work; the twelve figures shuffled forward.

"The same man," Cencio said, "who was with the two destructed leadies. But that's not Lantano with him; Lantano is a young man, in his twenties. That man there is middle-aged. I'll get the folio on him and show you." He disappeared. Webster Foote, alone, continued to watch the animated, developing episode; the twelve figures in motion, toiling along, the ex-tanker clearly quite tired, the man with him—certainly it was David Lantano. Yet, as Cencio said, clearly a man in his late middle-age. Strange, Webster Foote said to himself. The radiation must account for it. It's killing him and this is the fashion that his death is taking; a premature aging. Lantano had better get out of there before it's too late; before it doesn't matter.

"See?" Cencio said, returning with the Lantano folio; he switched on the room lights, halted the animation of the film segment. "Born in 2002; that makes him twenty-three. So how can that man there—" He shut the room lights off once more. "That is *not* David Lantano."

"His father?"

"According to the folio his father died before the war." Cencio, under a small lamp at the desk, examined the records which the corporation had gathered pertaining to the Yance-man David Lantano. "Evidently Lantano, interestingly, is an ex-tanker. Anyhow walked out of the San Francisco ruins one day, asked for asylum in one of Runcible's conapts. Sent, routinely, to the Berlin Psychiatric Waffen-Institute. Mrs. Morgen found him to be of unusual aptitude; recommended that he be admitted to the Agency on a trial basis. Began writing speeches; is doing so now. Brilliant speeches, it says here."

"That's him on that screen," Webster Foote said, "and the radiation is killing him. So due to his greed to acquire a demesne he's not going to live, and the Agency loses a brilliant speech writer and he his life."

"He's got a wife and two children. So he's not sterile. They all walked out of the S.F. ruins together, a little family. Touching."

"They'll probably die with him. Before the year's up. Start the animator going again, my boy."

Obligingly, Cencio started the animator once more into action. The tired ex-tanker still lagged behind. For an interval the two men were lost behind and within a great semi-standing building; then, once more, they emerged into the light of day, the leadies stringing in a file behind them.

Suddenly Webster Foote exclaimed, leaned forward: "My god. Stop the animator."

Again Cencio stopped the action of the scene; the figures froze as they were.

"Can you get a greater enlargement of just Lantano?" Foote asked.

With great skill Cencio maneuvered the magnifying stages of lenses, manipulated both coarse and fine focuses; the figure on the screen, the first, darker human grew until there was nothing but him on the screen. Only the one obviously youthful, vigorous man.

Both Cencio and Webster Foote gazed in disconcerted, agitated silence.

"Well, my boy," Foote said at last. "That knocks the radiation damage theory."

"That's how he ought to look. Like he does now. That fits his chronological age."

Foote said, "There is, in the advanced weapons archives at the New York Agency, some kind of time travel weapon which has been tinkered with until it's a scoop they can use for depositing objects into the past. Only Brose has access to it. But what we're seeing now suggests that Lantano has got his hands on either the original weapon or the adaptation made of it by the Agency. I think we would be well advised to have a perpetual vid monitor kept on Lantano if it's at all possible. Could we plant one on a leady of his immediate entourage? It's risky, I realize, but if he finds it all he can do is rip it off; he can't prove who put it there. And we only need a few more shots; just another handful.'' The animator, meanwhile, had run the sequence to its limit; unable to carry it any further it merely buzzed, while on the screen the figures once more were frozen. Cencio put on the room lights; both men moved about, stretching, pondering.

''What few more shots?'' Cencio asked.

''Of him as old as he gets in his oscillations,'' Foote said.

''Maybe we've seen it. Already.''

''But maybe not. Do you know,'' Foote said, suddenly gripped by his extrasensory hunch experience; it overpowered him—never had it struck him with such force. ''That man is not white; he's a Negro or an Indian or something.''

''But there aren't any more Indians,'' Cencio said. ''Remember that article circulated just before the war; the ethnic resettlement program established on Mars involved virtually all of them, and they were killed in the first year, when the fighting was confined to Mars; those who remained behind on Earth—''

''Well, this one's still here,'' Foote said. ''So that's that. We don't need twenty Indians; we need just one—overlooked, I mean.''

One of his lab technicians came to the door of the room, knocked respectfully. ''Mr. Foote, sir. A report of that portable TV set. That you wanted torn down.''

Foote said, ''You got it open and it's a standard model prewar Philco 3-D color TV portable with—''

''Can't open it.''

''What about those rexeroid bits?'' Rexeroid, a compound from Jupiter, generally could penetrate anything. And he had kept one in his London labs for just such occasions as this.

''The case of the object, sir, is rexeroid; the bit goes in a quarter inch and then—the substance took the edge off the bit so it won't cut. In other words we're out one rexeroid bit. We've sent for more, but they'll have to come from Luna; that's where the nearest available supply exists. None of the Yance-men have any, including Eisenbludt in Moscow. Or if they do have any they won't release them; you know how competitive the Yance-men are. Afraid if they lend you—"

"Don't sermonize," Foote said. "Just keep trying. Anyhow I took a look at that case; it's not an alloy at all—it's plastic."

"Then it's a plastic we've never before seen."

Foote said, "It's an advanced weapon, undoubtedly from the Agency's closed archives, although possibly someone dug it up. Anyhow developed at the end of the war and never used. Do you mean to say you don't recognize the fine German hand when you see it? That's a Gestalt-macher; I know it." He tapped his forehead. "This extra knob on my frontal lobe says so. *Without proof.* You get into it and you'll see; ejectors that spout blood, hair, words, brain waves, threads, handprints." And, he thought, a cyanide-tipped homeostatic, homotropic dart. The first and last; that most of all. "You've tried heating it, of course."

"Not too high. To about 240; afraid if we go higher—"

"Try up to 350. And report if it shows any sign of flow."

"All right, sir." The lab technician departed.

Foote said to Cencio, "They'll never get it open. It's not rexeroid; it's a thermoplastic. But that clever German thermoplastic that flows at one precise split half degree; above and below it's even harder than rexeroid. You have to get exactly the proper temperature; inside it's got a heating coil that melts it when it wants to change shape. If they keep trying long enough—"

"Or," Cencio said, "if they get it too hot there won't be anything left inside it but ash."

That was true. The Germans had even thought of that; the mechanism was built so that unusual pressures—such as heat, drills, probes of any sort—acted to trigger a demolition circuit. And the thing did not even burst in a visible way; its works simply disintegrated . . . so that one still continued to strive to gain entry—entry into a gadget which had already long, long ago fused itself into a shapeless nothing, workswise.

Those late wartime units, Foote thought, are too clever. Just too damn clever for us mortals; can you imagine what would have been dreamed up in another year? *If* the autofacs hadn't been destroyed, all the surface shops and labs and proving grounds . . . like that one, sole outfit that made artiforgs.

The intercom clicked on and Miss Grey said, "Sir, Yance-man David Lantano is on the line wanting you. Are you in?"

Foote glanced at Cencio. "Saw the satellite reenter. Knows we took extra-careful shots of him. He's going to ask why." Rapidly, he tried to think why. The ex-tanker? Good; he had something there, because, according to law Lantano had to turn over any tanker who bored through within his demesne area to the Berlin psychiatrists. Into the intercom he said, "Put Lantano on, Miss Grey."

On the big vidscreen the face of David Lantano appeared, and Webster Foote saw, fascinated, that it was the youthful phase of the age-oscillation or cycle; in any case it was the proper twenty-three-year-old man who confronted him.

"I have never had the pleasure of making your acquaintance," Foote said politely (Yance-men, as a general rule, enjoyed this sort of bending-the-knee). "However I know your reading matter. Extraordinary."

Lantano said, "We would like an artiforg. A pancreas."

"Oh dear."

"You can locate one. Dug up. We will pay highly."

"There aren't any." Foote thought, *Why? Who needs it? You? Did your ex-tanker friend bore to the surface for it? Probably the latter, and you are being charitable or anyhow going through the motions.* "Not a chance, Mr. Lantano." And then an idea came to him. "Allow me," he said, "to visit your villa, however, for a few moments. I have some maps, military maps from the war, which indicate areas not dug into which conceivably might contain stored artiforgs; these were U.S. Air Force hospitals in remote places. Alaska, North Canada. On the old picket line fringes and on the East Coast. Perhaps between us—"

"Fine," Lantano agreed. "What about nine p.m. at my villa? Nine as computed by my time-zone here. For you that would be—"

"Sir, I can count time," Foote said. "I'll be there. And I'm sure, with your extraordinary abilities, you'll be able to make use of these maps. You can dispatch your own leadies if you wish, or my corporation can—"

"At nine tonight, my time, then," Lantano said, and rang off.

"Why?" Cencio asked Foote, after a pause.

Foote said, "To plant the continual vid monitor."

"Of course." Cencio flushed.

"Run that animated sequence again," Foote said thoughtfully, "of Lantano at middle-age. Stop it at the point where he is aged the most. I noticed a quality about him, just now, on the vidscreen . . ."

As he again set up the magnifying equipment, the film, the animator, the projector, Cencio said, "What quality?"

"It seemed to me," Foote said, "that Lantano, as he aged, began to resemble someone. I could not place who, but someone I know well." As he had faced even the young Lantano on the big vidscreen he had experienced it, the *déjà vu*.

A moment later, in the darkened room, he was viewing a still of Lantano at middle-age, but seen from above; again the angle was bad, and always would be, when the photographing instrument was so vertically oriented, as a satellite naturally had to be. But—he could discern it anyhow, because, as the satellite made its pass, both Lantano and the ex-tanker came to a halt and peered up.

"I know who," Cencio said, suddenly. "Talbot Yancy."

"Except that he's dark," Foote said. "This man here."

"But if that skin-bleach were applied, that wartime dermal—"

"No, Yancy is considerably older. When we get a good shot of Lantano at say sixty-five, not fifty, then maybe we'll have something." *And when I have got inside his villa,* Foote knew, *we will thereafter have operating the equipment to produce that shot. And this will be tonight; only a few more hours.*

What is this Lantano? he asked himself.

And got no answer.

At least—not yet.

But over the years he had learned to be patient. He was a professional; he would, in Lantano's incomplete villa, establish a video monitor which sooner or later would tell him additional facts, and ultimately one day, hopefully not too long from now, the pivotal fact would emerge, and all would be tied together: the deaths of Davidson, Hig and Lindblom, the destruct of the two leadies, the peculiar aging of Lantano—and, as he aged, that even queerer fact that he grew more and more to resemble a plastic and metal dummy bolted to a wooden desk in New York City . . . oh, Foote thought; then that would explain that peculiar and up to now anomalous strip of film which showed the origin of the destruct beam that took out the two leadies. It was we had thought, someone *resembling* Talbot Yancy.

It was David Lantano at the extreme old end of his oscillation; *we have seen it already*. The key fact had already emerged.

Brose, he thought, you have made a major mismove; you have lost your monopoly on the contents of the advanced weapons archives. Someone else has gotten hold of time-travel equipment and he is using it to destroy you. How did he get hold of it? That doesn't matter; *that he has it:* that's the point.

"Gottlieb Fischer," he said aloud. "The idea for Yancy originated with him; so the crisis is actually in the past." And he who possesses the ability to travel in time has access to the past, he realized. There is a junction, a connection, between David Lantano, who or whatever he is, and Gottlieb Fischer, back in 1982 or '4 or right up to Fischer's death; but no later than his death . . . and probably slightly before Fischer began his work on the Yancy *Prinzip*, his variation on the *Führer Prinzip:* his new solution to the problem of who shall lead, since, if men are too blind to govern themselves, how can they be trusted to govern others? The answer is der Führer, as every German knows, and Gottlieb Fischer was a German. Brose then stole the idea from Fischer, as we all know, and turned that idea into an actuality; the dummy, one in Moscow and one in New York, bolted to the oak desk, programmed by the computer which in turn is fed speeches by well trained elite idea men—all that can be legitimately credited to Stanton Brose, but what we did not guess is that Gottlieb Fischer stole *his* part, the original germinal concept, from someone else.

Sometime near the year 1982, the German film producer *saw Talbot Yancy*. And derived his Führer, not from his own creativity, his artistic genius, but from simple observation. And who would Gottlieb Fischer, circa 1982, be seeing? Actors. Hundreds of them. Sorted over to play roles in his two vast phony documentaries—actors picked especially for their ability to portray world leaders. In other words, actors who had that *charisma*, the magic.

To Cencio he said slowly, thoughtfully, plucking his lower lip, "I think, if I comb versions A and B, the two Fischer works of invention, I will in one of the faked scenes, sooner or later, come across a Talbot Yancy. In makeup, of course; doing a character role." Playing Stalin, he decided. Or Roosevelt. Any of them—or all. What the documentaries lacked were proper credits; who played what great world leader: we need that list, and that list does not and never did exist; it was carefully *not* made.

Cencio said, "We own our own prints of the two versions, you realize."

"All right. Go through them and extract each of the faked scenes. Separate them from the authentic clips that—"

Cencio laughed sardonically. "Good lord. Save us." He shut his eyes, rocked back and forth. "Who, honestly, can *ever* do that? No one knew then, knows now, will know—"

True; a good point. The *whole* point, in fact. "All right," Foote said. "Just start running them. Until you catch a glimpse of the Protector. He'll be one of the great charismatic leaders, one of the big four; he won't be Mussolini or Chamberlain, so you can bypass them." God in heaven, he thought; suppose he's the "Hitler" who lands in the Boeing 707 fanjet at Washington, D.C. to hold secret conversations with F.D.R.? *Is that what rules the millions of tankers today*, the actor who struck Gottlieb Fischer as just right to undertake the task of impersonating Adolf Hitler?

It could, however, be a bit part. The role of some general. Even one of those "G.I. Joe" scenes in the foxholes.

"It'll take me weeks," Cencio said, obviously realizing the same thing. "And do we have weeks? If people are being killed—"

"Joseph Adams is protected," Foote said. "And Brose—too bad if he gets it; more power to his hidden enemy."

—His hidden enemy who is obviously and clearly David Lantano. But that merely led back to his original inquiry; who or what is David Lantano?

Anyhow now he had a partial answer—at least ad hoc. It had yet to be tested. David Lantano, at the extreme old age end of his oscillation, was hired by Gottlieb Fischer to play a part—or was at least interviewed—in one or the other versions of the 1982 documentaries; there, that was his hypothesis. And now to test it.

And the next step was going to be hard—the step which followed the positive identification of Yancy—that is, David Lantano—in one or both of the 1982 documentaries.

The next step, and this fitted the talents of Webster Foote, Limited of London, was to chisel with highly specialized equipment undetected and silently into the incomplete villa of David Lantano while Lantano was at the Agency in New York. And gain at least momentary possession of the time travel instrumentality which Lantano utilized.

It'll be tough, Foote knew. But we have the machines to track it down; it's been our job since 2014. And this time we're not merely doing a job for a client; this is for ourselves.

Because, he realized, our own lives are currently—and involuntarily—posted as stakes in this; it is, has already proven to be, the ultimate pot for which the players are wagering, striving, lying, faking and haggling.

"A law firm," he said aloud. "Wagering, Striving, Lying, Faking and Haggling. Associates. They can represent us before the Recon Dis-In Council when we sue Brose."

"On what grounds?"

"On the grounds," Foote said quietly, "that the duly elected world leader is the Protector, Talbot Yancy, as every tanker knows; as the Estes Park Government has asserted for fifteen consecutive straight years. And such a man really exists. Hence—*Brose holds no legal power*." Since the legal power, he said to himself, is Q.E.D. all Yancy's and Pac-Peop as well as Wes-Dem has been claiming, chanting, this.

And, I think, Yancy has begun to put forth a request for the validation of that claim, Foote decided. At last.

TWENTY-FOUR

The little dark-skinned boy said shyly, "My name is Timmy."

Beside him his smaller sister squirmed, smiled, whispered, "I'm Dora."

Nicholas said, "Timmy and Dora." To Mrs. Lantano, who stood off to one side, he said, "You two have nice children." And, seeing David Lantano's wife, he thought of his own, of Rita, still below; the doomed life of the ant tanks. Eternal, evidently; because even the decently inclined individuals who dwelt on the surface, men such as David Lantano and, if what he understood was correct, the conapt construction magnate, Louis Runcible: even these men had no plans, no hopes, nothing to offer the tankers. Except, as in Runcible's case, hygenic, pleasant prisons above ground instead of the darker, more cramped prisons below. And Lantano—

His leadies would have killed me, Nicholas realized. Except for Talbot Yancy's appearance on the scene, and with a usable weapon.

To Lantano he said, "How can they say Yancy is a fraud? Blair said so; all of them said so. You say so."

Enigmatically, Lantano said, "Every leader who has ever ruled—"

"This is different," Nicholas said. "And I think you know it. This isn't a question of the man versus his public image; this is an issue that has never been raised—as far as I know—in history. The possibility that there is no such person at all. And yet I saw him. He saved my life." I came up here, he realized, to learn two things: that Talbot Yancy does not exist, as we always believed, and—that he does; that he is real enough to destroy two feral, professional, veteran leadies who, in the absence of authoritative restraint, would revert, would kill without even serious debate. Kill a man as a perfectly natural act; part of their job. Perhaps even a major part.

"As a component in his makeup," Lantano said, "every world leader has had *some* fictional aspect. Especially during the last century. And of course in Roman times. What, for instance, was Nero really like? We don't know. *They* didn't know. And the same is true about Claudius. Was Claudius an idiot or a great, even saintly, man? And the prophets, the religious—"

"You'll never answer," Nicholas said. It was obvious.

Seated on the long wrought black iron and foam-rubber couch with the two children, Isabella Lantano said, "You are right, Mr. St. James; he won't answer. But he knows." Her eyes, powerful and immense, fixed them on her husband. They, she and David Lantano, exchanged glances, meaningful and silent; Nicholas, excluded, got to his feet and wandered about the high, beam-ceiling living room, aimlessly, feeling acutely helpless.

"Have a drink," Lantano said. "Tequila. We brought back a very fine stock from Mexico City/Amecameca." He added, "At that time I was speaking before the Recon Dis-In Council, discovering to my satisfaction just how disinterested they really are."

"What is this council?" Nicholas asked.

"The true high court of this, our only, world."

"What did you try to get from them?" Nicholas asked. "In the way of a ruling?"

After a long interval Lantano said, laconically, "A ruling on a very academic question. The precise legal status of the Protector. Versus the Agency. Versus General Holt and Marshal Harenzany—" He broke off, because one of his household staff of leadies had entered the living room and was approaching him deferentially. "Versus Stanton Brose," he finished. "What is it?" he asked the leady.

"Dominus, there is a Yance-man at the periphery of the guarded area," the leady said respectfully. "With his household retinue, thirty leadies in all; he is extremely agitated and wants to see you socially. With him in addition comes a group of humans referred to as Footemen commandos who protect his person against real or imaginary dangers, according to orders, he declares, from Geneva. He appears quite frightened and he said to tell you that his best friend is dead and 'he is next.' Those were his words as I recorded them, Mr. Lantano. He said, 'Unless Lantano'—he forgot the obligatory polite formality in his agitation. 'Unless Lantano can help me I am next.' Shall we admit him?"

To Nicholas, Lantano said, "That would be a Yance-man from Northern California named Joseph Adams. An admirer of certain aspects of my work." To the leady he said, after reflecting a moment, "Tell him to come in and sit down. But at nine I have a business meeting scheduled." He examined his watch. "It's almost nine now; make sure he understands he can't stay for long." As the leady departed Lantano said to Nicholas, "This one is not entirely without reputability. You may find him interesting; what he does at least produces conflicts within him. But—" Lantano gestured, with finality; for him it had been decided. "He goes along. After and during the doubts. He has them but—he goes along." Lantano's voice sank, and again shockingly, the ancient, wizened visage appeared, even older than before; this was not middle-age: this was the glimpse which Nicholas had witnessed as Lantano stepped into the Cheyenne basement, only now he saw it—briefly—close up. And then it was gone. As if it had been only a play of the fire's light; not a change in the man at all. And yet he knew, understood, that it really was within the man, and, as he glanced around at Lantano's wife and two children, he caught a fleeting impression, based on the three of them; he saw, as if from the corner of his eye, a waning within them, too—except that for the two children it was more a growth, an augmentation into maturity and vigor; they seemed, abruptly, temporarily, older. And then that passed, also.

But he had seen it. Seen the children as—adolescents. And Mrs. Lantano gray and nodding, in the doze of a timeless half-sleep, a hibernation that was a conservation of departing, former powers.

"Here they come," Isabella Lantano said.

Clanking noisily, a group of leadies filed into the living room, came to a halt; from within them, slipping out from behind, stepped four human beings who glanced about in a cautious, professional way. And then, after them, appeared one scared, lone man. Joseph Adams, Nicholas realized; the man vibrated with apprehension, as if gouged from within, already—not merely potentially—a victim of some liquid-agile, ubiquitous, death-disturbing force.

"Thanks," Adams said huskily to Lantano. "I won't stay long. I was a good friend of Verne Lindblom; we worked together. His death—I'm not so worried about myself." He gestured at first his corps of leadies, then the human commandos protecting him; his double shield. "It's the shock of *his* death. I mean, this is a lonely life anyhow, at best." Trembling, he seated himself near the fire, not far from Lantano, glancing at Isabella and the two children, then at Nicholas, with disoriented vagueness. "I went to his demesne, in Pennsylvania; they know me there, his leadies; they recognized me because he and I used to play chess together in the evenings. So they let me in."

"And what did you find?" Lantano said in a strangely harsh voice; Nicholas was surprised at the animosity of his tone.

Adams said, "The type VI leady in charge—it took the initiative of letting me have a reading which the brain-pattern recording apparatus in the wall had picked up. The killer's distinctive Alpha-wave. I took it to Megavac 6-V and ran it; the 'vac has cards of everyone in the Yance organization." His voice shook; his hands as well.

"And," Lantano said, "whose card did it pop?"

After a pause Adams said, "Stanton Brose's. Therefore I guess it must have been Brose who killed him. Killed my best friend."

"So now," Lantano said, "you not only have no best friend but you have instead an enemy."

"Yes; I suppose Brose will kill me next. As he did Arlene Davidson and then Hig and then Verne. These Footemen—" He gestured at the four of them. "Without them I'd be dead already."

Thoughtfully, Lantano nodded and said, "Very likely." He said it as if he knew.

"What I came here for," Adams said, "is to ask your help. From what I saw of you—nobody has your ability. Brose needs you; without such people, young brilliant new Yance-men like you coming into the Agency, we'll ultimately make a mistake—Brose himself will get more and more senile as that brain deteriorates; sooner or later he'll pass on a tape that's got a major flaw. Like the flaws in Fischer's two documentaries; something like the Boeing 707 or Josef Stalin conversing in English—you know about those."

"Yes," Lantano said. "I know. There are more, too. But generally still not detected. Both versions are marred in small, insidious ways. So I'm essential to Brose; well, so?" He glanced at Adams, waiting.

"You tell him," Adams said raggedly, as if having trouble breathing, "that if I'm killed, you'll pull your talents out of the Agency."

"And why should I do that?"

"Because," Adams said, "someday it'll be you. If Brose is allowed to get away with this."

"What do you think caused Brose to kill your friend Lindblom?"

He must have decided that the special project—" Adams halted, was silent, struggling with himself.

"You all had done your job," Lantano said. "And as soon as each of you had he was dispatched. Arlene Davidson, once the carefully articulated sketches—not properly sketches at all but superbly realistic drawings, perfected as to every detail—had been prepared. Hig, as soon as he had located the artifacts at the site of the Utah diggings. Lindblom, as soon as he had completed the actual artifacts themselves and they'd been shot back in time. You, at the point where your three articles for *Natural World* are finished. Are they finished?" He glanced up, acutely.

"Yes " Adams nodded. "I handed them over to the Agency today. To be processed. Printed up in fake back-dated editions, aged and so on; you seem to know. But—" He returned Lantano's acute gaze. "Hig died too soon. He did *not* call the artifacts to Runcible's attention, although he had the camera and tape going. There are other Brose agents on Runcible's payroll and they report—and the camera reports—that Runcible does not know; beyond doubt he's absolutely ignorant of the presence—former presence—of the artifacts. So . . ." His voice lowered, became a bewildered mumble. "Something went wrong."

"Yes," Lantano agreed, "something went wrong at the one really critical moment. You're right; Hig was killed an instant too soon. I'll tell you something more. Your friend Lindblom was murdered by a German wartime invention called a Gestalt-macher; it does two distinctly separate jobs: first, it assassinates its victim instantly and without inordinate pain, which, to the German mind, makes it ethically acceptable. And then it lays down a trail of—"

"Clues," Adams interrupted. "I know; we've heard of it. We know it exists in the advanced weapons archives, which naturally only Brose can get into. Then the Alpha-wave pattern that Verne's continuous action monitor picked up—" He was silent, clasping and unclasping his hands. "It was spurious. Laid down deliberately by the Gestalt-macher. Fakes. That's what makes up the Gestalt, clues like that, profile indicators. Did the other clues—"

"All delineated Brose; they agreed. Webster Foote, who will be here any moment, fed the seven data to the Moscow computer and it popped only Brose's card. Just as Megavac 6-V did for you, on the basis of just the single datum. But one—that one—was enough."

"Then," Adams said hoarsely, "Brose did not kill Verne; it was someone else. Who not only wanted Lindblom killed but wanted us to believe Brose did it. An enemy of Brose." His face worked frantically, and Nicholas, watching, realized that the man's world had disintegrated; momentarily, the man had no intellectual, idiocrastic basis by which to orient himself; psychologically he floated, lost in a toneless, untended sea.

Lantano, however, did not seem much moved by Adams' disorganization and despair. He said, sharply, "But the Gestalt-macher was nabbed at the death locus, kept from escaping by Lindblom's alert staff of leadies. The person who set up the macher, who dispatched it with those clue data in it, knew the Lindblom had a death rattle. *Don't virtually all Yance-men carry death rattles?* You do." He pointed at Adams' neck, and Nicholas saw a hair-thin loop of gold, a band of some unusual metal.

"That is—a fact," Adams admitted, bewildered now to the extent that speech for him was almost impossible.

"And so Brose saw a way of manufacturing a de facto case that he was not the authorizing source for the macher. Since its clues pointed to him, and it is axiomatic that the trail of clues deposited by a macher are spurious, then Foote, whose job it is to know this, knew, as Brose intended, that Brose was to be thought of as the killer—that this was what the killer wanted; and Brose was innocent." He paused. "However, Brose is not innocent. Brose programmed the macher. To indict himself and by that means certify to the police mind his innocence."

Adams said, "I don't understand." He shook his head. "I just do not understand, Lantano; don't say it again—I heard what you said. I know what the words mean. It's just too—"

"Too convoluted," Lantano agreed. "A machine that kills, that also lays down false clues; only in this case the false clues are authentic. We have here, Adams, *the ultimate in fakery*, the last stage in the evolution of an organization created for the purpose of manufacturing hoaxes. Convincingly. Here's Foote." Lantano rose, turned toward the door. It opened, and a single individual, without, Nicholas noted, a retinue of leadies plus human detectives to guard him, entered, a leather strapless binder-type case under his arm.

"Adams," Foote said. "I'm pleased to see they didn't get to you."

Somberly, with a peculiar weariness, David Lantano introduced everyone around; for the first time he acknowledged Nicholas' presence in regard to the distraught, frightened Yance-man, Joseph Adams.

"I'm sorry, Adams," Lantano said, "but I'm afraid my conference with Mr. Foote is confidential. You'll have to leave."

Huskily, Adams said, "Will you help me or not?" He rose, but did not move away. And his human, as well as artificial, bodyguard remained inert, watching the goings-on intently. "I need help, Lantano. There's no place I can go to hide from him; he'll get me because he has access to those advanced weapons; god knows what's in those archives." He appealed, then, with a silent, wild glance at Nicholas, seeking even *his* assistance.

Nicholas said, "There's one place he might not find you." He had been pondering this for several minutes, since he had first managed to grasp the nature of Adams' situation.

"Where?" Adams said.

"Down in an ant tank."

Adams regarded him, his expression too lax, too confused by conflict, to be made out.

"My tank," Nicholas said, deliberately—because so many other persons were present—not naming his tank. "I can relocate the vertical tunnel. I intend to go back, with or without the artiforg I came for; you could come with me."

Foote said, "Ah. The artiforg. It's for you. The pancreas." He seated himself, unzipped his leather binder. "Someone in your tank? A valuable person, a dearly beloved old aunt? Artiforgs, as Mr. Lantano has undoubtedly already told you—"

"I'm going to keep trying," Nicholas said.

TWENTY-FIVE

As he unzipped his leather binder, Webster Foote managed to let a roll of papers bounce out and onto the floor; he bent forward to retrieve them, and, in that moment, saw his chance and made use of it; as with his left hand he snatched back the decoy, the rolled-up blank documents, with his right he placed within the cushions of the couch on which he sat—a deliberately selected spot—an aud-vid transmitting monitor; it would not merely perceive and store data; it would instantaneously transmit all it picked up to a Footeman at the nearest tracking substation.

To Foote, the harassed Yance-man Joseph Adams said, "You fed the clue data to the Moscow computer and it popped Brose's card. So in your mind Brose is innocent, because the clues are spurious, laid down by a Gestalt-macher; someone hostile to both Lindblom and Brose did it."

Eying him, wondering how he knew this, Foote said, "Hmm."

"This is true," Adams said hoarsely. "I know because I fed the Alpha-wave pattern to Megavac 6-V myself and got the same card. But David Lantano—" He jerked his head toward the dark young Yance-man. "He points out that Brose could have programmed the macher, knowing it'd be caught; and you did catch it."

"Well," Foote said warily, "we have an object. But we haven't yet got into it; the thing resists entry. We assume it's a cammed stage of a German-made wartime device; yes, that's so." He saw no reason to deny it at this point; however, since Joseph Adams and David Lantano knew this, it now of course would have to be told Brose. And as soon as possible, Foote realized. *Brose must get it* from me *and not them. So I had better get out of here as soon as I can manage it, back into my flapple where I'll have access to vid-transmission by satellite relay* to Geneva. Because if Brose learns the news from them and not from me, my reputation will suffer permanent impairment; I can't afford this. He felt nettled, aggrieved.

Do you mean, he said to himself, *that I fell for a cover—or, more accurately, a* double *cover? The crime was committed by that portable TV receiver—so-called, so-appearing—but Brose really dispatched it, set it up to delineate* himself? *And to think that I never, even with my extrasensory ability, happened onto that idea.*

It's this Lantano, he realized; *the idea is his. Inspired. The man is dangerously so, dangerously gifted.*

In his ear a receiver-speaker, grafted subdermal so as to be invisible, piped, "We're picking up the aud-vid signals clearly, Mr. F. It's extremely well-placed. We'll get everything in that one room from now on."

Reflexively, still deep in thought, Foote unrolled his military maps, which showed ordinance dispositions of essential military stores; these had been top secret . . . classified, the old argot had been. Made available to him originally by General Holt, via the Agency. For purposes of a former job he had performed for Brose; the actual maps had been returned; these were Xeroxed copies. He studied them now, perfunctorily, prepared to begin the tedious cover discussion with Lantano . . . and then, without warning, summarily, his extrasensory faculty bumped him jarringly, flooded his mind with intimation, and he scanned closely, keenly, the top map. It showed an area near the Atlantic Coast of North Carolina. Three U.S. Army weapons arsenals were indicated, subsurface stores which had long ago been excavated by Brose's leadies and everything of value removed. This was so indicated by check-makers on the map. But—

The distribution of the arsenals indicated that they had been set up to supply highly mobile armored tactical surface units, probably engaged—or it had been so anticipated—in handling Soviet leadies landed by the giant troop carrier USSR transoceanic subs of the 1990s. And a quadripatrite division of such arsenals had been common in those days: three of weapons, fuel and repair parts for the heavy U.S. rexeroid-shielded tanks capable of surviving a direct hit by a ground-to-ground A-head missile . . . these were the three that had been dug up. But no fourth subsurface depot was indicated, and yet it should have existed fifty miles or so in the rear; that would have contained the medical supplies—if any had been provided for the personnel of the highly mobile mechanized defensive units drawing on the three weapons arsenals closer to the coastline.

With a pencil he drew lines connecting the three indicated arsenals, then, with the edge of a book plucked from a nearby table, he measured off a line which ended at the hypothetical locus which would transform the visible triangle into a square.

In five hours, Foote realized, I can have a work detail of leadies digging at that spot; they can sink a shaft and in fifteen minutes determine if a fourth depot, that of medical, hospital emergency equipment, exists there. The chances are—he calculated. About forty percent favorable. But—digs had been essayed on far slimmer evidence in the past, and by his corporation.

Some paid off; some did not. But it would be of incalculable value if he were to locate a store of artiforgs. Even a few, three or four . . . even that meager handful *would break Brose's monopoly*.

"At this spot," he said to Lantano, who had come over and seated himself beside him, "I plan to dig. You can see why." He indicated the three depots already excavated, then the lines he had drawn. "My Psionic hunch," he said, "tells me, water witchwise, that we will strike an undisclosed U.S. Army medical store, here. And perhaps luck will be with us. Artificial pancreaswise."

Joseph Adams said, "I'll go." Obviously he had given up; he signaled to his retinue of leadies; they and the four Footemen assigned to guard him began to collect around him and together the group of them all shuffled toward the door, an ensemble of defeat.

"Wait," Lantano said.

At the door Adams waited, his unhappy face still contorted; the suffering and confusion, pain at his friend's death, uncertainty as to who was responsible, what he himself ought to do—all was mingled, blended.

Lantano said, "Would you kill Stanton Brose?"

Staring at him, Adams said, "I—" His stare became blind, horrified. There was silence, then.

"You can't escape him, Adams. Probably not even by descending into an ant tank; not even by that. Because Brose's pol-coms are there waiting. If you went down into that tank with Nick—with their pol-com there, acting for Brose, who probably knows the exact conditions up here—" Lantano broke off. It was not necessary to say it.

"You'll have to decide for yourself, Adams," Lantano said, then. "It can be for any motive you care to assign yourself. Revenge for Lindblom's death, fear as regards your own life . . . for humanity itself. Take your choice. All three, if that appeals to you. But you do have the opportunity to see Brose. You could conceivably take him out. Although the chance, frankly, would be slim. However, it's a real chance. And look at your situation now; look at your fear. And it will get worse, Adams; I predict that and I think Mr. Foote here would predict the same."

"I—don't know," Adams muttered, at last.

"Morally," Lantano said, "it would be right. I am sure of that. Mr. Foote knows that. Nick here knows that—already. You know it, too, Adams. Don't you?" He waited; Adams did not answer. To Foote, Lantano said, "He knows it. He's one of the few Yance-men who does, who faces it. Especially now, after Lindblom's death."

"Kill him with what?" Adams said, then.

Lantano said, regarding Foote's military map intently, "I'll supply you with the weapon. Leave that part to me. I think we've arrived at the crux, here." He put his forefinger on the spot which Foote had indicated on the military map. "Go ahead and dig; I'll pay the costs." Once more he turned to Adams, who stood at the door entirely surrounded by his leadies and Footemen escort. "Brose has to be killed. It's only a matter of time. And by whom. And through what technical construct." To Foote he said, "What weapon would you recommend? Adams will encounter Brose at the Agency sometime later this week, in his own office. Adams' office. So he need not carry it on him; it can be in the office, cammed in place; he need only have the triggering mechanism on him or auto-arranged in advance."

Extraordinary, Foote thought. *Is this what I came here for?* It was supposedly a pretext, my visit here, to plant a monitoring device. By which I could learn more about David Lantano. But instead—I have been drawn into, or anyhow invited to enter, a conspiracy to kill the most powerful human being in the world. And the man with the greatest repertory of advanced weapons at his disposal.

The man, Foote realized, we all really terribly fear.

And this conversation, due to the aud-vid bug he had planted in the couch, *was being monitored.* And, by an incredible, maddening irony, by his own technicians. But his own corporation's experts, at the local tracking substation and then at the London office itself. Too late now, to shut it off; the data, the important message, had been sent out already. And, of course, somewhere in the corporation Webster Foote, Limited, Brose had his agents; eventually, although not perhaps right away, the news of this conversation in utter and complete bona fide detail, would arrive, through channels, at Geneva. And every man in this room, Foote realized, will be killed. Even if I say no; even if both Adams and I say no; *that will not be enough*. Because the old man, Stanton Brose, will not dare to take the chance; we will have to be dispatched. Just in case. To insure his absolute self-protection.

Aloud Foote said, "You have Brose's Alpha-wave pattern. In the wall monitor at Lindblom's demesne. And you have access to it—" He spoke, now, to Adams.

"Tropism," Lantano said, and nodded.

"Since Lindblom's leadies recognize you as the deceased's closest friend—" Foote hesitated and then he said, numbly, "I therefore recommend yes; the Alpha-wave pattern as the tropism. A conventional homeostatic high-velocity cyanide dart. Set to release from some recess in your Agency office the moment its dispatching mechanism receives and records that idiosyncratic Alpha-wave pattern as present."

There was silence.

"Could it be set up tonight?" Lantano asked Foote.

"It takes only a few minutes to install the barn for such a dart," Foote said. "And to program the dispatching mechanism within the barn housing. And to load the barn with the dart itself."

Adams said. "Do—you have such hardware?" He spoke to Foote.

"No," Foote said. Which was the truth. Unfortunately. He could not come through.

"I have," Lantano said.

Foote said, "There are hundreds of those wartime cyanide homeostatic high velocity darts left over from the days when the Communist international assassins were in business, and literally thousands of the low velocity ones that could be corrected after release, such as that which killed Verne Lindblom. But they're old. They exist but they can't be relied on; too many years have—"

"I said," Lantano said, "*that I have one*. The complete assembly: dart, barn, housing, dispatching mechanism. And in mint condition."

"Then," Foote said, "you must also have access to time travel equipment. This hardware you speak of, it must come directly from fifteen to twenty years ago."

Presently Lantano nodded. "I do." He clenched his hands together, violently. "But I don't know how to set up the assembly. The wartime and prewar CP assassins who used those were specially trained. But I think with your general knowledge of the field—" He glanced at Foote. "You could. Will you?"

"Tonight?" Foote said.

"Brose," Lantano said, "will visit Adams' office possibly as early as tomorrow. If it's installed tonight, Brose could be dead within the next twelve to twenty-four hours. The alternative of course, needless to say, is death for each and every human being in this room. Because within the next *forty-eight* hours, news of this discussion will be in Brose's hands." He added, "Due to some monitoring device, Foote, which you yourself brought; I don't know what it is, where it is, when and how you installed it, but I know it's in the room. And functioning."

"True," Foote said, at last.

"So we have to continue," Adams spoke up. "Tonight, as he says. All right, I'll fly to Lindblom's demesne and get the Alpha-wave pattern back; I returned it to the type VI chief leady, there." He hesitated, suddenly realizing something. "The Gestalt-macher possessed that pattern. How did it get it? The person who programmed it had the pattern; only Brose would have the pattern. So I guess you are right, Lantano. It had to be Brose who fed the data to the machine."

"Did you think," Lantano said quietly, "that perhaps I dispatched that machine to kill your friend?"

Adams hesitated. "I don't know. Someone did; that's all I knew. Except that I got that card popped; it seemed to me—"

"I think you did," Foote said.

Glancing at him, Latano smiled. It was not the smile of a young man; it had in it ancient, wild craft. An elliptic untamed wisdom which could afford to be gentle, could be tolerant because it had seen so much.

"You're an American Indian," Foote said, all at once understanding. "From the past. Who somehow, in the past, got hold of one of our modern-day time travel devices. How did you get it, Lantano? Did Brose send a scoop back to your era, *is that it?*"

After a time Lantano said, "The artifacts that Lindblom made. He utilized the ingredients of the original advanced prototype of the wartime weapon based on that principle. A geologist made an error; some of the artifacts appeared not subsurface but on the ground, in plain sight. I came along; I was leading a war party. You would not have recognized me, then; I was dressed differently. And all painted."

The ex-tanker, Nicholas St. James, said, "Cherokee."

"Yes." Lantano nodded. "By your reckoning, fifteenth century. So I've had a long time to prepare for this."

"Prepare for what?" Foote said.

Lantano said, "You know who I am, Foote. Or rather, who I've been in the past, in 1982, to be specific. And who I will be. Shortly. Your men are going over the documentaries. I'll save you some long and difficult research; you will find me in episode nineteen of version A. Briefly."

"And whom," Foote said levelly, "do you portray?"

"General Dwight David Eisenhower. In that spurious, utterly faked scene contrived by Gottlieb Fischer, in which Churchill, Roosevelt—or rather the actors impersonating them for Fischer's didactic purposes—confer with Eisenhower and the decision is reached as to exactly how long they can stall the invasion of the continent. D-day, it was called. I read a very interesting phony line . . . I will never forget it."

"I remember that," Nicholas said suddenly.

They turned toward him, all of them.

"You said," Nicholas said, " 'I think the weather is sufficiently rough. To hamper the landings and so account for our failure to establish our beachheads successfully.' Fischer had you say that."

"Yes." Lantano nodded. "That was the line. However, the landings were successful. Because, as version B shows—in an equally inspiredly spurious scene for Pac-Peop consumption—Hitler deliberately held back two panzer divisions in the Normandy area *so that the invasion would succeed*."

No one said anything for a time.

"Will the death of Brose," Nicholas said, "mean the end of the era which began with those two documentaries?" He addressed Lantano. "You say you have access to—"

"The death of Brose," Lantano said firmly, "will inaugurate the moment in which we, plus the Recon Dis-In Council, with whom I have already discussed this matter, will, in conjunction with Louis Runcible—who is essential in this—decide exactly what to tell the millions of underground dwellers."

"So they'll come up?" Nicholas said.

"If we want that," Lantano said.

"Hell," Nicholas protested, "of course we want that; it's the whole point. Isn't it?" He looked from Lantano to Adams, then to Foote.

Foote said, "I think so. I agree." And Runcible would agree.

"But only one man," Lantano said, "speaks *to* the tankers. And that man is Talbot Yancy. What will he decide to do?"

Adams, sputtering, said, "There is no Tal—"

"But there is," Foote said. To Lantano he said, 'What will Talbot Yancy decide to do?" *I believe you can authoritatively answer,* he said to himself. *Because you know; and I know why you know, and you realize this. We are no longer in the quagmire of fakes, now; this is real. What are you, what I am aware of, due to the photographic records taken by my satellite.*

After a pause Lantano said thoughtfully, "Talbot Yancy will announce, in the near future, if all goes well, that the war has terminated. But that the surface is still radioactive. So the ant tanks must be emptied on a gradual basis. On strict allocation, step by step."

"And this is true?" Nicholas said. "They really will be brought up gradually? Or is this just another—"

Looking at his watch, Lantano said, "We have to get busy. Adams, you get the Alpha-wave pattern from Pennsylvania. I'll bring the assembly that comprises the terminal weapon we've decided on; Foote, you come with me—we'll meet Adams at his office in the Agency, and you can install the weapon, program it, have it ready for tomorrow." He rose, then, moved agilely toward the door.

"What about me?" Nicholas said.

Lantano picked up Foote's military map, carried it to Nicholas, presented him with it. "My leadies are at your disposal. And an express flapple that'll get you and nine or ten leadies to North Carolina. This is the spot for them to excavate. And good luck," Lantano said tersely. "Because from now on you're on homeo—on your own. Tonight we have other matters to take care of."

Foote said, "I wish we didn't have to—rush into this; I wish we could discuss it further." He felt fear. Precog, extrasensory, as well as the ordinary instinctive fear. "If only we had more time," he said.

To him Lantano said, "Do you think we have?"

"No," Foote said.

TWENTY-SIX

With his cumbersome human and leady entourage surrounding him, Joseph Adams left the living room of the villa; Foote and Lantano followed, the two of them together.

"Did Brose program the macher?" Foote said to the dark young man—young now, but as he had seen on the animated sequences of the satellite-obtained photographic record, capable of or victim of an oscillation into any section of his life track.

Lantano said, "Since the machine came equipped with the Alpha-wave pattern of—"

"Which can be obtained by any Yance-man from any of the three major computers," Foote said, in a voice that did not carry to Joseph Adams, who was insulated by the clankings of his entourage. "And Lantano, let's face it; *you know that*. Are you responsible for Lindblom's death? I'd like to know before we go into this."

"Is it important? Does it really make a difference?"

Foote said, "Yes. But I'll go ahead anyhow." Because of the danger of not going ahead, the menace to their lives; the moral issue had no bearing, not at this late point. Not since he had installed the aud-vid bug. If ever anyone became the victim of his own professional ingenuity . . .

"I programmed the macher," Lantano said, then.

"Why? What had Lindblom done?"

"Nothing. In fact I was deeply in his debt, since through him I obtained the time travel rig; I wouldn't be here now without him. And before him I—" The most brief, short-lingering hesitation. "I killed Hig."

"Why?"

"Hig I killed," Lantano said matter-of-factly, "to stop the special project. To save Runcible. So the special project would misfire. Which it did."

"But why Lindblom? Hig I can understand. But—" He gestured.

Lantano said, "For this. To indict Brose. To provide delineation that would convince Adams that Brose had killed his best friend, the only friend, as near as I can make out, that Adams had left in the world. I expected the macher to escape; I didn't think Lindblom's leadies were that efficient, had been trained to move that fast. Evidently Lindblom suspected something, but perhaps from some other quarter."

"And what does this accomplish, this death?"

"It forces Adams to act. Brose is wary; Brose, without having a rational, conscious reason, distrusts me and avoids me. *Brose has never come within weapons distance of me, will never;* I couldn't have reached him alone, by myself, without Adams' help. I've looked ahead; I know. Brose either dies tomorrow morning when he visits Adams' office—which is one of the few places Brose will go—or Brose continues on, if you can accept and believe this, *another twenty years*."

"In that case," Foote said, "you did the proper thing." *If* this was true. And no way existed by which he could check. Twenty years. Until Brose was one-hundred-and-two years old. A nightmare, Foote said to himself. And we are not out of it yet; we still must awake.

"What Adams does not know," Lantano said, "will never find out, is a deplorable fact that should never have come into existence. Lindblom, up to the time of his death, was agonizing over a decision. Had actually reached a decision; he was finally prepared to report on Adams' moral reservations toward the special project. He knew that Adams was on the verge of leaking enough information to Louis Runcible to keep Runcible from being gaffed, from falling onto the hook; Runcible would have, based on Adam's tip, made the archeological finds public. He would have lost his Utah land, but not his overall economic syndrome. Nor his political freedom. Lindblom—he was loyal, when it came down to it, to the Agency. To Brose. Not to his friend. I have seen this, Foote; believe me. Within the next day Lindblom would go through channels—and he knew exactly how, exactly which mediatory agency to make use of—to approach Brose at his *Festung* in Geneva, and Adams himself was afraid of this; he knew that Lindblom held his life in his hands . . . Adams' life. Due to Adams' rather unusual—among Yance-men—higher inclinations, his scruples. His awareness of the evil underlying the special project from start to finish.'' He was silent as Joseph Adams, in his overloaded commercial model flapple, managed to get off the ground, to depart into the night sky.

Foote said, ''If it had been me I wouldn't have done it. Killed Hig or Lindblom. Anybody.'' In his business he had seen enough of killing.

''But,'' Lantano said, ''you are willing to participate in this now. In Brose's death. So even you, at a point, feel—recognize—that no other resource can be turned to, except the ultimate one. I've lived six hundred years, Foote; I know when it is and isn't necessary to kill.''

Yes, Foote thought. Evidently you do.

But where, he wondered, does this sequence terminate? Will Brose be the last? There's no guarantee extended, here.

His intuition told him that there would be more. Once this sort of thinking, this method of problem solving, began it tended to develop its own momentum. Lantano—or Talbot Yancy as he would soon be calling himself, and not, evidently, for the first time—had worked centuries to achieve this. Obviously after Brose might come Runcible or Adams and, as he had thought from the start of this, himself. Whoever, as Lantano had put it, was ''necessary.''

A favorite word, Foote reflected, of those driven by a yearning for power. The only necessity was an internal one, that of fulfilling their drives. Brose had it; Lantano had it; countless little Yance-men and would-be Yance-men had it; hundreds if not thousands of pol-coms down in the ant tanks below, Foote realized, are ruling as true tyrants, through their link with the surface, through their possession of the *gnosis*, the secret knowledge of the actual state of affairs that obtain here.

But with this particular man the drive spans centuries.

Who, then, Foote asked himself as he followed Lantano toward a parked and waiting express flapple, is the greater menace? Six-hundred-year-old Lantano/Yancy/Running Red Feather or whatever his original Cherokee name was, who in the dotage stage of his cycle will become what is now merely a synthetic dummy based on him, bolted to an oak desk—a dummy which, and this will convulse a fairly extensive number of Agency people, of demesne domini, all at once will become ambulatory and real . . . this, or the rule by an aging, genuinely senile monstrosity who hides out in Geneva, blubbering over with plans to heighten and strengthen the dikes which support his existence—how can a sane man choose between these and still stay sane? We are cursed as a race, all right, Foote said to himself; Genesis is right. If this is the decision we are stuck with; if there are no choices but this, in which we must all become instruments of one or the other, units which either Lantano or Stanton Brose picks up and moves about, according to the direction of his grand design.

But is this all? Foote asked himself as, reflexively, he entered the flapple, seated himself beside Lantano, who at once started up the engine; the flapple rose into the gloom, leaving the hot-spot of Cheyenne behind, and the half-completed villa with its glowing lights . . . which, no doubt, would after all see completion.

"The assembly," Lantano said, "which constitutes the weapon, is in the back seat. Carefully packaged in its original autofac carton."

Foote said, "Then you knew what I would choose."

"Time travel," Lantano said, "is valuable." That was the extent of his laconic reply; they flew on in silence.

There is a third choice, Foote said to himself. A third person, of enormous power, who is not a unit moved about by Lantano and not by Stanton Brose either. In his Capetown resort villa, sunning himself in his vine-walled villa patio, lies Louis Runcible, and if we are out to locate sane men and sane decisions we may find both there in Capetown.

"I'll go through with it, as I said," Foote said aloud. "The setting up of the weapon assembly in Adams' office in New York." *And then,* he decided, *I'm heading for Capetown. For Louis Runcible.*

I'm physically sick, he realized, *made so by the aura of "necessity" that surrounds this man beside me—an order of political and moral reality which I'm too simple to fathom; after all, I've lived only forty-two years. Not six hundred.*

And as soon as I've arrived safely in Capetown, Foote said to himself, *I will get my ear up against news transmitters of every kind, waiting without break, without interruption, to hear, out of New York, that Stanton Brose, fat and putty-like and senile-cunning, is dead—if the coup from within the Agency itself by its youngest (good god, six hundred years was young?) brightest idea man, speech writer, has been successful.*

After that perhaps I—and, hopefully, Louis Runcible, if we can make a deal—will have some idea of what to do. Will see our "necessity."

Because at the moment, lord knew, he did not.

Aloud he said, "You personally are ready, the moment Brose is dead, to claim, before the Recon Dis-In Council, to constitute the sole legitimate governing body? The planetwide Protector, outranking General Holt here in Wes-Dem and Marshal—"

"Doesn't every one of the several hundreds of millions of tankers know that? Hasn't the Protector's supreme authority been established for years back?"

"And the leadies," Foote said. "They'll obey you? Not Holt or Harenzany? If it comes to that?"

"What you are overlooking is this: my legal access to the simulacrum, that *thing* at the oak desk; I program it—I feed reading matter to it by way of Megavac 6-V. So I've in a sense begun to make the transition already; I will simply blend with it, not by an abrupt abolition of it, but by—" Lantano gestured spasmodically. "The word is—*fusion*."

Foote said, "You won't enjoy it, being bolted to that desk."

"I think that part can happily be eliminated. Yancy may in fact begin visiting representative ant tanks. As Churchill did the bombed-out areas of England in World War Two. Gottlieb Fischer did not have to counterfeit *those* sequences."

"Did you, in your centuries of past life, limit your public appearance to one faked scene in Gottlieb Fischer's documentary? One impersonation of an American general of World War Two? Or—" And his extrasensory insight was keen, now; it had sniffed something into the light. "Did you at one or more times already hold power—power to some extent . . . not like this, not that of the planetwide supreme Protector—"

"I have to some extent been active. On a number of occasions. There is an evolutionary, historic continuity of my role."

"Any name I would recognize?"

The man beside him said, "Yes. Several." He did not amplify, and it was obvious that he was not going to; he remained silent as the express flapple flew above the unlit surface of Earth, toward New York City.

"Not too long ago," Foote said cautiously, not really expecting to obtain an answer to this direct query, "some of my better interrogators, working with tankers who had bored through to the surface, extracted the—to me—fascinating fact that a weak TV signal, not the normal one from Estes Park, carried by the coax, had elliptically alluded, shall we say, to certain irregularities in previous official, supposedly authentic—''

''There I erred,'' Lantano said.

''Then it was you.'' So now he knew the origin of that. Once more a hunch of his had proved correct.

''Yes, it was my mistake,'' Lantano said. ''And I almost cost Runcible his free existence, which for him would have meant his physical life. It was obvious I had to stop—once I discovered that Brose blamed the splice and the transmission on Runcible. All I was really doing was to set up Runcible for extinction by Brose's agents. And I didn't want that. I removed the lash-up cut into one of the peripheral shielded coax cables—but I was too late. Brose had already in that weird, worn-out, crafty, infantile brain hatched up the special project. The gear teeth had begun to turn, and it was my—mine, all my—fault; I was obsessed by what I had initiated. And at that point—''

''You managed,'' Foote said tartly, ''to impede it rather well.''

''I had to; the responsibility was so clearly mine. I had transformed a latent suspicion on Brose's part into a crisis. Of course, it goes without saying, I couldn't come forth. So I started with Hig. That seemed the only way to approach it at that late date; the only way to handle it so that it came to a stop, a real stop—not just a temporary one.''

''And without, as you say, exposing yourself.''

Lantano said, ''It was a difficult situation and dangerous, not only to Runcible—'' He glanced at Foote. ''But to me. And I did not intend to have that.''

God help me, Foote thought, *to get away from this man. And out over the Atlantic in a flapple, alone, in contact with Runcible by vidphone, telling him I'm on my way.*

Suppose Runcible didn't listen.

That anxiety-inducing thought, with every one of its ramifications, remained central in Foote's mind, all the way across the United States to the Agency buildings and the office of Joseph Adams in New York City.

The office was dark. Adams had not yet arrived.

''Naturally it'll take him a little while,'' Lantano said, ''to get the

Alpha-wave pattern.'' Nervously, looking—for him unusually—taut, he examined his wristwatch, checked the dial which gave New York time. ''Maybe, we should get the Alpha-wave pattern from Megavac 6-V instead. You begin setting up the assembly.'' The two of them stood briefly in the hallway outside Adams' office at 580 Fifth Avenue. ''Go on in while I get the pattern.'' Lantano started off, rapidly.

Foote said, ''There's no way I can get in. Adams and Brose have, as far as I know, the only keys.''

Staring at him, Lantano said, ''Can't you—''

''My corporation,'' Foote said, ''possesses tools to obviate any lock in the world, no matter how intricate or obstinate. But—'' He had none with him; they were all in London or scattered at field stations around the world.

''Then we might as well just stand here and wait,'' Lantano said, not pleased at all, but accommodating himself to the fact; they had to have Adams, not only for the Alpha-pattern of Stanton Brose by which to render the weapon tropic but simply and literally to gain access to the premises, the office, which evidently fat, huge, aging Brose would enter bright and early in the morning, ahead of its owner. One of the few places outside of Geneva where he apparently felt safe. And Geneva itself was impossible; if they had to alter their plans and make a try at Brose there they were already finished.

They waited.

''Suppose,'' Foote said presently, ''Adams changes his mind. And does not come.''

Lantano glared at him. ''He'll come.'' The black deep-set eyes were envenomed even at mention of the possibility.

''I'm waiting exactly fifeen more minutes,'' Foote said, with quiet dignity, unafraid of the furious dark eyes, ''and then I'm getting out of here.''

The two of them continued to wait, minute after minute.

And, as each minute ticked past, Foote thought, he's not coming; he's backed out. And if he's backed out we must assume he's contacted Geneva: we can't afford to make any other assumption than that we're waiting here for Brose's killers. Waiting in this hall for our deaths.

''The future,'' he said to Lantano, ''it's a series of alternatives, is it? Some more probable than others?''

Lantano grunted.

"Do you foresee, as one alternative future, Adams informing Brose and saving himself at our expense?"

Lantano said, tightly, "Yes. But it's unlikely. About one chance in forty."

"I have my extrasensory hunch faculty," Foote said. And, he thought, it tells me that those are not the odds; the odds are far, far greater that we are trapped like pink-eared baby mice, floating, drowning, in a dish of honey. Served up for extermination. For greedy, lip-smacking consumption.

It was a very arduous, and, psychosomatically, very unfortunate wait.

And, despite what Lantano's watch said, very long.

Foote wondered if he could endure it.

Could—or, in the face of Brose's ability to move his agents about rapidly from this place to that, would.

TWENTY-SEVEN

After he had stopped by Verne Lindblom's demesne and had picked up the Alpha-wave pattern of Stanton Brose's brain once more from the type VI senior leady, Joseph Adams with his retinue of personal leadies and his bodyguard from the Foote organization flew aimlessly, not toward New York; not in any particular direction.

He got away with that for just a few minutes. And then one of the four Footemen leaned toward him from the seat behind and said distinctly and grimly, "Go the Agency in New York. Without delay. Or I'll kill you with my laser beam." He thereupon placed the cold, round muzzle of his laser pistol to the back of Joseph Adams' head.

"Some bodyguard," Adams said, bitterly.

"You have an appointment with Mr. Foote and Mr. Lantano at your office," the Footeman commando said. "Please keep it."

On Joseph Adams' person, in the form of a dead man's throttle strapped to his left wrist, he possessed—had rigged this up as a result of Verne Lindblom's death—an emergency signaling device that connected him by microwave with his retinue of leadies now squeezed in on each side of him here in this oversized flapple. He wondered, if he were to trigger the signal, which would come first; would the Footeman commando, an expert, kill him, or would his leadies, who were war veterans, take out the four Footemen?

An interesting question.

And on it nothing more or less than his life depended.

But why *not* fly on to the Agency? What held him back?

I'm afraid of Lantano, he realized. Lantano knew too much, had too many pieces of detailed knowledge about Verne Lindblom's death at his disposal. But I'm afraid, he realized, of Stanton Brose, too; I'm afraid of both of them, but of the two Brose is the known fear and Lantano the unknown. So for me, Lantano creates an even greater sense of that grisly all-encompassing devouring inner and outer fog that sweeps life away from me . . . and god knows, Brose has been bad enough. His special project was the epitome of wickedness and cynicism, plus Brose's own unique blend of senile cunning, of drooling, glint-eyed, almost childishly mischievous doing-of-wrong *and enjoying it.*

And Brose, he realized, will get worse. As that brain rots more and more, as those miscroscopic strictures of minute blood vessels continue to occur. As bit after bit of brain tissue, clogged, deprived of oxygen and nutrition, perishes. And leaves the remnants just that more revolting, that much less to be depended on, ethically and pragmatically.

The next twenty years, under the decaying rule of Stanton Brose, would be even more profoundly ghastly as the decay of the central, guiding organ penetrated deeper, ceaselessly deeper, and lured the world along with it. And he—all the Yance-men—all of them would be jerked and dangled by the conclusive twitches on the deranged master string; as Brose's brain degenerated, as extensions of Brose, would all of them degenerate in resonance. God, what a prospect . . .

The force which Lantano had unique control over—time—was the force which was corrupting the organic tissue of Stanton Brose. Hence—

With one stroke, the release of one high velocity homeostatic Alpha-wave-tropic cyanide dart, that corrupting force would he abolish from their lives. And wasn't that the whole rational reason for this flight to New York, to his office, where Lantano and Foote waited?

But Joseph Adams' body, unconvinced, threw its metabolic secretions of fear through and through his sympathetic nervous system. Struggling for relief—in other words, he realized, for escape. *I want to get away.*

And Foote, too, he realized acutely, if that look on his face meant anything, felt something of this. Only not as strongly as I'm feeling it now, because if he did he would not be in New York; he'd be out here long ago. Webster Foote would know how. And, he realized, I don't; I'm not equipped, as he is, for this.

"Okay," Adams said to the Footeman commando behind him who held the laser pistol to Adams' head. "I was disoriented for a minute; now I'm all right." He turned the flapple then toward New York.

Behind him the Footeman commando withdrew the laser pistol, restored it to its shoulder holster as the flapple streaked northeast.

At his left wrist Joseph Adams released the dead man's throttle signaling device. The microwave impulse, to his leadies, automatically and instantly became perceptible, although his own sense receptors picked up nothing. Nor did those of the four Footemen.

As Adams stared fixedly at the control before him, his leadies in a brief skirmish—almost gruesomely silent—killed the four Footemen. The noise, after a time so short that Adams could not really believe or accept that the act had been accomplished, came to its termination; a rear door of the flapple was opened, and with much straining and groaning and clanking, the leadies dumped out the bodies of the four Footemen, out into the emptiness of space and the remoteness of a night, which, it seemed to Adams had begun but would never end.

Adams said, "I just couldn't go to New York." He shuts his eyes. *In nomine Domini*, he thought. Four men dead; awful, and he would always wear, carry with him, the mark: *he* had ordered it—and without using his own hands. Which made it just that much worse. *But they put that gun to my head,* he realized, *and in my fear I went insane; they threatened to kill me if I didn't go to New York, and since I can't do that—god help each of us,* he thought. *That to live we have to destroy; this price has to be paid, this bad bargain: four lives for one.*

Anyhow it was done. And so he turned the flapple toward the south; it moved southeast, now, toward the Carolinas. Instead of toward New York. Which he would never see again.

It took him hours to sight the illuminated blotch in the darkness below which was the scene of the diggings.

The flapple, at Adams' instruction, began its spiral down. Toward the spot where Nicholas St. James, the ex-tanker, dug with the assistance of David Lantano's leadies, seeking the possible buried U.S. Army prewar medical storehouse and the artiforgs—if they existed, and if this was the correct spot—somewhere below the surface.

Once landed, Adams made his way toward the diggings. Off to one side, the ex-tanker Nicholas St. James sat among cartons and boxes and Adams realized that the location had proved correct. The U.S. Army dump had been located; already prewar supplies were being recovered. It was, in Yance-man argot, christmas morning.

Glancing up at the sight of the first leady, Nicholas peered. "Who is it?" he said. Simultaneously, Lantano's leadies ceased their toiling; without command they moved toward Nicholas, to protect him; their manual extensors dropped so as to make contact with the weapons which they, at their mid-sections, carried. It was done swiftly, smoothly, and of course at once.

Adams gave an order and his own leadies moved about him, too, in an equally defensive pattern. The two men, now, were separated each by his own leadies; only leady faced leady—neither man could see the other.

"St. James—remember me? Joe Adams; I met you at Dave Lantano's demesne. I've come by to see what luck you had. In getting your artiforg."

"Real luck," Nicholas yelled back. "But what's this deploying of these leadies for? Who's fighting who and what for?"

"I don't want to fight," Adams said. "Can I retire my leadies? Will you do the same with yours and give me your word there won't be any hostile interaction?"

Sounding genuinely puzzled, Nicholas said, "But there's no war; Blair said so, and I saw the demesnes. Why should there by any 'hostile interaction' between you and me?"

"No reasons." Adams signaled his leadies; they withdrew reluctantly, because after all, each of them was a veteran of the war, the true war which had been fought thirteen years ago.

Alone, as a single human, Adams approached the ex-tanker. "Did you find the particular artiforg you need?"

Excitedly, like an overjoyed, enthralled small boy, Nicholas said, "Yes! Three artiforgs, a heart, a kidney, I found it—an artiforg pancreas, still in its original protective carton—it's sealed in an aluminum drum." He displayed it proudly. "Plastic-dipped to keep out air; undoubtedly it's as good as when it was first made. This container was built to protect its contents for, look, right here; for fifty years."

"Then you did it," Adams said. *You got it,* he thought to himself, *what you emerged into the light of day for. Your journey is over. You lucky guy,* he thought. *If only it were that simple for me. If what I needed, lacked, required so that I might live, could be held in the hand, inspected, its ink markings read. Picked up and manually gripped; some object, material and hard—and my fears equally concrete. Limited, as has been your case, to the fear of not finding one specific clearly defined wartime construct, and that construct now found and possessed, as much as we can in this life ever possess anything, really retain and keep it. And look what I have lost,* he thought. *My demesne, my job; I am going to give up the surface of Earth. In order not to follow Verne Lindblom. Because,* he said to himself, *I know it was David Lantano who did it. I knew that the moment Lantano admitted that he had the weapon assembly in his possession. The components that make up the killing agent known to us all: the high velocity—or as in Verne's case, low velocity—cyanide-tipped homeostatic dart. And not rusty but in working order . . . as was the one which reached Verne Lindblom's heart.*

Mint condition, as Lantano had said. Derived directly from the war-years, from thirteen years ago, by means of Lantano's time-travel equipment. And to be set up in my office to kill Brose exactly as Verne was killed; admittedly it will be instantaneous and painless, but it is still murder, as was mine of the four Footemen commandos. But—this is how we stand. And I'm leaving. Descending. If I can.

"You're going back to your tank?" he asked Nicholas.

"Right away. The shorter a time old Souza is in freeze the better; there's always the chance of some brain decay. I'm going to leave Lantano's leadies here to keep on digging, get the rest up; I guess Lantano and Foote can split it or anyhow come to an agreement."

"They seem," Adams said, "able to agree. Foote supplied the map; Lantano the leadies and the digging equipment. They'll find some way to divide the trove." *What's amazing,* he thought, *is that you are getting your pancreas without conditions. They've asked nothing in exchange. So they're not* bad men, *not in any typical, ordinary sense; together Foote and Lantano, with dignity and* caritas, *arranged for you to obtain what Brose has deprived you—and everyone else on the planet—of, what he has hoarded for himself. Brose—who was absolutely without* caritas.

"I thought you were supposed to meet them in New York," Nicholas said to Adams.

"They'll make out." From Megavac 6-V they could get Stanton Brose's Alpha-wave pattern; they would think of that sooner or later, when he did not show—in fact probably already had. And, if they could not mount the dart weapon in his office, if they, using Foote's tools and skills, could not pick the intricate door lock, could not enter, they could—and would—find a serviceable place in the corridor, the sole passage to the office, the route which Stanton Brose would have to follow to reach the office. He knew, intuited on a very deep, absolute level, that together Foote and Lantano would manage somehow to work it out.

They would never forget, however, that he had failed to show. If they did not get Brose then the old, half-senile mass of fat would no doubt destroy them, and possibly Adams as well; if they did—well, probably at some convenient later date, when Foote and Lantano, especially Lantano, had gained power, replaced Brose, they would track him down. There would be plenty of time for vengeance. Ultimately, in either case, *it would come*. Whatever the outcome of the weapon planting which at this moment was taking place in the agency hallway or office at 580 Fifth Avenue, New York City.

"Did you ever tell Lantano," he asked Nicholas, "which ant tank you came from?"

"Hell no," Nicholas said. "I have to protect the people down there; I've got a wife and a kid brother, down in—" He broke off. "I told that ex-tanker in the Cheyenne ruins, though. That Jack Blair." He shrugged stoically. "But Blair probably won't remember; they all, there in those ruins, seemed a little scrambled witwise." Soberly, he said to Adams then, "I'm the elected President of the tank. I carry a terrific responsibility. That's why it was me they sent up to the surface to get this artiforg." He turned, started toward the parked flapple.

Adams said, "Can I go along?"

"To—" Nicholas looked startled, but principally preoccupied; it was the artiforg that concerned him—the object and the task of getting it back intact with him to his tank. "You want to go below with me, you mean? Why?"

"I want to hide," Adams said, simply.

After a pause Nicholas said, "You mean Lantano."

"I mean," Adams said, "everyone. They got my one and only living friend; they'll get me. But if I'm down below, and they won't know which tank, maybe, unles your pol-com happens to report—"

"My pol-com," Nicholas said tonelessly, "came from the surface, from Estes Park, after the end of the war. He knew. So there isn't going to be any pol-com at the Tom Mix. Anyhow, not that one."

Another death, Adams realized. And also "necessary." Like each of the others; like mine will be, eventually. And yet—this rule, this necessity, has always existed, and for everything that has ever lived.

What we've got here is only a special case, only a hastening of the natural, organic process.

"Sure," Nicholas said. "You're welcome. I know from what you said at Lantano's demesne you're as unhappy as hell up here."

" 'Hell,' " Adams echoed. Yes, it was, literally, the burning place of the dead; the place of fires, the flicker of red, the charred background, the pits, summed up and summoned up by the war of thirteen years ago—he had been living it, first in the scorching blaze of the war itself, then in its other, later form, the cool, approaching mist, and then once more in its more awful searing aspect; igniting him, cramming him with this time a new, entirely new, agony: from the moment he had learned of Verne Lindblom's death.

"You'll have to get used to the overcrowding down there," Nicholas said as the two of them made their way toward the parked flapple, Adams' leadies trailing behind. "And you can't bring them—" He gestured at the retinue of leadies. "—with you; you'll have to come alone. There's no room; in fact in our cubby we share the bathroom—"

"Good enough," Adams said. He would agree to anything, give up his last leady, be stripped of that, too, and gladly. And—he would be more than willing to share the bathroom with those inhabiting the adjoining room. He would not endure it; he would thrive. Because it would make up for the loneliness of his years as dominus of his vast, silent, forest-surrounded demesne, with its ocean fog; the gruesome, empty Pacific fog.

The tankers would not understand that. Maybe they would even marvel at his ability to adjust to such crowded conditions—after having been a functionary, as he would tell them, *have* to tell them, of the Estes Park Wes-Dem Government. Like the pol-coms he had descended into their tank to share their deprivations with them . . . or so they would think.

Ironic.

TWENTY-EIGHT

They were, presently, airborne. The flapple, in the night's darkness, headed northwest, toward the Cheyenne hot-spot. With only the two men aboard. All leadies, both Adams' and Lantano's, had been left behind to dig. Adams wondered if they had begun to scrap, yet, if the fracas that was latent between the two factions had broken out overtly. Probably so.

To reopen the vertical tunnel to the Tom Mix tank proved a major problem. It was not until dawn that the two of them at last managed, with equipment brought from Adams' demesne on the Pacific Coast, to cut away the hard, fused crust which Lantano's two leadies had installed as a barrier to further use of the shaft. Nicholas and Adams had been lucky to find the spot at all; however the thoroughness of the leadies' job had assisted them. The spot had been conspicuous, even at night, by its temporary barrenness, by the smooth and lifeless artificial surface, an almost obsidian-like disfiguration among the tufted weeds and rubble.

Now the entrance once again gaped. The professional work of the no longer extant leadies had been undone. But it had taken hours.

Setting it on auto, Joseph Adams dispatched the flapple; it rose, disappeared into the gray, early morning light. Left here it would have acted as a clear giveaway. And the problem still remained of resealing the tunnel's entrance after them in such a manner that it would not even with instruments be detected.

For this purpose he and Adams had composed a plug. A section of hard dirt, weed-covered, sheared to fit the tunnel-mouth exactly. This, in actuality, was relatively a simple aspect of the job; he and Adams now squeezed down into the tunnel, and then, by means of a series of small-link chains attached to steel stakes driven into the underside of the plug, they dragged the piece of hard earth and weeds after them and over them; all at once the gray light of morning vanished and they had only their lanterns. By pulling the chains taut they wedged the plug securely in place.

And then, with great care, they detached all metal pieces from the plug, the stakes and the chains . . . detectors, used later on, would have registered the presence of the metal; that would have been the tropism that would have distinguished their trail of escape, for the hounds who would one day be coming.

Five minutes later Nicholas, with his boots, kicked loose the seal at the base of the tunnel; the tank's committee of activists, acting under Jorgenson's expert direction, had carefully made the seal susceptible to easy removal from above—after all, if Nicholas returned, with or without the artiforg, he would have to come by this route.

Squeezed into the small storeroom of floor one the entire leadership of the committee, Haller and Flanders and Jorgenson, all of them waited with their strange little hand-made laser pistols which they had turned out in the ant tank's shops.

"We've been listening to you for an hour," Jorgenson said. "Banging and rattling around up there, reopening the tunnel. Naturally we have a full-time alarm system rigged; it woke us at exactly four a.m. How did you make out?" He saw then, in Nicholas' hands, the aluminum cylinder.

"He got it," Haller said.

Nicholas said, "I got it." He handed the cylinder to Jorgenson, turned then to help Adams out of the tunnel and into the crowded storeroom. "What about Dale Nunes? Did he file a report up to—"

"Nunes," Jorgenson said, "is dead. An industrial accident. In the bottom-floor shops; he was—you know. Exhorting us to greater productivity. And he got too near a power cable. And for some reason—I forget now—but anyhow the cable wasn't properly shielded."

Haller said, "And some oaf pushed Nunes backward so that he fell onto the cable. And it wiped him out." He added, "We already buried him. It was either that or have him report to up above on your absence."

"And in your name," Jorgenson said, "like you were still here, we sent an official report to the surface, to Estes Park. Asking for another pol-com to replace Commissioner Nunes, and of course expressing our regrets."

There was silence.

Nicholas said, "I'll take the artiforg to Carol." And then he said to them all, "I didn't bring this back so we could make our quota. I brought it for Souza's sake as such. For his life. But the quota is over."

"How come?" Jorgenson said, perceptively. "What is it, up there?" He saw Adams, then, realized all at once that Nicholas had not returned alone. "Who's this? You better explain."

Nicholas said, "I will when the mood strikes me."

"He's still President of the tank," Flanders reminded Jorgenson. "He can wait as long as he wants; chrissakes, he brought the pancreas; I mean, does he have to deliver a speech in addition?"

"I was just curious," Jorgenson, backing down, said lamely.

"Where's Carol?" Nicholas said, as with Joseph Adams, he passed through the gang of committee members toward the door of the storeroom. He reached the door, took hold of the knob—

The door was locked.

Jorgenson said, "We can't leave here, Mr. President. None of us."

"Who says so?" Nicholas said, after a pause.

"Carol herself," Haller said. "Because of you. The Bag Plague or the Stink of Shrink or any other bacterial contamination that you—" He gestured at Adams. "—and this fella may have on you. And we're all of us we're stuck, too, because we said, christ, we got to be at the bottom of the tunnel. In case it *isn't* Nick that we heard, that set off the alarm. And if it was—" He hesitated. "Well, we felt we ought to be here. To sort of, you know; officially be on hand. To greet you." He glanced down in embarrassment. "Even if you didn't have the artiforg. Because after all you tried."

"You risked your life," Jorgenson said, in agreement.

Nicholas said acidly, "Under the threat of being blown up by you shop boys; and my wife and brother along with me."

"Maybe so," Jorgenson said, "but you did go, and you got it, so you didn't just poke your head out, then slide back down again and say, 'Sorry, fellas; no luck.' As you could have done. Hell, we couldn't have disproved it. Proved you hadn't tried." They all seemed embarrassed, now. Guilty, Nicholas thought; that was more it. Ashamed of the terror tactic they had used to get him to go. Now, he realized their President has returned, with the artiforg; old Maury Souza will be revived, restored to his position. Our production of leadies will resume and we will meet our quotas. Except that their ant tank

President knows the truth, now. Which he did not when he originally left, climbed the tunnel, emerged on Earth's surface—to learn what Commissioner Dale Nunes had known all the time.

No wonder Nunes had insisted everyone act solely through channels—that is, through Nunes. Make no *direct* contact with the world above.

No wonder a pol-com in each ant tank was essential.

It had always been obvious the the pol-com performed a vital function for *somebody*—presumably for the Estes Park Government. But only by journeying to the surface himself—and coming back here again—had he seen just how vital, and for whose benefit, that function had been.

"Okay," Nicholas said to the committee; he let go of the doorknob, gave up. "And what did Carol intend next? A decontamination process of some sort?" To 'cide bacteria, microbes and viruses which he knew to be nonexistent; it was a temptation to tell them now—but he refrained. The time, he knew; it has to be exactly right. This must not be mishandled, because if it is there will be too great a reaction. Too much—justified—anger. They will burst up, through the large chute, the leady chutes, break out, carrying their handmade laser pistols . . . and the veteran, expert leadies will massacre them as they emerge. And, for us, it will be over.

Jorgenson said, "We've already notified Carol by intercom that it is you; she ought to be here any second. Be patient. Souza's deep in the freeze; he can wait another hour. She'll graft in the pancreas sometime around midday. Meanwhile we're all supposed to take off all our clothes, pile them up, then outside the door there's this chamber we built down in the shops; we'll pass through it, naked, one by one, and jets of 'cide of different types will—"

To Nicholas, Adams said, "I never, I just never realized. How completely they accept it. It's incredible." He seemed dazed. "We thought of it I guess as an intellectual acceptance. But *this*." He gestured.

"All the way," Nicholas said, nodding. "In every emotional level. Down to the basic phobic animal level; to the very deepest layer." He began to remove his clothes, resignedly. Until the time arrived to tell them, there was no choice; the ritual had to be gone through.

At last, as if prodded by a remote reflex of some dim, uncertain source, Adams, too, began unbuttoning his shirt.

TWENTY-NINE

At one o'clock that afternoon Carol Tigh performed—successfully—the pancreas insertion operation on the still-frozen dead Maury Souza, and then, using the tank's most precious medical equipment, the old man's circulation, heartbeat, respiration were artificially, externally restored; the heart began to pump blood, then, on its own, and following that one the artificial function stimulators were cautiously and expertly detached from him.

The EEG and EKG records, during the next, critical hours, indicated that body processes were occurring normally; old Souza had a good chance—a very good chance—of recovering and living out a few more good, important years.

So that was that. Nicholas, after standing at the bedside of the old mechanic for a long time, watching the monitoring machinery spill out their ribbons of tape, at last turned away, satisfied.

It was time at last for him once again to face his little overcrowded, jammed-together family in their adjoining cubbies with their shared, quarreled-over-daily bathroom. Once more he would resume the old life of the tank.

For a while.

And then, he said to himself as he walked alone down the clinic corridor and to the terminal ramp which led to his own floor, his residential floor, the trumpet shall sound and—not the dead—but the deceived shall be raised. And not incorruptible, sad to say, but highly mortal, perishable, and—mad.

A nest of hot, scorched wasps, rising to attack. This tank first, but by then we will have established contact with our neighboring tanks, will have told them, too. Pass it on, we'll say, he said to himself.

Until everyone knows. And finally a worldwide network of angry wasps; and if they all swarm simultaneously, no army of leadies can get them. Just *some* of them. A third, perhaps. But no more.

However, it all depended on the TV transmissions during the next twenty-four hours. What Talbot Yancy, either real or imaginary, had to say to them.

He would wait, first, on that.

And which would it be, Brose or Lantano? Who, at this hour, lived and held power, and who had died?

The next Yancy speech, the next dose of reading matter, would tell him. Probably within the first ten words uttered by the face on the screen.

And which, he asked himself as he arrived at the door of his little cubby, do we want to see emerge? Adams would know better than I; David Lantano was good to me, made it possible for me to obtain the artiforg. But David Lantano's leadies before that, began the act of killing me . . . would have, if the man himself, in his older, artificially lighter skinned Yancy phase, hadn't intervened. Or perhaps something else had emerged up there or will emerge in time; neither Lantano nor Brose but a combination—Joseph Adams, as they had worked together to reopen the tunnel, had conjectured about this—a new alignment, of Webster Foote and his worldwide police corporation with Louis Runcible and his unwieldy economic supergigantic overgrown satrapy. Pitted against the Agency and its army of leadies, many of them wise old tomcats with kinks in their tails, left over from the war and ready at any pretext to fight again . . . whether commanded by Stanton Brose or David Lantano.

He opened the door of his cubby.

There sat Rita, composed, waiting. "Hi," she said quietly.

"Hi." He stood awkwardly in the doorway, not knowing whether to enter or not, trying to read her attitude.

Rising, Rita said, "It's nice to have you back. To see you. How are you?" She came toward him, then, hesitantly, also uncertain, as he was. "You didn't get the Bag Plague, then. That's what I was most afraid of. From what I've heard and seen on TV and what Dale Nunes said before he—disappeared."

He put his arms around her, hugged her.

"This is fine," Rita said, hugging him fiercely back. "But Nick, an all-points came through just a few seconds ago; we're supposed to be in Wheeling Hall right now, listening to the Protector, but I'm not going—Nunes, as you know, is dead, and so right now there's nobody to *make* us go. So I'll stay here. With you." She held him against her; however, he very swiftly disengaged her arms. "What is it?" she said, then, bewildered.

"I'm going to Wheeling Hall." He strode to the door.

"What does it matter—"

He did not take time to answer; he sprinted down the hall, to the ramp.

A moment later, with perhaps no more than a fifth or sixth of the citizens of the tank, Nicholas St. James entered Wheeling Hall. Catching sight of Joseph Adams he made his way over to him, seated himself rapidly beside him.

The giant floor-to-ceiling TV screen was lit and active; it pulsed but showed nothing.

Adams, briefly, said, "We're waiting. There has been what the announcer just now called a 'delay.' " His face was pale, stark. "He, that is, Yancy—he started to appear; then the image was cut off. As if—" He glanced at Nicholas. "the coax had been cut."

"Jesus," Nicholas said, and felt his heart beat, retrieve its rhythm, at last continue to labor on after a fashion. "So they're still fighting it out."

"We'll know," Adams said, speaking coolly, professionally. "It won't be long." His tension seemed deliberately technical. And kept so.

"Was he at his big oak desk? With the flag behind?"

"Couldn't tell. Too fragmentary; it lasted—they were able to keep it on—just a split second. I think—" Adams' voice was low but quite clearly audible as, around them, tankers leisurely, with no particular concern, took their seats, yawned, murmured, chatted. They did not know; they just did not know what this meant, to them, to their future collective and intimate, personally lived, individual lives. "—to tell you the truth, the showdown evidently did *not* come at nine o'clock a.m. New York Time. Apparently it's just coming now." He examined his watch. "It's six p.m. at the Agency. So something, god knows what, has been going on all day long." He turned his attention back to the big TV screen, then. And became silent. Waiting.

"The dart," Nicholas said, "missed, then."

"Perhaps. But that wouldn't be the end. Lantano wouldn't give up and die. Let's take this step by step. First of all, that particular weapon assembly, if it fails to meet its target, so notifies its installer owner. So no matter where he may be say a thousand miles away, Lantano would know instantly the bad news. And Foote—he'd be up to something in the meantime anyhow; I hope at Capetown. If he has the brains I know he has, definitely at Capetown. And would have disclosed to Runcible the whole business about the special project. And remember this: there are, in those conapts of Runcible's, thousands upon thousands of ex-tankers who Runcible might already have trained, armed, prepared for—" He broke off.

On the screen appeared the enormous, three-dimensional, full-color familiar ruddy but tanned, healthy, hard-cut features of Talbot Yancy.

"My fellow Americans," Yancy said, in his grave and firm, momentous yet considerate, even gracious voice. "I am humble before the sight of God to announce to you a matter of such infinite significance that I can only pray to the Almighty and thank Him that we, you and I together, have lived to see this day. My friends—" The voice, now, had choked with emotion; contained, however, by the iron, military inspired stoicism of the man. Masculine always, yet nonetheless overwhelmed; that was Talbot Yancy at this instant, and Nicholas simply could not fathom this that he saw: was this the simulacrum which had always confronted them from the TV screen, or was this—

The camera retreated. Now the oak desk. The flag. As always.

Nicholas said to Joseph Adams, "Brose got them. Before they got him." He felt leaden, dulled. It was over.

Well, that was that. And—maybe for the better. Who knew? Who would ever know? And still the great real task lay ahead, for him, for all the tankers. Nothing less than a total, absolute war to the end, to try to break through and stay broken through to the Earth's surface.

On the screen in a trembling, overcome voice Talbot Yancy said, "Today I can inform you, every one of you down beneath the ground where you have for so long labored, year in, year out—"

Adams grated, *"Get to it."*

"—without complaint, enduring and suffering, and always having faith . . . now, my friends, that faith which has so long been tested can be justified. The war, my friends, is over."

After a moment—Wheeling Hall and the people scattered here and there in it were dead-still—Nicholas turned; he and Adams looked at each other.

"And soon, my friends," Yancy continued in his heavy, solemn way, "you shall come up to your own sunlit world once again. You will be shocked, at first, by what you see; it will not be easy, and this will be slow, I must tell you; slow in coming; it must be done bit by bit. But it is here now. All fighting has ceased. The Soviet Union, Cuba, all members of Pac-Peop, has as an entitey resigned itself, agreed, at last, to—"

"Lantano," Adams said, unbelievingly.

Getting to his feet, Nicholas walked up the aisle, out of Wheeling Hall.

In the corridor, alone, he stood in silence, thinking. Evidently Lantano, with or without Webster Foote, had after all gotten Brose, either early in the morning with the high velocity dart, or, if not then and by that weapon, later on. And in some other but absolutely professional, equally serviceable way. Aimed, of necessity, at the old brain itself, because that alone could not be replaced. When that organ was gone it was over. And it is over.

Brose, he realized, is dead. There is no doubt of it. This was the proof—what we were waiting for. The one, the only sign we down here would receive. The reign of the Yance-man, the fraud of thirteen years, or forty-three if you start with Fischer's documentaries—all over.

For better or worse.

Appearing beside him Adams stood for a moment; neither of them spoke and then Adams said, "It all depends on Runcible and Foote, at this point. Maybe they can drag Lantano into a stalemate. Moderate him. What in the old U.S. Government was called 'balance of power.' Possibly through an appearance before the Recon Dis-In Council; insist on—" He gestured. "God knows. I hope *they* do. It's a mess, Nick; honest to god—I know without being up there and seeing; it's a terrible mess and it'll be a mess for a long time."

"But," Nicholas said, "we're going to start emerging."

Adams said, "What I'm waiting to see is how Lantano or whoever it is that's running the simulacrum now, or however they're transmitting—I want to see how they explain those thousands of miles of grass and trees. Instead of an endless waste surface of radioactive rubble." He grinned, grimaced, twitched rapidly; half a dozen, then steadily deeper, stronger and more profound conflicting ideas and emotions flew across his features as, in his mind, he saw swiftly into one possibility after another: the idea man, the Yance-man in him, the person that he was, came, under these conditions, the excitement, the fear and stress, back into being. "What the hell," he said, "can they—whoever 'they' are—possibly say? *Could* there be a plausible cover story? Lord, I can't think of one. Anyhow right now, right on the spot. Lantano, though. You have no realization, Nick; he might. He's brilliant. Yes, he very possibly might."

"You think," Nicholas said, "that the biggest lie is still to come?"

After a long, visibly tormented pause Adams said, "Yes."

"They can't just tell the truth?"

"The what? Listen, Nick; whoever they are, whatever combination out of all the possible crazy bedfellow conniving, double-dealing deals and deal-outs, whatever group or person has gotten its paws, temporarily anyhow, on the winning cards, after his long day of—whatever took place; they have a job, Nick: they have *the* job, now. Of explaining away an entire planet of green, neatly trimmed, leady-gardener cared-for park. *This is it*. And not just satisfactorily explaining it to you or me or a couple of ex-tankers here or there but to hundreds and hundreds of millions of hostile, really furious skeptics who are going to scrutinize every single word that ever issues out of a TV set—by anybody!—from this moment forever into the future. Would you like that job, Nick? Just exactly how well would you like to have to do that?"

"I wouldn't," Nicholas said.

Adams said, "I would." His face writhed, in suffering, and with what seemed to Nicholas as authentic and unmistakable devouring yearning. "I wish to god I were in on it; I wish I were sitting in my office at the Agency right now, at 580 Fifth Avenue, New York, monitoring this transmission as it goes out over the coax. It's my job. *Was* my job. But the fog scared me, the loneliness; I let it get me. But I could go back now and it wouldn't get me; I wouldn't let it. Because this is so important; we were working up to this all the time, this moment when we had to account for it all. Even if we didn't know. It added up to this *and I'm not there*, now that this moment's finally come; I'm off and hiding—I ran." His suffering, the sense of loss, the knowing he was severed from them and it, palpably grew, made him gag as if he had been brutally butted in the depths of his stomach; as if physically thrust back so that now he was falling, and helplessly, with nothing to cling to: Adams caught at the empty air, flailing, futile. And yet still he was trying.

"It's over," Nicholas said to him, and not trying or wanting to be kind. "Over for you personally and over for all of them." *Because*, he said to himself, *I'm going to tell them the truth.*

They looked at each other, silently. Adams blinking out of the recess into which he fell and fell. Both of them without friendliness, and utterly without warmth. Divided, each from the other. Absolutely.

And, second by second, the hollowness, the space between, enlarged. Until finally even Nicholas felt it, felt the grip of what Joseph Adams had always called—the fog. The inner, soundless fog.

"Okay," Adams gasped. "You blab the truth; you rig up some dinky little ten-watt shortwave radio transmitter and raise the next tank, pass your Word along—but I'm going back up to my demesne and I'm going to hole up in my library where I have to be right now and write a speech. Beyond doubt, without qualifications, the best one I ever did in all my years. The culmination. Because that's what we need. Even better than Lantano can do; when I really have to I can surpass even him—there isn't anyone who can get beyond me at my job; I know I have it. So we'll see, Nick; we'll wait a while and see who wins, who believes what and whom when all this is finally over; you have your chance and I'm not going to let mine slip by—I'm not going to be left. Discarded." He stared at Nicholas.

Rita, breathless and excited, hurried up the hall to her husband. "Nicholas, I just heard—the war's over and we're going to be able to go back up. We can finally start to—"

"But not quite yet," Nicholas said. "They haven't quite got it ready; conditions on the surface aren't quite right, yet." He returned Adams' fixed, goaded, suffering stare. "Are they?"

"No, not yet," Adams said in slow, mechanical response, as if he had already gone and little, very little of him, remained here now, by which to answer. "But conditions will be," he said. "Like you said. Okay in time."

"But it's true," Rita said, gasping. "We won; they, Pac-Peop; they surrendered to our armies of leadies. Yancy said so; it was piped to every cubby in the tank, I heard it down below." Seeing the expression of her husband's face she said falteringly. "It's not just a rumor. Yancy himself, the Protector, personally said it."

To Adams, Nicholas said, "What about this. You could tell them—tell us—that it's a surprise. For our birthday."

"No," Adams said vigorously, thinking once more at high speed, weighing each of Nicholas' words. "Not good enough; it won't do."

"The radiation level," Nicholas said. He felt tired, considering, and not too pessimistic, not by any manner of means despairing. Despite what both he and Adams saw: the task which had step by step approached unnoticed, all of these waiting, and for each of them, unproductive years. "The radioactivity," Nicholas said.

At that, Adams' eyes flickered intensely.

"The radioactivity," Nicholas said, "has just now finally, after all this time, at last dropped to a tolerable level. There it is; what about that? And throughout all these years you were forced to say—you had no choice, just no choice at all in the matter; it was morally and practically *necessary* to say—that the war was still going on. Or otherwise people, and you know how they always do, would have rushed to the surface."

"Foolishly," Adams agreed, nodding slowly.

"Too soon," Nicholas said. "The way they naturally act in their stupidity, and the radiation; it would have killed them. So actually when you get right down to it, this was self-sacrificing. The sort of moral responsibility that your leadership entailed. How about that?"

"I know," Adams said quietly, "that we can come up with something."

Nicholas said, "I know you can, too." Except for that one thing, he said to himself, and put his arm around his wife to draw her closer.

You're not going to.

Because we will not allow you.

Philip K. Dick was born in 1928. His twin sister, Jane, died in infancy. He started his writing career publishing short stories in magazines. The first of these was 'Beyond Lies the Wub' in 1952. While publishing science fiction prolifically during the 1950s, Dick also wrote a series of mainstream novels, only one of which, *Confessions of a Crap Artist*, was published during his lifetime. These included titles such as *Mary and the Giant* and *In Milton Lumky Territory*. During the 1960s, Dick produced an extraordinary succession of novels, including *The Man in the High Castle*, which won a Hugo award, *Martian Time-Slip*, *Dr. Bloodmoney*, *The Three Stigmata of Palmer Eldritch*, *Do Androids Dream of Electric Sheep?* and *UBIK*. In the 1970s, Dick started to concern himself more directly with metaphysical and theological issues, experiencing a moment of revelation - or breakdown - in March 1974, which became the basis for much of his subsequent writing, in particular *Valis*, as he strove to make sense of what had happened. He died in 1982, a few weeks before the film *Bladerunner* opened and introduced his vision to a wider audience.